WILD MAGIC

Wild Magic

A VICTORIAN FAERIE TALE

E.B. WHEELER

Rowan Ridge
Press

ISBN: 978-1-960033-07-9

First printing: October 2023

Published by Rowan Ridge Press, Utah

Cover design by Lauren Makena

Cover and interior design © Rowan Ridge Press

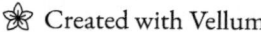 Created with Vellum

For everyone searching for where they belong

Chapter One

Amy couldn't get the blood off her hands. She'd scoured them against her skirts, but the dead girl was part Fay. Just like all the other recent murder victims. Now, the latent magic in the blood prickled on Amy's palms.

Amy had left the girl's body where she discovered it in Covent Garden and hurried for the Pimlico district of London. Hurried for Domin and her other friends. Men in bowler hats and women with bustled dresses crowded the coffee shops and storefronts, bumping her as she passed. The jumble of emotions on the street made her dizzy: excitement, nervousness, worry, pride, insecurity. Normally, she could filter out other people's emotions, but her racing pulse and the tight choking in her chest distracted her, ripped her open and left her vulnerable. She kept her head down, tucking her blonde curls beneath her hood.

Don't look at me. You don't want to look at me. You don't want to be involved.

She pushed her shock and horror outward like a shield, and the passersby veered away from her and hurried on to their errands. Emotions were dangerous for the Fay—it made their magic unpredictable—but Amy didn't care at the moment.

All she could see was the dying girl, fawn-like, brown eyes wide and frightened as they turned glassy. Blood. So much blood carrying a trace of Faerie power. The girl probably had no idea. Maybe just some extra charm or musical ability that she attributed to good fortune. And the Grigori had killed her for it.

The Grigori had to be involved. It fit too well. The Grigori's obsession with magical blood. Their experiments on those whose veins flowed with it, trying to unlock magic's secrets. And Mr. Rushford, their leader, had proven his willingness to kill in his attempt to sacrifice Amy's friends the previous year. But the Grigori couldn't be acting alone. How did they know which humans had Faerie blood?

Domin, Henry, and Jairus had found other victims of the Grigori already dead, but this girl had fought back. And right there in crowded Covent Garden, they'd killed her. The Grigori were becoming bolder.

Were they hunting Amy at that moment?

Her breath caught. She glanced over her shoulder at the faceless crowds and broke into a run.

Domin would know what to do. Amy's thoughts swirled like blood pouring onto stone, pooling, the stink thick and choking... She shook her head, trying to clear it. Domin always knew what was best. The girl's death wouldn't be entirely in vain if it provided a clue that led them to her killer.

Amy reached the private house in Pimlico where the men had apartments. The sign in the front window said, "Rooms to let to Respectable Gentlemen." Not a place for ladies. Amy glanced down at her skirts spotted with blood from kneeling next to the dying girl. Which was more improper, visiting a gentleman's boarding house, or walking about London with blood on her dress? A humorless, hysterical giggle rose in her throat, but she swallowed it. None of the rules of Society mattered while the Grigori hunted the Fay.

She knocked, and a woman with steely gray hair tucked under a widow's cap answered. The landlady, no doubt. The woman's gaze swept down to Amy's ruined skirts. Disgust radiated from the woman, and Amy absorbed it, flushing hot with shame.

"What do you want?" the landlady snapped.

"There's been an...an incident," Amy said. "I need to tell some of your tenants. Nothing to concern you. I'm a respectable lady."

Take no notice. You don't want to see or know.

The landlady returned a skeptical glare. Amy hardly believed what she'd said herself—no conviction—and her glamour rolled right over the woman.

"If you write a message, I'll pass it on," the landlady countered.

Amy's blood-stained hands itched—almost burned. This couldn't wait on a go-between. Amy's plans tended to go wrong, and every minute made it easier for the Grigori to cover their tracks and escape. But every excuse Amy thought of caught on her tongue. Even after being banished from her mother's realm, she was still a Seelie Fay and could not lie. Nor could she slip around back and enter the house without permission.

The landlady's impatience pressed against Amy.

"Henry Stewart!" Amy burst out. "He's my brother, practically." They had been raised together, at least, and her affection for him was sisterly. "There's been a tragedy. I must speak to him immediately." The warm tears that came to her eyes were genuine, as were the panic and sorrow she pushed at the woman.

The landlady's face softened. She grunted and stepped back, relenting either through magic or simple compassion. "I'm not sure if he's in at the moment, but he and his friends have rooms on the second floor."

Amy hurried up the stairs. The door to the sitting room stood open, exuding an eerie emptiness like a house long abandoned. Nothing stirred, no distant sounds of life. Goose bumps prickled up Amy's arms.

"Domin?" she half-whispered. "Henry? Mr. Hale?"

She slowly pushed the door wide, opening herself to whatever emotions lingered there. The room was dark and cold and smelled slightly smoky. She couldn't sense anyone inside, and in fact, she felt few traces of emotion. A lingering restlessness itched at her, but no indication that violence had been done there, and not much feeling of home about the place. It was just a room in a boarding house, after all. And only a middle-of-the-road one at that.

Amy stepped into the dark room. Her foot hit something soft. A body? No, only a fallen pillow. Jairus and Henry might be lazy housekeepers, but Domin would not leave things lying about. She felt her way across the room to open the curtains and turned around. She gasped at the mess. Chairs overturned, pillows cut apart, items knocked from the desk to the floor. The spilled candle wax had cooled and hardened into strange ripples on the desk.

Amy's pulse hammered in her throat. Think, think—she

had to stay calm and rational. She paced the room. A silver-plated food cover on the side table caught her eye. She lifted it warily, revealing a stack of sandwiches, the bread beginning to mold. So, it had been there several days, but the men had planned to come back for it soon. They'd been neat, hadn't left in a hurry. And they hadn't returned.

Yet the damage must have been done recently or a housemaid would have found the damage, reported it, and probably cleaned it up. So, someone else had come, maybe only shortly before Amy arrived. To rob the room? Amy studied the chaos. Some pillows had been slit open, spilling their feathers on the floor, but not all of them. A thief would have been more systematic. And would have taken the food cover, even if it was only silver-plated.

She closed her eyes, took a deep breath, and let the cold and the stillness and the stuffy scents flow into her. Yes, it was there. A trace of emotion she had not picked up initially: frustration.

Someone had broken in and lost their temper when Domin and the others were not there. The evidence of a tantrum made her think of the Fay, but most Fay had to be invited in, and her friends were not so foolish. The Grigori, then? Amy's stomach turned. Thank goodness her friends were gone! But how would the Grigori have gotten past the landlady?

Amy went to the window. It was cracked open. That explained the cold and the smoky scent. Someone could have climbed in and out, but it was a straight drop down into the garden below. She looked up to the roof. She wasn't entirely familiar with the extent of human skills, but she didn't think most men could climb that way. A creature that could fly? Maybe. Banshees could go wherever death was coming.

A crow cawed in the garden.

Amy shivered and slammed the window shut, latching it.

Amy looked again at the blood staining her skirt and hands. Her head swam, and she felt like she might be sick. This was too much. The Grigori were too dangerous, and she could be the next victim. Or one of her friends could be. Yet she was alone now, and in the past, her choices tended to result in people she cared about being hurt. Or killed.

Chapter Two

Mary raised her small crossbow and took her time sighting the center of the target. It was shaped roughly like the armored figure of the Morrigan. The spirit of battle. The red-haired Fay woman who could dissolve into a flock of crows and reanimate corpses fallen in battle. Who led the banshees, heralds of death. Mary's pulse pounded in her ears. She squeezed her eyes shut, and the Morrigan's sword flashed in her mind.

No. Mary had to be brave like Amy and Cassandra. She focused on the target, exhaled slowly, and squeezed the trigger. The iron-tipped bolt sprang forward and thumped into the Morrigan-target's midsection. One of the crow feathers added for effect drifted to the ground.

"Bravo!" Cassandra called behind her.

"It was too low," Mary said, frowning at the firing mechanism.

She made an adjustment to the trigger, but the problem wasn't the crossbow—it was her. She'd originally designed the crossbows for Cassandra, whose weak right hand struggled with pulling a regular bow, and Mary had woven magic into each of the weapons so they would fire true. She'd modeled them on a pistol crossbow her father had once repaired—smaller and lighter than the old types used by knights, so they didn't fire as far, but they were easy to hide in a picnic hamper. Yet no matter how well she designed the crossbows, they didn't make her brave enough for a sure aim.

"It was still a killing blow on most creatures. Fay or not, I mean," Cassandra said, limping over to push the bolt through the target and remove it. "And I daresay even *she* would be hurt by it."

They didn't speak the names of the Fay, not so close to the Old Woods and the stream that flowed from Elfland along the edge of the Weaver's property.

"I did use iron and rowan wood," Mary said, trying to mimic Cassandra's optimism. She tried to mimic as much as she could about Cassandra—with the exceptions of her limp and her admiration of Henry Stewart and Domin, whose blunt temperaments intimidated her. As a Faerie changeling, Mary would never be at home in the human world like Cassandra was, but she could try.

Cassandra returned the bolt. "Even a little iron hurts them."

Mary nodded and took the bolt. The iron was uncomfortable for her, too, but she didn't want Cassandra to count her among "them." She ignored the cold sting of the iron's nearness as she reloaded the crossbow, willing the bolt to sail straight. A buzz hummed through her fingers—her changeling magic at work. She aimed again, the bolt pointing at the target's heart. The only sounds were the rush of the stream and the distant chirp of birds. Mary imagined a bristling of wings behind her and jumped. The bolt sailed through the target's throat.

"That's...effective," Cassandra said.

"I was startled." Mary swung the crossbow down and ground her teeth. "When it matters, I want to hit her in the heart."

Cassandra raised her eyebrows. Mary wasn't certain why she looked surprised. They were supposed to be learning to protect themselves from the Fay. That was why Domin taught them, why Cassandra lied to her family about collecting flowers in the woods, and why Mary snuck away from her father's shop when she was supposed to be polishing the clocks.

"Maybe they'll leave us alone," Cassandra said, but her words rang hollow.

"Maybe," Mary lied in return.

Lying was a human art Mary could indulge in since the Fay had cast her off. But, a lie it was. After all, Cassandra had wounded the Queen of the Unseelie Fay, an insult not likely to be forgiven or forgotten.

Cassandra muffled a yawn with her good hand. Dark circles underlined her hazel eyes.

"You're not sleeping well," Mary said.

"I've been plagued by nightmares of late." Cassandra glanced down at the palm of her weak right hand—the one that the Grigori had branded with a demon's mark. "Sometimes I wonder—"

A rustle sounded in the woods. Both girls jumped. Something moved through the trees. Mary froze, but Cassandra had her crossbow up in less than a heartbeat.

Mary raised her weapon, fighting the tremble in her hands. But Cassandra lowered hers, reaching out to push Mary's down as well.

"The white stag," Cassandra whispered.

They sometimes caught glimpses of the creature in the

woods—an ancient spirit, according to Domin, and one that had helped them when they were lost in the Unseelie realm the previous year. It had not approached them since. This time, it limped up to the edge of the stream, turning its dark eyes from Cassandra to Mary.

Mary held very still, her heartbeat thrumming in her ears. She doubted the spirit meant them harm, but its antlers could easily gore them. Its leg still bore a wound where Mr. Rushford had shot it the previous fall. It had neither healed nor festered. Mary wondered how Rushford had dealt it such a lasting injury. Perhaps knowing was the key to helping the creature. The stag was broken, and Mary liked to fix broken things.

"Good afternoon?" Cassandra said, addressing the stag with an awkward curtsey.

Mary couldn't tell if the stag understood, but Domin had taught them to always be polite when dealing with magical creatures.

The stag lowered its head in return. Then, it turned and bounded away without looking back.

"Should we follow it?" Cassandra asked.

"I don't know," Mary whispered. She would follow wherever Cassandra led.

Cassandra took a step in the stag's direction. A tinkling of bells stopped her. She and Mary shared worried looks. The bells strung at points along the property boundary were a gift from Domin—or, more likely, from Domin's changeling half-brother Telesm. They only rang when a creature from the Faerie courts crossed onto the Weaver's property.

"Domin?" Mary asked.

Cassandra shook her head. "They don't ring for him—he's neither Seelie nor Unseelie."

Mary shivered. That could mean the Dark Lady or the

Unseelie elf Fitzhugh had returned. It also meant that the bells wouldn't ring to warn them of the Morrigan; like Domin and the white stag, she belonged to neither court.

Cassandra put a reassuring hand on Mary's shoulder. "Whatever it is, we're ready for it."

Mary doubted she would ever be able to lie that bravely. She managed a shadow of a smile.

Cassandra rested her crossbow in the crook in of her arm, and Mary followed her example, though her mouth had gone dry, and she wished she could curl up and hide. It was easier to shoot at a target made of wood and cloth. Pixies or hellhounds would be something different. Or the Morrigan herself. Mary's heart thudded too hard in her thin chest.

They snuck across the property, cutting through the Weaver's orchard. An overripe apple thumped to the ground, making Mary jump, but she didn't see anything else stirring until they neared the house. A cloaked figure—a woman— slipped through the front gate. She looked over her shoulder toward the road, then crept closer to the house.

Mary sucked in a sharp breath. She raised her crossbow, fingers stiff and slow. The cloaked figure paused to touch the last of the white roses draped around the garden gate.

"Wait—the roses!" Cassandra said. "She must be Seelie. I think... Yes, it's Amy!"

Cassandra and Mary hurried to greet their friend. Amy had written to them from London, but they hadn't seen her since the previous fall when they stopped the Dark Lady's sacrifice.

"Amy!" Cassandra called.

Amy's head jerked in their direction, and the hood fell away from her face. Cassandra and Mary stopped short. Amy was unnaturally lovely, even for the Fay, with her heart-shaped face, large blue eyes, and perfect ringlets of blonde hair. Today, however, her face looked drawn and haggard, and an ashen gray tone stole the bloom from her cheeks. Amy's eyes brimmed with tears when she saw her friends.

She rushed forward to embrace Cassandra, almost knocking her off her feet, and took Mary's arm in a firm grip.

"Thank goodness you're here," Amy said, her voice faint and shaky.

"What happened?" Cassandra asked.

Amy squeezed Mary's arm, and Mary fought the urge to wiggle away from the nails digging through her sleeve.

"They're gone," Amy choked out. "Not anywhere in London. Please tell me you know where we can find Domin?"

Chapter Three

Amy could sense nothing of Mary's emotions, and only snatches of Cassandra's, between the lingering effects of the train ride and Cassandra's protection from Faerie magic as one of the Sabbath-born. But what Amy did catch was enough: confusion, followed by alarm.

Cassandra gripped her cane. "Domin usually visits to tutor us, but I haven't seen him for several weeks. What do you mean 'they're gone?' You can't mean Domin and...and the others?" She touched the locket she always wore—the one Henry had given her.

Amy sagged. So tired. Too tired to explain. Cassandra caught her arm and guided her to a bench in the garden. Mary hovered beside them, her gray eyes wide.

Amy dropped her face into her hands. "I don't know what to do."

"You're frightening me." Cassandra sat beside her. "Come, we're speaking of Domin. It cannot be so terrible. What about Mr. Stewart? Have you asked him?"

Amy drew a shaky breath. "You imagine I didn't think of that? He's missing, too."

Cassandra stiffened, and her hand went to Henry's locket at her throat.

"And so is Mr. Hale." Amy shook her head and gave the elder tree in the garden a wary glance. Its clusters of almost-black berries hung low as if trying to overhear their conversation. Elder kept dark creatures away, but it attracted the Seelie Fay. "It's not safe to talk here. Take me to a rowan tree."

Amy pushed herself to her feet.

Cassandra took her arm again. "Are you injured?"

"I took the train. The iron—it hurt." Those rails, cutting her off from the earth and its magic.

Cassandra nodded her understanding, and she and Mary helped Amy hobble across the orchard to one of the many rowan trees in the hedgerow.

Amy sank into its shade and looked up with gratitude at the red berries dangling in bunches overhead. "That's better." She groaned and rubbed her eyes. The energy of the Old Woods was near, unobstructed by any iron. It flowed around her like healing waters.

Mary settled close by, moving carefully as if not certain if she was welcome and afraid she would be sent away like a naughty child trying to eavesdrop. Cassandra sat beside Mary, and the Faerie changeling gave her a grateful, almost worshipful, glance.

"Mr. Hale is missing, too?" Cassandra asked. "Along with Domin and H—Mr. Stewart?"

Amy nodded. "At least, I can't find any trace of them. Their lodgings are abandoned, and I've had no word from any of them."

"They are all very capable," Cassandra said. "Perhaps they're chasing some Faerie creature in a remote area."

Cassandra grasped Henry's locket. Amy's mind settled enough to realize that Cassandra had probably not spoken directly to Henry since he left to keep the Fay away from Cassandra and her family. Even if Henry didn't know that men could not write letters to women they weren't related or betrothed to, Cassandra's parents certainly would have. Domin must have been Henry and Cassandra's only link, and he would make a poor matchmaker.

"I hope they're merely detained," Amy said. "But there's more. There have been problems in London."

"Problems?" Cassandra urged, her weak hand tightening against her skirt.

"Murders," Amy said. She looked around and dropped her voice further. "It looks like the Grigori are killing people with Faerie blood."

Mary sucked in a sharp breath, and Cassandra's eyes widened.

"Are there many Fay in London?" Cassandra asked. "I thought, with iron being used more..."

Amy drew a deep breath laced with the scent of autumn leaves. The lingering effects of the train ride had almost cleared from her head. "Yes, iron makes parts of the city uncomfortable for pure Fay. But many areas of London are not so modern, and many humans have Faerie blood. Since the Fay usually cannot have children among themselves, they take human consorts, and those children sometimes live out their lives in the human world, having more children. It's not uncommon for humans to have traces of Faerie blood, and certain individuals— especially aristocratic ones—have more than others."

Cassandra wet her lips. "If many people have Faerie blood, might the murders be unrelated?"

"No. The victims are definitely those with more Faerie blood." Amy sighed. "And they're not normal killings. The bodies are...unusual. Drained of blood, and some are desiccated, like they've been mummified."

"Ah," Cassandra said slowly. "That explains why my father has been burning the newspapers when he's done reading them. But could the Grigori do that to a body?"

Amy rubbed her forehead. "I think they must have a supernatural ally. Though, the Fay normally do not hunt one another. Humans like the Grigori have been our most determined enemies."

Amy's skin prickled at memories of long-ago witch hunts. That was why she had joined in the Gunpowder Plot. That was why she'd betrayed Domin's trust and almost wiped out a significant portion of the Stuart line he guarded.

She picked dried grass from the hem of her skirt, trying to leave it clean again. "Whatever or whoever is helping them, they can sense Faerie blood, and they're deliberately hunting those who are not part of a court. Not the solitary Fay, who are powerful enough not to need the courts, but those beneath the notice of the Faerie Lords and Ladies—those who are most vulnerable."

Mary paled at that, and Amy didn't blame her. The Grigori threatened all those who shared Faerie blood.

Cassandra glanced between her friends. "Then Domin and...and the others are probably hunting the hunter?"

"That was what I assumed at first, but they have been gone for some time. I had hoped they might be here, or that Domin had said something."

Cassandra shook her head, her eyes dark with worry. "I

don't think Domin planned to be gone so long." Her expression brightened, and she glanced toward the Old Woods. "But I know who might be able to tell us more. At least about Domin."

"Who?" Amy asked, then her eyes widened as she realized what Cassandra meant. "Oh, I don't think it's wise to go back there. He'll be angry. The last time, I awakened his guardians."

"But Telesm is Domin's brother. He will probably know where Domin is or how to find him."

Amy shivered. Telesm was a Faerie changeling powerful enough to live as a solitary Fay, and his collection of magical artifacts made him both the envy and the fear of the Seelie and Unseelie Courts. Worse, Telesm knew what Amy had done— her past betrayal of Domin and her more recent robbery of his cache of artifacts. And having been cast out of the protection of her mother, the Lady of the Woods, Amy was at least as vulnerable in Elfland as she was in the human world.

"Have you seen Telesm since, uh, that day?" Amy asked.

Cassandra shifted and stared down at the polished handle of her rowan wood cane. "Well, no. I haven't seen him. But Domin speaks of him from time to time." She met Amy's eyes uncertainly. "And we need help, don't we?"

They needed help. Their friends needed help. There was no way around it: Cassandra was right.

Amy steeled herself and nodded. "Very well. We will return to Elfland."

Amy remembered well the way to Telesm's cottage. Last time she had traveled this path, it had been at a gallop with a fiery lion on her trail. Domin had rescued that plan from complete failure. Hopefully, her decision to come looking for Domin wouldn't also be a disaster.

They followed the stream to the cave where it flowed from Elfland. The dark cavern entrance breathed cool, damp air over them. Cassandra hesitated, nodding to herself and straightening her shoulders before guiding them through. Mary skittered after her.

Amy stared into the darkness, sensing Elfland more than seeing it ahead of her. She'd had little to fear from other Fay while under her mother's protection, but now that she was cast out, she would have to find a way to protect herself. Taking her cue from Cassandra, she stiffened her back and walked into the darkness, the stream burbling beside her.

She passed through the veil between the worlds and emerged into a thicket of hawthorns always in bloom. Cassandra and Mary waited for her, and across the stream, Telesm's lion sentinels stood guard. They were stone now, but each could transform into a different element to attack intruders.

"Ready?" Cassandra asked.

Mary shivered and gave a weak nod.

"Yes," Amy said. "Onward."

They lifted their skirts to keep them dry and splashed across the ankle-deep stream into Telesm's clearing. His cottage looked peaceful, half-smothered in the embrace of rambling roses. A breeze wafted the sweet scent over them, nearly lulling Amy into complacency. But the stone gaze of the lions roused her, and she hunched her shoulders as she passed them, half expecting them to remember her past transgressions and shimmer to life.

The ladies reached the front door of the cottage without incident. Last time, Domin had brought them inside, but Amy was fairly certain Telesm would have rescinded the invitation his brother had offered their party. She wouldn't be able to go inside without permission.

"It sounds very quiet," Cassandra whispered. "Do we knock?"

"I'm sure that will alert him we're here, even if he's not in the house." Amy glanced back at the lions, watching for any sign of movement.

Cassandra nodded and rapped her knuckles lightly on the door.

It creaked open. Cassandra jumped back, lifting her cane as if ready to swing it. Nothing moved. Across the threshold, Telesm's mess of treasure and bric-a-brac glinted in the filtered light from the windows. Just inside the door stood a statue of a young woman in armor—a statue, they had learned, that was actually a living person frozen in stone.

The ladies exchanged wary looks.

"Can we go in?" Cassandra asked.

"I think that would be unwise." Amy cleared her throat and spoke to the room. "Good afternoon? We have come seeking an audience with Telesm."

"I'm not some kind of oracle, you know," said a male voice behind them. "I don't give audiences."

They whirled to find Telesm standing behind them, a basket full of rose petals in one hand. He was dressed casually in silk robes that no doubt reflected his origins: his father was a Persian prince, he had boasted. He bore a brotherly resemblance to Domin—aside from the scar marking one side of his face—but while Domin looked serious and wise beyond his apparent years, Telesm wore a smirk.

Telesm dismissed Cassandra and Mary with a glance and focused on Amy. "Why are you disturbing me this time?"

"We're looking for Domin," Amy said, her voice pitched a little too high.

Telesm shrugged one shoulder. "You wasted a journey. He's not here."

"He's missing," Amy said. "We need to find him."

"My brother is capable of watching out for himself."

Amy pressed her lips into a thin line. "But he may be in danger."

"So?" Telesm cocked an eyebrow. "You are confusing me with my brother. He is part daemon. A natural protector. I am human and Fay. Utterly selfish."

Cassandra studied him through narrowed eyes. "Not entirely selfish." She pointed to the statue next to the door. "You care about her."

Telesm froze, his eyes wide as though Cassandra had slapped him.

Amy glanced at the statue and, as before, she sensed emotions trapped beneath the stone. She reached toward the statue and, to her surprise, the threshold did not stop her. It was as if the statue invited the contact. She gently touched the stone girl's arm—something Domin had forbidden. The stone didn't yield, but it was warm beneath her fingers. Longing and frustration flooded Amy, and tears welled in her eyes.

"She cares about you, too," Amy said. "It's like she's asleep, but dreaming."

"A dream or a nightmare?" Telesm's blasé demeanor softened for a moment, and he looked sincerely curious. But then he shook his head. "No, don't touch her. Don't invade her dreams without her permission. Sometimes it is better to let the past rest, and she has suffered enough at the hands of the Fay."

Amy reluctantly moved her hand.

"They turned her to stone?" Cassandra asked.

"Of course not. A basilisk did that."

"But you do care," Amy said. "You care about Domin as well."

"My elder brother does not need me. Now, kindly move away from my doorway."

Mary scuttled back, and Amy's shoulders sagged in defeat. There was a note of command in Telesm's words, and he could chase them away if he wished. They were out of options for finding Domin, Henry, and Jairus.

"Come," Amy whispered to Cassandra. "He will not help. We'll...we'll think of something to help our friends."

Cassandra leveled a challenging gaze at Telesm. She stuck her cane out so it blocked the door with a thud. "Can you find him?"

"I am capable of it, if that's what you're asking."

"Then I'm not leaving until you tell us where he is."

"I will have my lions eat you."

"You will not. You're not a monster," Cassandra said, though she didn't look entirely certain.

Mary shuddered and glanced at the lions.

Telesm rolled his eyes. "Then you may sit there until you starve."

Cassandra smiled and lowered herself to the ground in a rustle of skirts, blocking his doorway. Amy suppressed a laugh.

Telesm looked much less amused. "Would you—"

"You did say that I may sit here until I starve," Cassandra said. "I'm sure it will be inconvenient for you, but a Fay must keep his word."

Telesm glared, but then his expression softened, and he chuckled. "What stubborn creatures human women are! Very well, if you wish to go on the hunt for my brother, I will put you on his scent and let him deal with you. Fitting punishment for him giving away the location of my sanctuary."

Cassandra grinned. Amy offered a hand to help her up.

Telesm sized them up, then said, "The elf has permission to enter this time, but I do not extend an ongoing invitation." Amy pursed her lips, but Telesm added, "Oh, I don't fear you, though I know who you are—what you've done. I just don't want to be bothered again. If only I could keep humans and changelings away as easily." His gaze rested on Mary for a moment with faint curiosity, then he led them inside.

Chapter Four

Cassandra stepped carefully into Telesm's cottage, remembering Domin's prior injunction not to disturb anything. This was where she had learned that Henry was a human changeling. It seemed like much more than a year had passed since that time. She noticed the enchanted shield she had wielded against the hell hounds and was tempted to touch it again—to feel strong and brave—but Telesm's presence convinced her not to. Amy cast a furtive glance at the magical harp she had stolen from the cottage, then determinedly avoided looking at it.

"Now," Telesm said, rummaging through one of his piles of treasure. A set of iron gauntlets clanked to the floor. "Tell me where you last saw my brother. Scrying is a finicky art, and any direction you have will make the process faster."

He pulled out an oval wrapped in linen and whisked the cloth aside to reveal a polished silver mirror. Cassandra craned her neck to see what the mirror showed, but she caught only a flash of reflected light.

Amy's gaze fixed on the mirror, then she blinked rapidly and met Telesm's eyes. "The last I knew, Domin was in London hunting the Grigori."

Telesm's forehead wrinkled. "Hunting the what?"

"Who, not what," Amy said. "A group of occultists."

Telesm shook his head, looking bemused. "That's his business, I suppose."

"They may be murdering the Fay."

"Good for them," Telesm muttered.

Amy gasped. "You don't mean that!"

Telesm grinned wickedly and stared into the mirror. He traced his finger over it and leaned closer. Silence settled over the cottage. Telesm's grin faded, and his lips curled into a frown. A cold dread stirred in Cassandra's stomach.

"Well?" Amy asked.

Telesm shifted the mirror, catching the light from the window. Finally, he pressed his lips together and looked up. "I cannot find him."

"What does that mean?" Cassandra asked.

Telesm lowered the mirror and stared out the window. "I do not believe he is dead, though I cannot rule it out. But it troubles me. Bah! I don't wish to be involved in Faerie troubles. Why must Domin always drag me into them?"

"You are going to help us find him, then?" Amy asked.

"Of course I am. It would be novel to be the one who saved him for once, and I do not allow anyone to trifle with my family."

Cassandra's lips twitched at that. She felt much the same, though she had far less ability to do anything about it.

"Tell me about these Grigori," Telesm said.

Amy looked to Cassandra, who—unwillingly—had the most contact with them.

"Their leader is a man named Rushford," Cassandra said. "They are studying Faerie powers to see if they can replicate them for themselves. Last Michaelmas, they tried to perform a ritual to summon a creature called a Leannan."

Telesm's eyes widened, and then he laughed. "I am amazed Domin has to bother hunting them. It sounds like they will eliminate themselves in short order. Didn't one of your human mages speak of this? Natural selection?"

Cassandra chuckled. "You mean Darwin? He's a scientist, not a mage."

"I see little difference." Telesm shrugged. "Regardless, perhaps I can find this Rushford. Tell me about him."

"Well," Cassandra said. "He's very unpleasant, and he wears horrid clothing."

"That describes so many humans. I will need more. No." Telesm tilted his head and studied Cassandra. "I will let you look for him."

"Me? I'm not Fay!"

"Not much, at least—your blood is strongly human. But my scrying mirror doesn't require Faerie blood. It does require someone who can see truly, and I think you are one of them."

Cassandra hesitated. Domin had mentioned that Georgina had a gift for seeing, and that Cassandra's youngest sister, the seventh daughter of a seventh daughter, might be a seer as well. It could run in her family. But Cassandra didn't want to think she might see truly. Not after the dreams that had haunted her of late: dark nightmares of her friends and things she didn't understand that left her in a cold sweat.

Yet Henry and their other friends might be in danger.

"I'll try," Cassandra said. "Tell me how."

"Just look into the mirror and concentrate on the person you are seeking."

Cassandra nodded and peered into the mirror. It did not show her own reflection, which gave her an odd, queasy feeling. She concentrated on her memories of Rushford with his little brown mustache that hung on his lip like a shriveled worm. His desire to "repair" her and make her his project. His face shadowed as he led the other Grigori in their dark ritual.

The mirror rippled like a pond disturbed by a stone. She caught a glimpse of Rushford in the reflection. He was in the library of some grand house, perusing the shelves of leather-bound books, but she didn't know whose house or where.

"I see him, but I can't tell where he is."

"Broaden your mind, human," Telesm said. "Don't be afraid of your feelings. They lend power to magic."

Cassandra frowned. It was unladylike to give in to strong emotions, but sometimes doing the right thing meant flouting polite conventions. She reached down to where a knot of fear, anger, and disgust hid beneath her heart. Outrage that someone like Rushford was free to harm others because his money and position gave him a veneer of respectability. She gripped the edge of the mirror, tilted it from Telesm's grasp, and he released it to her. The silver was cold against her fingers. The reflection blurred then whirled like a maelstrom through different images. Her stomach lurched, but she tried to focus on what she saw.

Was that London? Yes, there was Westminster. Rushford was there, then—somewhere. Did that mean Henry was still in the city as well? Last she had pried any news from Domin, Henry had been studying medicine in London between hunting for monsters.

The dizzy spiral of images came to a sudden stop on Henry's reflection. His suit was battered, his curly brown hair, always a little wild, was thoroughly disheveled, and his face bore the sick-colored marks of half-healed bruises. Shadows lay over his image. He was somewhere dark.

Cassandra's sympathy flared, and along with it her anger at Rushford and his Grigori.

The silver mirror hummed under her fingertips, and the reflection blurred to another image of Henry. This one, Cassandra knew from her dreams. She wanted to look away, but her gaze seemed frozen to the mirror. Henry, younger than he appeared now, stood on a cliff overlooking a seaside village. Storm clouds simmered on the horizon. He gestured for the storm, his face impassive. Wind and water responded to his call, bringing a huge funnel of water dancing up from the sea. Fishermen in the harbor scattered as the waterspout approached, their boats tossed and battered against the docks. Then the deadly funnel rushed into the village. Henry watched, no emotion on his face, as wind and water crashed into homes—

Cassandra gasped. The mirror slipped from her weak hand.

Telesm swore and caught it before it hit the floor.

"What did you see?" Amy asked.

Cassandra's pulse hammered in her throat. She blinked several times, trying to bring herself back into the here-and-now. She wrapped her fingers around Henry's locket, still warm from resting against her skin.

"I think Rushford is in London," she managed. "And... and I saw Mr. Stewart. He did not look well. Looked as though he had been beaten."

"Was Domin with him?" Amy asked. "Or Mr. Hale?"

"I didn't see them," Cassandra said. "I couldn't tell much, though. It was dark."

"Tell me more of these Grigori," Telesm said. "What are their abilities?"

"They are deep in the dark arts," Amy said. "They were allied with the Dark Lady. We don't know what they are capable of."

"They could not capture Domin," Telesm said, though he didn't sound certain.

"I would like to think not," Cassandra said. "But I wouldn't bet anyone's life on it."

Telesm glared at Cassandra, then he rolled his eyes and turned away. "Very well. I will come to London with you."

Cassandra gave a start and looked to Amy and Mary. "I don't know... We didn't necessarily mean—"

"It doesn't matter what you meant." Telesm selected a satchel and looked thoughtfully around his collection. "And what you don't know could fill volumes, I'm sure. That's why you need me. If Domin is well, I have words for him about how he trains his human pets. And if he's not well, then I'm not leaving his rescue up to you."

Cassandra flushed at that, but she couldn't argue. If Henry, Domin, and Jairus were in trouble, they would need all the help they could muster.

"Yes, that's settled." Telesm snapped open the satchel and dropped in a knife that appeared to have a large ruby on the hilt. He frowned at the chaos of his cottage. "Do any of you have anything personal of Domin's?"

"The men left some of their things behind in their London lodgings," Amy said.

Telesm considered that. "It would need to be something with a sympathetic connection to him. It would help me trace him."

Amy looked skeptical. "Domin is not very materialistic."

"Wait!" Cassandra grasped Henry's locket, her cheeks

burning. "I have this. It's Mr. Stewart's. He asked me to keep it for him."

"And Mr. Stewart is Domin's current charge?" Telesm asked. "Ah, and that trinket is silver. Yes, that will do nicely. Bring it along."

Cassandra sighed. "I just hope it won't be difficult to convince my parents to let me travel to London."

Cassandra disliked the idea of Amy using magic on her parents, but she also couldn't be left behind. Mary had gone to pack a bandbox—apparently still angry enough at her father for keeping her true nature hidden that she wasn't concerned with his permission. Telesm had ordered them to meet in the orchard in the morning.

On the walk back to her house, Cassandra eyed the yellows and browns creeping over the leaves in the Old Woods. Michaelmas had passed without incident, but All Hallow's Eve would be upon them soon—one of the days when the veil between worlds was thinnest. When magic would be strongest. When her family—and her friends—were in the most danger. How was she supposed to protect them all? Dried leaves crunched under her boots, and she recalled the bone fragments littering the ground of the Unseelie Kingdom. Her steps slowed.

"Cassandra?" Amy asked.

"I'm... I'm worried about my family," she said.

"I can't influence your parents to do anything against their nature," Amy reminded her gently.

"I know," Cassandra said.

But when it came to Cassandra's social opportunities, her

parents were unpredictable. They could be glad to send Cassandra off to London to increase her chances of finding a suitor willing to overlook her physical limitations. On the other hand, they might worry that Cassandra would embarrass the family with her clumsiness or rambling tongue.

In the garden, they ran across Cassandra's old nurse, Nancy, who had brought little one-year-old Anne out in her pram for some fresh air. Nancy stiffened and watched Amy warily. Thanks to a Faerie ointment placed on her eyes, she could see the Fay for what they were, and she knew the Unseelie Queen had tried to kidnap baby Anne the previous year. Nancy pulled the pram away from Amy, closer to the elder tree. Amy looked down at the gravel path, pink warming her cheeks.

But little Anne smiled at Amy and reached out her chubby hands. Amy grinned and waved her fingers at the child, who giggled with the unabashed joy of young children. Cassandra smiled, too. Nancy had reason to fear the Fay, but Anne helped Cassandra remember that not all Fay were the same, and their magic was not always bad.

Cassandra stepped through the back door of her house without renewing her invitation for Amy to enter—she had never rescinded her previous one, and she wanted her friend to know it. The voices and laughter of her young sisters drifted from upstairs, but she and Amy found Cassandra's parents and her more mature sisters, Sophie and Georgina, in the drawing room.

"Lady St. Clair," Cassandra said, using the title Amy had gained from a short and unwanted marriage to a human lord arranged by her scheming mother, Titania. "You remember my parents, Mr. and Mrs. Weaver. And my sisters, Sophie and Georgina."

Cassandra's mother stared with admiration, and her father

puffed out his chest and straightened his waistcoat. Cassandra's worries eased. They would not take much convincing.

Sophie, who had been sitting on the sofa doing embroidery, looked torn between jealousy and a desire to ingratiate herself. Only Georgina, who had to lip-read the conversation, seemed unmoved. She looked up from her sketch pad and studied Amy like she might wish to include her in a painting later.

"How do you do?" Amy said, turning on her most charming smile. "I have missed Cassandra's company since I was here last year visiting the Ashby's. We have been corresponding, you know. But now, I insist on her company. I must take her to be my guest in London."

Cassandra watched her parents carefully. They had to allow her to go, but she didn't want to see their eyes glaze and lose focus as everyone had when the village was enchanted.

Her parents exchanged glances. Cassandra couldn't actually sense Faerie magic—not usually—but she imaged she felt the nudge Amy sent her parents.

"Very well," her father said. "Lady St. Clair, we're happy to trust our Cassie to your chaperonage."

"I assume you will be attending parties?" her mother said too eagerly.

"It's not the Season, but I'm sure we'll enjoy some social occasions," Amy said.

The careful wording wasn't lost on Cassandra—the Fay couldn't lie—but her parents seemed pleased. If only they knew that Amy's chaperonage would likely involve traipsing about with men in very unladylike places.

Her parents offered Amy a guest room for the night— which meant that some of Cassandra's sisters would be doubling up to make space for Amy—and soon Cassandra was alone with the sound of Georgina's sketching and the almost-physical force of Sophie's jealous pout.

"I'm sorry you're not coming to London this time," Cassandra said, sitting beside her older sister. She meant it sincerely. Sophie longed for a London Season, but this visit to London would not be what Sophie wished for.

Sophie cut her a sideways glance. "It doesn't seem that you tried very hard to include me."

"I can hardly ask Amy to invite you," Cassandra said gently.

"Oh, it's Amy now?" Sophie snapped. "Well, I hope you and *Amy* enjoy all your London flirtations while I rot away here without a single eligible gentleman." Sophie's gaze fell. "I'm beginning to think Robert Ashby is never returning."

No, they had not seen anything of the Ashbys since Sir Walter Ashby had fallen to the Dark Lady's blade. Robert had witnesses his father's death and knew more of the dark world of the Fay than Sophie could even guess at.

Georgina cut in. "Maybe if Cassie's visit is successful, Papa will let us go next Season. I would love to study with a London art master."

Sophie hmphed but looked speculative at that idea. Little would they understand that Cassandra's idea of a successful visit to London was much different from their own.

Chapter Five

The Grigori were clever, Henry had to give them credit for that. An iron-framed mill made a good place for them to hide from the Fay. Unluckily for the Grigori, it didn't keep all of their enemies at bay. Henry smiled grimly, though the still-healing bruises on his face made the action stiff and painful. They'd confronted the Grigori in London and had a brawl, but the men had escaped, and Henry and his companions had been too late to save the woman the Grigori had dumped into the Thames. She had been long past saving. Henry grimaced. No, he and the Grigori weren't finished yet.

He shifted positions, leaning against the iron frame of the empty cotton mill to peer down at the space below. From their perch, they had the perfect position to ambush the Grigori. The only disadvantage was that Henry couldn't use his magic with the iron around. It felt odd and fuzzy to be cut off from the energy of the land. Domin had shifted into a panther and laid low in the brick window frame, not able to touch the iron without pain.

Jairus, however, seemed almost cheerful about their perch. The American tossed a silver bullet from hand to hand and whistled a battle tune. The sound echoed through the empty building.

"Maybe a little more stealth is in order?" Henry said. "We don't know when the Grigori will return."

Jairus caught the bullet and grinned. "Well, we beat them here." He tapped the side of his head. "God tells me things are turning our way."

Henry grunted, never sure if Jairus was inspired or crazy, and not wanting to argue when the Grigori might be close. Rushford and his men always seemed to be a step ahead, and Henry didn't dare hope that they had finally gained an advantage. It had only been Domin's tracking skills that led them to the mill. A Grigori workshop, based on the glass tubes, thermometers, barometers, and racks of chemicals below. There was no trace of death on the grounds, so this was not where the Grigori were killing those with Faerie blood. But this was the only lead Henry had so far.

Domin growled a warning that someone was approaching. He flattened himself against the window, nothing more than a shadow. Jairus drew his pistol, and Henry pressed against the iron beam.

The door below banged opened like a shot fired, and a group of men shuffled inside. They carried lanterns against the afternoon gloom and wore well-tailored suits at odds with the bundle they struggled to maneuver. Henry's chest tightened. Was it a body? Had they missed another murder?

"I hope she likes this one," one of the men said, his voice polished by London's drawing rooms. "He doesn't have much fight in him."

"She's hungry," another replied. "She'll be glad for what she can get."

The pit in Henry's stomach deepened. He didn't know who "she" was, but the Grigori were not above dealing with dark creatures—or sacrificing people to them. Hopefully, that meant the person the Grigori carried was still alive and could be saved. He went to move, to jump down and fight, but a hand held him back: Domin in human form again.

"We must discover whom they're serving," Domin breathed.

Henry frowned but nodded once. This was more than they'd learned in the last year about the Grigori, and they needed to find out all they could. But not at the cost of another life. Henry drew the line there.

The men set their burden on one of the tables. Henry strained to see. It was definitely a person, apparently bound and gagged. Not a large person. The Grigori's victims were generally young. Children from the worst parts of London. Perhaps cast-off, illegitimate Faerie children. Those whose deaths wouldn't rouse the police or Parliament to action. Murders that shocked and titillated the newspaper subscribers but didn't threaten them.

"Time to find out what we can learn from him."

That was Rushford. Henry bristled. He would never forget that voice. A warning hand rested on his shoulder, but he shrugged it off.

Below, illuminated by the lanterns like actors on a stage, the Grigori gathered around the victim. Rushford drew a vial of blood from the young man, who didn't make a noise in protest. Was he unconscious? Henry couldn't tell. Rushford poured the blood into vials and mixed the samples with chemicals. The men watched in anxious silence—a scene Henry knew too well from having lived it the year before.

"Interesting!" Rushford's voice echoed in the empty mill. "This one has high levels of magic in his blood."

"Is he one of them?" a man with a nasal voice asked nervously. "They might come looking for him."

"I don't think so." Rushford turned back to stare at the young man. "He demonstrated no magical abilities, and he seems undefended. At any rate, our friend might extract useful information from him when she feeds."

Henry shook his head. Rushford was not going to win this one. Whomever they were feeding, Rushford could be her next meal. It wouldn't be that lad down there.

Henry glanced over his shoulder and saw the same sentiment echoed in Jairus and Domin's expressions.

"When they get outside," Henry whispered. He couldn't use his abilities inside the iron-framed mill.

The wait ground against Henry, making him wish he could pace or do...something. Anything. He settled for tapping his fingers against the scar on his shoulder where the Grigori had burned him with a cigar. He hadn't broken then, and he wouldn't let them break anyone else now.

The sun set while the Grigori took more measurements and talked about blood and magical reactions. They prodded the boy, trying to get a reaction from him, and Henry dug his fingers into his scarred shoulder.

"We could untie him," one of the men suggested. "See what he's capable of."

"So he can demonstrate his talents on us?" Rushford asked. "No, he stays bound until we have him caged."

Finally, they hauled the boy up and headed back into the gathering dark.

"Go!" Henry whispered.

He and Jairus snuck down the stairs and out the front door. Jairus had his pistols ready, and Henry called on the wind as soon as he was outside of the building. It blew cold and fierce with the scent of ice, and thunder rumbled in the clouds. The Grigori glanced at the sky and hurried toward a waiting carriage.

Jairus's first shot took one man through the leg. The other Grigori spun to face them, holding the boy in front of them as a shield. Cowards. The lad's eyes were wide, but a gag silenced him. Rushford grabbed a shotgun from the carriage.

Jairus shot again, aiming low enough to avoid hitting the boy, but that only forced the Grigori to back closer to their carriage. Henry lashed the Grigori from behind with hail. The men flinched, protecting their heads, and the horses whinnied and thrashed in terror, making the carriage rock dangerously. Rushford stepped forward and raised the shotgun.

A crash above drew everyone's attention. Domin leaped from the window in panther form, claws extended for Rushford. Rushford fired his shotgun. Domin crumpled to the ground like a torn rag, a hole through his abdomen. Henry shouted and ran forward.

"Two shots!" Jairus warned.

Before Henry understood his meaning, Rushford pulled the second trigger.

Shot sliced into Henry's left side and arm. He hissed, the pain stunning him to a stop. The energy around him turned fuzzy, hard to grasp. Wind blasted over them, out of control.

Rushford had hit him with iron shot. Henry couldn't use magic, and Domin was trapped in his panther shape, unable to heal. The Grigori must have picked up the trick from Jairus.

Jairus fired at Rushford, but his shot went wide.

"Go!" Rushford ordered his men, dashing for the carriage.

They grabbed their injured companion and fled.

Jairus fired again, splintering the top of the carriage and spooking the horses. He glanced over his shoulder, obviously torn between chasing the Grigori and helping his companions.

"Get the boy!" Henry shouted, trying to ignore the pain searing his side, the disorientation of the iron lodged in his flesh, as he made his way to Domin's fallen form.

One of the Grigori turned to fire from the door of the carriage. Jairus threw himself to the ground and fired back, but the Grigori's carriage rumbled away.

Jairus swore eloquently and ran over to Henry and Domin.

"Iron?" he asked.

Henry nodded.

Jairus swore again. "What should I do?"

"We have to pick the iron out." Henry flexed his hand, which tingled with pain from his injury.

Domin would be difficult to kill, even with iron, but blood flowed from the gaping wound in his black fur, and he couldn't heal himself.

Henry unsheathed the knife he always kept sharp and knelt by Domin. Jairus drew his own blade, and they dug pieces of iron from skin and flesh. Henry's hands grew sticky with blood, and he was desperately aware of the carriage rolling farther away with each moment.

"Is that all of it?" Jairus asked. "I don't see any more."

"If it was, he would heal himself."

Jairus rose to his feet and backed up, giving Henry space. Henry looked over the gaping wound. It would be fatal on a mortal, and Henry didn't know the limits of Domin's supernatural strength, especially if he cut any deeper. Domin's ribs still rose and fell, but his green eyes were glassy. He'd never heal in this condition. Henry had to hope that the daemon magic binding Domin's life to Henry's bloodline was strong enough to endure a little more. He took a deep breath.

"I'm sorry."

He cut into Domin's rib cage. Domin jerked, and his breathing stopped. Henry forced his hands steady, working fast. As soon as the iron was out, Domin could heal. Henry plucked a piece of iron from deep in his friend's flesh.

Domin lay deathly still for a long moment, then he groaned. His form shivered, first into a whole panther and then into his human form.

Henry sagged in relief and looked up to send Jairus after the Grigori, but the American had already vanished.

"Thank you," Domin said, pushing himself up.

Henry wiped his hands clean, then clenched his fists to stop them from shaking. "I'm not certain you should thank me for that torment."

"Better that than having a permanent window for my liver." Domin's eyes narrowed. "They hit you, too."

Henry touched his side, which oozed blood. "The shot only grazed me, but it did leave a few pieces of iron behind. That's a nasty trick Rushford learned."

"Indeed."

Jairus jogged out of the mill, a sheaf of papers tucked under his arm. He smiled at Domin. "Good to see you breathing. I ain't a veterinarian, so I went with my strengths and conducted a little raid."

A boom from the mill vibrated in Henry's chest and shattered the glass in the lower windows. An orange glow shone from the empty frames.

"Did you set it on fire?" Henry asked.

"After last time, I thought that was our tactic," Jairus said with his best mock-innocent grin. He waved the papers he'd taken from the building. "They ain't coming back here anyway, but don't worry, I took these. Maybe they'll tell us what the Grigori are planning."

Domin nodded. "Good thinking."

"Let's go after them," Henry said. "We might still be able to save that boy."

"What about you?" Domin asked.

Henry shook his head. If they cut into him, he wouldn't heal so quickly. He would do without magic. "It's not a dangerous injury, and we need to catch that carriage."

Chapter Six

Henry leaned his head against the cool window of the third-class train compartment. They'd had no chance of cutting off Rushford's hired carriage, but at least they'd been able to catch the same train as the Grigori, taking a compartment farther to the back to avoid being seen. The compartment could have seated six, but they had it to themselves. Probably anyone glancing in had decided not to sit with the three men who looked like they'd come out of the wrong side of a boxing match —or rather two men, since Domin appeared uninjured.

Henry's side throbbed where the iron shot had struck him, and being cut off from magic made him feel off balance. Fuzzy around the edges. A reminder of how far he was from being human.

Domin's expression was impassive, but his stiffer-than-usual posture showed that sitting in the train, whisking along on iron tracks in an iron-reinforced wooden box, was uncomfortable for him as well. Jairus's face was as bruised as Henry's, but he wore a huge grin. The outrageous American was actually enjoying this. Henry shook his head. If he was being honest, it did give Henry a thrill to think they might stop the Grigori this time. They just had to rescue the boy before the Grigori killed him.

Jairus flipped through the papers he had taken, and his expression turned serious. "Hmm."

Henry stirred from his thoughts and turned away from the moonlit countryside flying by outside. "What did you find?"

"Ramblings, mostly. But there are several references to a dark muse. Any idea what that might be?"

"Bad poetry," Domin mumbled.

Jairus guffawed. "Is that a joke? Did Stewart find your sense of humor when he pulled that iron out?"

Domin's mouth quirked in a smile. "Rushford is given to dramatics, and the Grigori are trying to find a 'dark muse' to teach them magic. Any number of creatures might fit that role, but perhaps that is the 'she' they intend to sacrifice the boy to."

"We won't let them, of course," Henry said. "Do we rescue the boy at the next stop?"

Jairus shook his head. "That gives them too many options. We strike while they're trapped on the train."

"They'll be expecting us," Domin said.

"At the stop, maybe, but not on the train." Jairus glanced up at the communication cord that ran through each compartment, allowing the occupants to signal to the guards if there was trouble. "We cut that cord, get the advantage through surprise. Domin, you grab the kid and jump. Stewart and I will follow."

Henry laughed, though it made his side twinge in pain. "Jump from a moving train? Domin will survive it, but not us."

Jairus smiled. "We wait for a hill or a curve so the train has to slow. It's too bad we ain't got horses, but otherwise, it's like a good old train robbery."

"Train robbery! What an American idea." Henry shook his head at being the sensible one. That was a new role for him. "You're going to get us transported."

"I'm sure there are monsters to fight in Australia, too," Jairus said cheerfully.

Henry wasn't leaving England, though. He didn't think his magic would work in a place where he didn't have a tie to the land—cutting himself off from that magic might even kill him. He still owed a debt to its people for his failure to stand up to Titania for so long. And she would never let him go so far away. He might be free to fight the Grigori and rescue children and stage train robberies, but his life was not his own.

Then there was Cassandra. He wouldn't leave her, either, though he saw no opportunity to offer her anything that she deserved.

He blinked away memories of her bright eyes and warm smile. He didn't like Jairus's plan, but he didn't have a better one.

"I assume you expect us to go along the roof," Henry said. "There will be a guard on each end of the train."

"We move slow, stay low," Jairus said with an unconcerned shrug.

Henry ran his fingers through his disheveled hair. "I suppose it's the best we have. We want to strike before they're ready for us."

Domin nodded grudging agreement.

Climbing out of the carriage was not as easy as Henry had expected. Domin, of course, had no trouble, but Henry and Jairus struggled to get footholds on the exterior of the carriage. Henry was careful not to look down at the tracks flying past beneath him. He kept his focus on the wooden train carriage and the rolling green fields in the distance.

"Almost as though they don't want people climbing them," Jairus puffed.

Once Domin helped haul them up, it was not as difficult to sneak across the tops. Moving slowly and quietly so as not to alert the other passengers, and staying low so the guards near the front of the train didn't see them, they crept across the rooftops. The winds whipped by, and Jairus kept his head tucked, but Henry did not fear the wind. It sang of freedom. Its rush slackened as they approached a hill, and he missed its bracing effect.

"This is it," Domin whispered.

"We go in on each side," Jairus said. "Domin grabs the kid and leaps out while Stewart and I keep the men busy. Once you're away, Domin, we'll jump off, too."

Domin nodded. Jairus cut the communication cord for the car with a knife and pulled his pistol.

They braced themselves on either side of the compartment. The train jolted and slowed as the tracks climbed the hill.

Domin swung down, kicked open the door, and landed smoothly in the compartment. Henry followed directly behind him. He landed in the doorway, bracing himself against the shattered frame. The ground rolled on beneath him—slower than before, but still dizzying. Six Grigori crowded into the compartment with the boy, whose hands were tied and mouth gagged. The Grigori shouted and sprang to their feet, blocking their prisoner. One yanked the communication cord, which came loose in his hand.

Jairus burst through the other side, his pistol leveled at Rushford and a wicked grin on his face. Rushford grabbed the boy and held him as a shield. Henry threw a punch at the nearest Grigori, while Domin shoved another Grigori aside and grabbed Rushford by the hair to yank his head back.

A caw broke through the shouting, and a crow dove through the carriage behind Jairus. Jairus ducked, but the crow went straight for Rushford.

Domin used the distraction to grab the prisoner and leap from the compartment.

"Stop him!" Rushford called.

Henry stepped in their way. He tried to summon ice, but the iron shot in his arm interfered. Instead, he settled for punching one of the men as Jairus hammered another back against the wooden seats.

The men fell into a tangled mess.

"Go!" Jairus shouted.

Henry turned and jumped from the train, curling up so he rolled when he hit the ground. He looked back to see one of the men framed in the light of the carriage.

A flock of crows streamed overhead.

Henry scrambled to his feet, holding a bruised elbow. The crows flew at the men in the carriage, who fell back and slammed the door on them. Then, the crows circled back to Henry. He braced himself. These were not ordinary crows. The Morrigan or one of her banshees was near.

The crows drew close, and Henry didn't have his usual magic to fight them.

An arrow blasted through the crows. The flock cried out with a single pained voice, and the birds whirled higher into the night.

Henry turned to see where the arrow had come from. Domin and Jairus didn't have bows. A group of figures moved in the moonlight, three of them women. More of the Fay? But one of them walked with a limp.

He stepped closer, and his heartbeat picked up before he consciously understood who he was seeing.

"Cassandra," he whispered to himself, enjoying the sweet taste of her name.

Then, cold rushed over him. He didn't understand how she could be there, but the crows still flapped overhead, their cries echoing death.

Chapter Seven

Amy grabbed Cassandra's arm to keep her from rushing to Henry. It would make a touching reunion, but the crows circling in the moonlight were either a banshee or the Morrigan.

Cassandra saw the threat, and her dreamy gaze hardened. She raised her crossbow. Amy wished she had something to fight with as well. For the moment, she stepped back to allow Cassandra and Mary to take aim. She had helped bring her friends together, but she was no use in this fight.

Cassandra fired through the crows. Mary fumbled her crossbow, and the bolt fell into the long grass.

Jairus stepped up next to Henry, his sawed-off shotgun in hand. Henry wielded only an iron knife. Amy wondered why he didn't call magic to his aid.

The crows whirled together into a cyclone of feathers. A piercing shriek rang through the air. Everyone covered their ears, but it did no good. The wail was more than a sound—it sunk deep within Amy, stirring up a grief so heavy it threatened to drag her down into a hopeless night with no dawn.

A snarl broke through her frozen despair. Domin. He charged in panther form and leaped through the circling crows. They scattered, breaking apart the banshee's cry.

The black birds whirled higher and melted into the form of an old woman with an ash-gray cloak that spread around her like tattered wings. Her hood hung low over her face, so Amy could not see her eyes.

"You are marked for death," the banshee's call echoed in the night.

It pierced Amy, making her heart tremble. Did the banshee mean her? Fay were not easy to kill, but they were not immortal.

"Not today," Jairus drawled.

He raised his gun and fired.

The Faerie woman dissolved into shrieking crows. They plummeted for Jairus, but Cassandra fired her crossbow, shattering the birds' formation. Jairus raised his gun and pulled the second trigger, and the remaining birds dissolved into a mist that settled to the ground. Amy shuddered when the chill passed over her, then she shifted her feet as though she could avoid touching the ground where the mist had dissipated.

Henry jogged over to the women, his gait uneven as though he were in pain, but his eyes fixed on Cassandra. "Excellent timing." He held her gaze for a moment, then, with visible effort, took in Mary and Amy. "What brought all of you here?"

"Domin disappeared," Amy said. "And so did you and Mr. Hale. Even when we tried to scry for you…"

"How did you manage that?" Henry asked.

"With my help, of course," Telesm said, walking up from the shadows behind them.

"You got *him* involved?" Henry asked, looking impressed.

"*He* is right here," Telesm said, "and he wants to know what happened to his brother."

Henry's forehead furrowed. "After he attacked the banshee, he must have gone back after the prisoner we rescued from the Grigori."

"What are the Grigori doing?" Cassandra asked. "Amy told me that they're killing people with Faerie blood, but why?"

Henry shook his head. "We still don't know."

"It's more than just killing them, though," Jairus said behind him. He tipped his hat. "Ladies," he added with a nod. "The papers have the stories all wrong, but there are some things they're not far off about. The bodies aren't normal. They remind me of the hell hounds we hunted after they were dead. Like mummies."

"Some kind of ritual, then?" Cassandra asked quietly, gripping the hand the Grigori had scarred.

"I'm afraid that's likely," Henry said. "What we don't know is what they're trying to accomplish."

Amy shuddered. It was bad enough that they were murdering people, but if the deaths were part of a ritual, they could be leading to something far worse.

Domin still hadn't rejoined them. Amy scanned the dark fields, spotting his form in the distance. She walked toward him, and the others followed her lead.

They found Domin sitting across from a boy who looked about sixteen—the Grigori's victim, Amy assumed. The young man had light brown skin and black hair that sprung from his head in loose curls like a messy crown. He glared sulkily at Domin.

"He doesn't wish to come with us," Domin explained, taking in the ladies and his brother without even a blink of surprise.

"Then leave him," Telesm suggested. "It seems to me we've all had enough trouble over this changeling."

"Changeling?" Henry asked. "What makes you think he's a changeling?"

Telesm rolled his eyes. "The fact that he's still glittering with magic, to start."

"Unseelie magic," Amy whispered, her eyes wide with sympathy. The magic created by suffering hung heavy around the young man. Not the innate power of Faerie changelings like Telesm and Mary Leland, but the binding cords of power that marked a human changeling. Like Henry.

Domin nodded. "I don't think he's been away from Elfland long, but he won't tell me anything about himself."

Amy sighed. "You're probably being too cross with him."

She knelt near the young man, arranging her skirts so she didn't crush them against the dewy grass.

The young man looked at her but did not seem phased by her beauty. A sure sign that he had spent too much time among the Fay and was used to their otherworldly appearances. He looked instead to Henry and Cassandra.

"You should let me go," he said, his voice smooth and silvery. "You don't want anything to do with me. You should forget you ever rescued me."

Amy frowned at the boy. What a strange thing to say.

"We could let him go," Cassandra said. Then she tilted her head and her forehead wrinkled as if confused at her own words.

Telesm laughed. "Oh, they gave him a silver tongue! Poor lad, you're standing before the worst crowd outside of Elfland for your skills."

Amy assessed the young man again. The Fay's magic gave human changelings abilities that corresponded with their natural talents. Henry's royal blood created a connection with the land that let him use its powers. This young man must have been a gifted speaker, and the Fay had given him the ability to manipulate with his words. Not manipulate the Fay, of course —but humans.

The young man grunted and hunkered down. "You really don't want anything to do with me."

"We'll decide that," Jairus said.

Amy smiled at the boy. "My name is Amy. I'm the daughter of the Lady of the Woods, but she has banished me from her realm, so I live in this world now."

The boy studied her, his dark eyes sharp in the moonlight. "Can you lie, then?" he asked. His voice had the faintest trace of a French accent. He pointed at Domin. "He changed appearances. I don't trust him."

Amy smiled. "I'm still Seelie, so I cannot lie. Nor do I wish to at the moment. I don't want to be like the other Fay. My friends here don't want to hurt you. Henry is a human changeling. Like you."

The young man's eyes brightened for a moment, and he turned to Henry. "Are you free from the Fay, then? Is it possible?"

Henry glanced at Domin and then at Cassandra. "I have negotiated a sort of freedom from the Fay, but it has been so long since they took me from the human world that I need their magic to stay alive."

The young man's expression fell back into gloom. "I think it has been a long time since I was taken, too. I don't remember much, but it seems very different. There was a guillotine."

"The French Revolution," Amy said, her heart sinking. "Yes, that was some decades ago." Too long for him to return to the human world except perhaps as a very elderly man. It was

surprising he remembered anything of his life before Elfland—
the Fay usually took infants too young to recall their human
families. They had wanted this young man for something in
particular to make an exception.

"Then my maman is dead," he said flatly.

"She was human?" Amy asked.

"Of course." He glared as though the idea of being anything
else was offensive.

"Then I'm afraid she must be gone. Yet you did manage to
escape the Fay," Amy added. "That's impressive."

He shook his head. "I didn't escape. The...the terrible lady
cast me out. She meant for me to die. I have some Faerie blood,
you see, but not enough to have my own magic."

"Yet she didn't pull away your magic, so you are still alive,"
Amy said, torn between optimism and confusion.

"You don't understand," he said, his voice low. "She wanted
those men to hunt and capture me."

Jairus swore under his breath.

"Monsters!" Cassandra gasped.

"You mean she's sending them changelings as prey?" Amy
said.

"I was the only one. I think it was supposed to be a trap."
He looked like he wanted to say more, but instead took them all
in in a sweeping, slightly confused glance. "She will be angry
that you interfered. Why did you bother?"

"We're not going to let the Grigori kill you," Jairus said.

The boy shrugged and stared off into the darkness as if he
had already accepted his fate. Amy wanted to shake him, tell
him not to give up, but he wasn't going to trust the advice of
a Fay.

"We're going to keep you safe from her," Henry said,

ignoring a warning look from Domin. "And we're going to find out what her plan was."

The boy shook his head. "Who are you? All of you?"

"Monster hunters," Jairus said with a grin.

Amy brightened. "In fact, Miss Weaver here injured the Dark Lady last fall."

Cassandra's eyes widened, and Amy winced, realizing too late it might be unwise to alert anyone with Unseelie connections to Cassandra's whereabouts.

But the boy gawked at Cassandra. "*She* is the Iron Lady?"

Cassandra looked astonished and embarrassed, but Henry smiled at her. "I think Iron Lady a fitting title for Miss Weaver. Do the Fay fear her?"

"My...the Dark Lady wants to kill her. But the changelings whisper about her—about all of the outcasts. You. We have wondered if the stories were true. If there was hope."

The moonlight betrayed Cassandra's bright red cheeks.

Amy stood and extended a hand. "There is hope. Come with us and see."

The boy looked at her hand like she had offered a dead fish. He stood on his own, keeping a wary distance.

"What is your name?" Henry asked the boy.

"Lucien," the boy said sullenly.

Amy realized she would need to find room in her house for all these guests. They had to stay together to stay safe. She might have to use the attic, but she would rather avoid all the unpleasant memories stored there—relics from past decades she wished she could forget as easily as she locked away the old fashions and furniture.

And watching Lucien, she wondered what new problems she was bringing into her home. She'd been among the Fay long enough to recognize deception, and this changeling was hiding something.

Chapter Eight

Mary had never seen a home as fine as Amy's London townhouse. The Grigori's manor house had been imposing but not exactly comfortable—and then she'd helped burn it down. But even under the cover of night, Mary could tell Amy's London house was immaculate. It stood on a neat square in Mayfair, its light stone face and columns rising several stories through the foggy night like an enchanted castle. A sunken basement lightwell separated the house from the street like a moat, and Mary shrank away from the sharp points of the wrought iron fence as she scurried up the stairs after the others.

"I had gas lighting installed," Amy announced once they were in the high-ceilinged foyer, and she lit the fixtures.

Mary blinked at the brightness of the lights, which revealed fine wool carpets, oil paintings, richly colored window hangings, and a statue that might have actually come from ancient Greece. All this finery was no doubt meant to show off Amy's position and make her guests feel important by extension, but Mary felt small and lost.

The others showed no such qualms. Telesm scrutinized the statue. Jairus wandered into the sitting room off the foyer and flopped down in a chair to talk with Domin. Henry drew Cassandra aside, and they whispered together, no thoughts for anyone else. Only Lucien looked uncomfortable, hunching his shoulders and slouching into a corner.

Amy watched him with a frown, then sighed and turned to Mary. "I'll have to find rooms for everyone. You don't mind sharing with Cassandra, I hope?"

"That's fine," Mary whispered, not wanting her words to ring off the high walls.

"I keep my servants to a minimum," Amy said. "I don't like to keep people enchanted, and I don't want word to get out about any oddities they might notice. Some brownies used to help, but since my mother banished me... Well, at the moment, there's just an old woman who doubles as a cook and a maid-of-all-work. I normally have a lady's maid who could help you undress, but I sent her to visit her sister while I was gone. Can you manage for yourself?"

Mary looked down at her plain dress and almost laughed. "Yes."

Amy rubbed her forehead. "Do you suppose Telesm will agree to room with Domin? And what am I supposed to do with Lucien? I don't want to leave him unattended. Henry might be a good companion for him—they're both human changelings."

Mary had no answers for Amy. The excitement of the last several days—tracking the men through the countryside and facing the banshee—had worn her thin, and Amy's problems weren't the types of things Mary could repair.

Amy led her up a wide staircase softened with a carpet runner and opened a heavy oak door. "This will be your room.

It hasn't been aired, I'm afraid, so I hope the sheets aren't musty."

Raised voices echoed from downstairs. Telesm was arguing with someone.

"Oh, good heavens," Amy said, rushing to light a candle for Mary. "I'm sorry to leave you to settle in alone."

She hurried off, freeing Mary to wander around the room, gawking at everything. The closet was bigger than Mary's bedroom at home. The beds were as soft as the fluffy coat of a lamb, and the sheets smelled of fresh rose petals. Despite the lingering worry that she would leave clock grease or sawdust on the finery, Mary curled up in the smaller bed and quickly fell asleep.

She woke with a start to the sound of someone in the room. Her first thought was of Faerie enemies, but she peeked out from under the blankets to see the pale light of dawn. A gray-haired woman knelt by the hearth to light the fire. Starting the fire was Mary's chore at home. Only when she was very ill had she enjoyed the luxury of watching someone else do it. When the maid looked up, Mary pretended to be asleep, not wanting the woman to know that she had disturbed Mary's slumber.

Once the door clicked behind the maid, Mary shucked off the blankets and dressed. Cassandra slept soundly in the other bed, but Mary wasn't accustomed to sleeping in. She crept downstairs to see more of the house.

Mary gaped anew at each room—all full of light and gilding. There was even a ballroom. Mary shuddered at the thought of attending a ball. She loved music, but who would dance with her? Jairus Hale, no doubt, but only to be kind. Mary hurried away. Amy had a garden behind her house, too. Not just a dirty alleyway like Mary's father, but a real garden with roses, a small gazebo, and a hawthorn tree, now laden with little red berries.

Mary slipped outside, then stopped short to see Lucien there. He sat on a bench, staring at the hawthorn tree with a troubled expression. Mary regarded him with suspicion. She thought he knew things that he wasn't telling. She considered sneaking back inside, but he looked over and saw her. His face immediately became guarded, but he nodded at her.

She'd had enough people turn their backs on her that she couldn't do it to someone else. She slowly walked over and sat on the other end of the bench. The cold of the stone quickly seeped through her dress. Lucien wore a blanket around his shoulders, and his dark curls stuck out in every direction as if he had just woken up.

"Did you sleep out here?" she asked.

He nodded curtly and pulled the blanket tighter. "There's no place for me in there."

"Amy would have found you a room." Mary bit her lip. "That's not what you meant."

He gave her a snide look. Mary studied his profile. There was something vaguely familiar in his face, but even more, something about him *felt* familiar, as though he wore a cologne that she knew.

"I don't feel like I belong, either," Mary admitted, "but they helped me, and they will keep you safe, too."

"They can barely keep themselves safe, from what I've seen. No one can stand up to *Her*."

The Dark Lady. Mary shivered. "She frightens me, too."

"You should be afraid—more afraid than you are. You're lucky you've been living in this world. You had a taste of peace. I hope you enjoyed it, because it won't last. She'll extend her hold over everyone."

"Do you know her plans?"

He laughed bitterly. "Does anyone? I certainly don't. But I've seen enough pieces to know it's terrifying. She makes all of us help her. Building our own gallows."

A shock of understanding jolted through Mary.

"It was you!"

He gave her a withering look. "What was me?"

"The machine. The one with the electricity."

He turned to look at her fully for the first time, his brown eyes wary. "How do you know about that?"

"The machine felt the same way you do. Your anger."

"Why shouldn't I be angry? Yes, she made me and several other changelings help build a machine to force people to use magic. And then she tested it on us."

"That's terrible!"

"She feeds on suffering. Everything she does is terrible. But what do you mean the machine felt like me? What's your magic?"

She looked down at her hands, her cheeks warm. "I can fix things. Sometimes, it's as if machines talk to me."

"Strange." He wrinkled his forehead. "I talked to the machine. Whispered to it as I worked, told it how much I hated the elves and everything they do. I don't think my abilities are supposed to work on machines, but they wove magic into it, so the magic must have listened to me."

"Well, I changed the machine. I made it hurt the person who used it instead of the person in the chair."

His eyes sparkled. "Did you? That's clever. I would like to hurt them."

"You shouldn't want to hurt anyone if you don't have to," Mary said, feeling like a hypocrite. Because she wanted to hurt the elves, too.

Lucien scoffed and turned a distrustful gaze on the roses lining the garden. "Easy to say for someone who didn't have to live in Elfland."

"You think the human world was easy?"

"No, but I think it taught you something besides pain. We heard rumors about the other Faerie kingdoms and the human world—about sunshine and starlight and green things growing. That made it worse, knowing there was something better we could never touch. Everywhere I looked, all I saw was suffering. It's hard to even imagine anything else."

"Don't you have friends—other human changelings?"

"They don't allow us to have friends."

Mary thought of her parents' lost child—the one the Fay exchanged her for. "Are there many other changelings, though?"

His lips twisted down. "An army. An army of enslaved children."

Mary's stomach twisted. "Could you find someone there? In Elfland?" This was the revenge she most wanted on the Fay, especially because it would ease her own conscience as well.

"Find one of the changelings?"

"Yes. A girl. I don't know what age she would be. Probably younger than me."

"Why are you looking for her?" He regarded her suspiciously.

"She's...the one I was traded with. My sister."

His eyebrows rose. "What do you want with her?"

"I want to set her free."

He scowled and threw a pebble at the hawthorn tree. "None of us can be free."

"Cassandra told me the stories—that the years catch up with humans if they're cast out of Elfland and cut off from the magic that sustained them. But this girl would only be my age in the human world."

Lucien pursed his lips, some of the cynicism in his eyes replaced by interest. Mary had given him a problem to be solved, and she sensed that it overcame even his deep anger. "Without knowing her name or what she looks like, it would be impossible to know which changeling you were traded with."

Mary took a deep breath and reached into the pocket she wore under her skirts. She pulled out a few scraps of time-worn fabric that she had discovered packed away in her father's room when searching for more answers about herself—remnants of soft colors punctuated with tiny flowers. "I wonder if these might help. They are full of love and hope. I suspect my mother made a baby quilt from them for the child she was expecting, and since we have no such quilt in our home... My mother is dead, so I can't ask her, but might the Fay have taken the blanket along with the child?"

Lucien took the scraps—gently, she noted—and held them up. He studied them with skepticism, but something flickered in his eyes, and he pointed to one of the blue scraps with little white daisies. "You're in luck. I think I have seen a kitchen girl wearing a square of this same pattern covering her hair."

"Then we can save her?"

He handed the scraps of fabric back. "I might know where to find her—*might*. But that doesn't mean it would be easy to steal her from the most terrible of the Faerie queens."

Chapter Nine

Cassandra awoke with the words from her nightmare still echoing in her mind: She'd seen Amy dressed in an old-fashioned gown with wide skirts and a ruff. Amy's eyes had sparkled with anger, and she said, "If they have to die, then so be it."

It was a dream, nothing else. Amy was kind, always trying to help. She'd been part of the Gunpowder Plot long ago, but that was the past. So, why did Cassandra dream of it—an event that occurred long before her lifetime?

She shuddered and scrambled out of bed to put the bad dream behind her. Mary was already gone. Cassandra wished her shy friend didn't feel such a need to be unobtrusive, but she didn't know how to make Mary feel welcome and wanted.

Cassandra managed to button up her dress without ringing for help. The long mirror caught her attention, and she made certain the dress was flattering and her hair was arranged just so. Henry's locket glinted at her neck. Her stomach fluttered with excitement, and her fingers felt shaky and awkward as she finished making herself presentable. More than presentable. Henry was there, possibly downstairs already.

Finally, her excitement to see him overcame her worry about how she looked, and she limped for the stairs. She kept her gloves off. This was a place that she didn't have to hide her scars.

Henry loitered near the bottom of the stairs. As if waiting for her. Her heart gave a little jump at seeing him. He looked up and smiled, his whole face brightening, and she felt like her insides might melt at that warm welcome.

"Good morning," Cassandra said.

"Good morning. Did you sleep well?"

Her sleep was full of nightmares, as it had been since the following year. Some of them were about Henry serving the Fay, but all of that was forgotten when she saw him there, in person and warm and friendly—not at all terrible.

"Well enough," she said. "You?"

He laughed, a rumble in his chest. "We've been sleeping rough for a while, so this was quite luxurious. And I was glad thinking I would see you again today." A faint red tinged his cheeks. "I have thought of you often, but it wasn't safe to visit you."

Her heart fell a little at that reminder. "At least we're safe for now. And here. Both of us, I mean." Curse her fumbling tongue. "It's good to see you again. I have thought of you, too."

She touched her neck and found the chain of the locket he had given her to carry for him. She pulled it out and showed him.

His eyes lit, and he stepped closer, close enough that she could feel his warmth, and he put his hand around hers to study the locket.

"Thank you for keeping it safe." He met her eyes, and she

found she had nothing to say to him. She only wanted to stare into his eyes. To lean a little closer.

He traced the back of her hand with his thumb. "Keep holding onto it. I like knowing it's with you. Until some point in the future. When things are different."

"Is it possible?" Cassandra whispered. "For things to be different?"

"It has to be." He tightened his grip on her hand. "I'll either arrange a bargain so the Lady of the Woods can't control me any longer, or I'll gain enough power that she cannot keep her hold on me. I will find a way to be free. I've continued my studies. I'll be able to work as a surgeon. I haven't stopped hoping."

"Nor have I." When they both said it—longed for it—Cassandra believed it was possible, somehow, for Henry to be free.

"A-hem." Someone cleared his throat behind them.

Cassandra's face warmed, and she turned to see Jairus watching them with an amused glint in his eyes. Henry did not let go of her hand or let her pull away, and he gave Jairus a withering look.

"I hate to interrupt," Jairus said, a chuckle in his voice. "But Lady St. Clair wants to see everyone in the dining room. I believe we're discussing tactics and strategies."

Henry sighed. "I thought we might have a few hours respite."

Jairus shook his head, his expression turning serious. "Not when the Grigori are out there. War waits for no one."

"Of course," Henry said, releasing Cassandra's hand.

She immediately missed his touch, but he offered his arm to escort her, and she was happy to take it. Jairus led them back to the dining room, where tea and scones waited for them on the sideboard and Domin studied a map of London spread out on the table. He was placing chess pieces on it in various locations while Amy watched. Telesm lounged in a corner, and Mary stood by the sideboard as if trying to hide from the conversation.

"You're forgetting Lord Sanders," Amy said, pointing to a spot on the map just outside of Westminster in Pall Mall.

Domin raised an eyebrow. "I thought he was killed in a robbery after a late night at his club. You think he's a victim of the Grigori?"

"I do. I happen to know his grandmother was of Faerie blood. Another of my mother's schemes."

Domin nodded, looking grim, and added a pawn in the place where Lord Sanders had been found dead.

"Is that common?" Jairus asked. "For humans to have Faerie blood?"

Domin shrugged one shoulder. "It is not uncommon, especially among the upper classes. They often knowingly or unknowingly married members of the Faerie courts in the past, and some of the bloodlines persist."

"Fay are more likely to have children with a human consort," Amy said. "My father was a human prince with Faerie blood—enough Faerie blood that I inherited my mother's Faerie abilities."

"As did I," Telesm added.

Cassandra was surprised Telesm didn't remind them once again that his father was also a prince. Her family was respectable, but she felt the lowness of her station compared to her companions.

Henry shifted. "And if the child has more human blood than Faerie, he is human by any observable measure."

"Like Lucien," Mary said quietly.

Domin frowned, toying with the chess piece in his hand.

"Precisely. I think he represents an instance where the Dark Lady was hoping to breed another powerful Fay. He did not inherit enough magic from his Faerie parent, so he is a human changeling instead."

Henry shuddered and looked disgusted. Cassandra was disgusted, too, that the Fay treated humans and even their own children like animals.

"Why not let the Grigori kill the Fay?" Lucien asked from the doorway. "They're demons."

Cassandra jumped at the young man's voice and turned to face him. "The Grigori are monsters, too. And they're not just assassinating Fay who are guilty of atrocities. They're hunting innocent people who might not even know what crimes their ancestors could have committed."

"Is anyone innocent?" Lucien muttered.

"They don't deserve to be murdered," Cassandra countered.

Henry put a warm hand on her back and gave Lucien a warning look. "And since most of us in this room have some Faerie blood—yourself included—we're not going to sit and wait for them to come slaughter us. Or other innocent people. Children, even. We're not like the Grigori or the Fay."

Cassandra nodded. Of the people in the room, only she and Jairus had no connection to the Fay, and they were both demon-marked by the Grigori, which Domin said also attracted magical attention. They all had reason to fear Rushford and his followers.

"Then where do we look?" Amy asked.

"Many of the bodies have turned up in Drury Lane," Henry said. "But we don't think they were taken from there. Many appeared to have come from rough circumstances."

Domin pointed to the map. "We've been scouring the East

End. It's so full of poverty and criminal activity that it's hard to know where to search next."

"A little discouraging," Jairus admitted.

Henry glanced quickly at Cassandra. "I don't think we should take the women to the East End. At least, not some of the areas we've been searching. It would be unsafe."

Cassandra wanted to protest, but she realized he was probably right. If they were hunting killers, they needed to be inconspicuous, and a group of well-dressed women wandering in the worst parts of London would attract the wrong kind of attention—a distraction from the real problem. Yet she was determined to find a way to help. To protect her family, her friends, and all the people who didn't understand the threats lurking on the edges of their world.

Henry's eyes widened, and he put his hand to his chest.

"Henry?" Domin asked.

"It's the Lady of the Woods." His voice was tight. "She's summoning me."

Chapter Ten

Henry gritted his teeth, fighting Titania's pull, but he wouldn't be able to resist forever. He could yank back against her magic, ease the pain, or push magic at her and throw her off balance, but it was exhausting. And futile. She was near, and the only reason she didn't kill Henry was fear of Domin's reprisal. She couldn't enter the house—not unless Amy invited her—but she knew where they were, and she held the ends of Henry's chains.

"A Faerie Queen is here?" Jairus asked, reaching for his pistol.

"Nearby," Henry said.

"You'd best go outside," Amy said.

Henry shot her a withering look. "Thank you."

"My mother banished me, if you recall," Amy said. "I don't intend to invite her into my home. She'll come to the garden. There's a gateway to her kingdom by the hawthorn tree there."

Henry sighed and headed for the garden. He couldn't blame Amy. None of them could afford to defy Titania, but they didn't have to invite interaction with her. He looked up to find Domin by his side. He gave his friend a nod of gratitude. At least he didn't have to face Titania alone.

When he opened the door to the gardens, he realized Jairus and Cassandra had also followed, though they hung back. Jairus had his shotgun, and Cassandra had her crossbow, her lips set in fierce determination. He smiled to himself. Not alone at all. Though, he hated to think Cassandra was going to witness whatever humiliation Titania was likely to heap upon him.

He squared his shoulders and walked to the back of the garden, gazing up at the hawthorn tree. An arched wooden trellis laden with climbing roses stood beside it—a gateway that would open to Elfland if the right person touched it with magic. It wasn't long before a breeze blew around him, and the air filled with white hawthorn petals, though spring was long past in London.

Titania, the Lady of the Woods, stepped through the arch to stand before him. A crown of oak leaves adorned her long, flowing hair, and her dress shimmered with the colors of an autumn forest. The hawthorn petals continued their swirl behind her. She would have looked inhumanly beautiful, but Henry knew her too well to admire her. Her gaze flicked over Domin, but she didn't even acknowledge Jairus and Cassandra.

"Henry Stewart," she said.

He inclined his head in an almost-bow. Respectful, but not obsequious.

"I have need of your skills."

He folded his arms. "If you recall, I choose how my skills are used."

Something dangerous flashed in her eyes, but then she made a dismissive gesture. "It has not escaped your attention that the Fay are under attack in London."

Henry raised an eyebrow, aware of the bruise still healing on his forehead and the scabs on his arm where the iron shot had pierced him. "It has not."

"The Faerie courts have held council. The Lords and Ladies agreed to work together to combat this threat against our kind. We will not allow humans to hunt any Fay again, so we are assembling our resources against them."

Henry frowned at that. He did not want to be a resource, but they did need to stop the Grigori. "Very well. I will cooperate."

"And you have already begun hunting these Grigori vermin?"

"I have. Though I have not succeeded in stopping them."

"Of course not," said a deep, male voice from behind Titania. "You cannot do it without my help."

Fitzhugh stepped through the wall of twirling petals. He was careful not to touch the roses, but he wore a mocking grin. The Unseelie elf was dressed in human fashion, with a dark suit, top hat, and silver-topped cane that Henry knew concealed a sword blade.

"Fitzhugh!" Henry said through gritted teeth. He turned questioning eyes to Titania.

She smiled coldly. "I did tell you that all the Faerie courts are working together."

"The Unseelie, though?" Henry asked.

He risked a quick look at Domin. Domin's expression was as stoic as usual, but his mouth was set in a firm line. For the Seelie and Unseelie courts to work together was unprecedented.

"The Seelie courts know they cannot win without Unseelie strength," Fitzhugh said.

The Lady of the Woods gave Fitzhugh a quelling look. "If your lady had not consorted with these low humans, we would not be in this situation. You are only paying your dues."

"The Unseelie do not pay their dues," Henry said. "They find others to pay their dues for them."

"No doubt that is why their queen sent Fitzhugh," the Lady of the Woods said. "He will pay the price for her failure."

Fitzhugh shrugged one shoulder. "I will not fail. And I am not alone. May I present Jane?"

"Princess Jane," said a voice from the curtain of petals behind him.

A young lady stepped through the divide between their worlds. She was short, with blond hair fastened up beneath a tiara that sparkled...not with jewels, Henry realized, but with beads of water that caught the light. There was a hungry gleam in her eyes that Henry did not like.

"Fitzhugh and Jane represent the Unseelie Court," Titania said, her nose wrinkled in disdain. "You and my daughter represent the Seelie Courts."

"Amy?" Henry asked, surprised.

"Indeed. She is banished from my presence and my favor, but I know she is sheltering you, and this way I do not lose more resources on the matter. I'm certain you can handle the Grigori, especially with Domin's aid. I know you still have his loyalty."

She glared at Domin and raised a hand, revealing the blue tattoo swirling around her wrist, a reminder of the vow binding her, Henry, and Domin—Domin would kill her if she caused Henry's death. It did not free Henry, but it certainly gave him some latitude. It also meant that she did not consider the Grigori a serious threat. She would not assign Henry to a dangerous task if it might endanger his life—and therefore hers. Or she hoped the Grigori would rid her of Henry and Domin both.

"So, if I understand, you want me to try to stop the Grigori from kidnapping and killing those of Faerie blood?" Henry asked.

"Precisely. I consider them an Unseelie problem, but the courts agreed to work together since the problem is an insult to us all. The Unseelie will take the lead in it because they are at fault for it. You need only support them in their efforts. In fact, I require an oath that you will do so."

Henry glanced at Fitzhugh, who raised an eyebrow and smirked.

Henry shook his head. He had to be very careful what he promised the Fay. "I will swear to use my abilities to try to stop the Grigori from harming anyone else. Nothing more."

Titania glared at him, then her gaze slipped to Domin. "Very well. I will accept this of you."

Henry felt the shiver of the oath taking hold, but he didn't flinch from it. It was what he had already planned to do.

"Now," Titania said, "I leave you to your work."

She stepped back into the swirling petals under the hawthorn tree and vanished. The archway was a mere trellis once more.

Fitzhugh grinned. "Well, won't this be a pleasant little house party?"

Chapter Eleven

"Absolutely not," Amy said, crossing her arms and glaring at Fitzhugh from the garden door. "You're not making it past the threshold."

Cassandra couldn't blame her. She didn't want Fitzhugh and Jane in the house, either. And it was probably best if the Unseelie Court didn't know that Telesm or Lucien was there.

Fitzhugh grinned at Amy. "Amy, dearest, we're all working together now. You want to stop the Grigori, don't you?" He tilted his head. "And I believe you're already harboring one fugitive from the Unseelie Court."

Cassandra went cold at that. They did know, then. No doubt the Dark Lady was aware of Cassandra as well. She stepped closer to the shelter of the house.

Amy pursed her lips, then slowly smiled. "Domin, Mr. Hale, do you think you could bring the dining table out into the garden?"

Jairus grinned. "Sure thing, Lady St. Clair."

Domin nodded and went inside with Jairus.

Jane's blue eyes widened, and she turned on Fitzhugh. "If they won't let us inside, then where are we supposed to sleep?"

"I can have a bed brought out as well," Amy said with a smirk.

Jane's eyes flashed. "I am of royal blood. I do not sleep in the garden! Especially not one with roses." She stomped her foot like an angry child, and a bitter wind whipped through the garden, ripping petals from the last fall roses and carrying them away.

Henry held out a hand, and the wind stopped. He glared at Jane. "You're the Unseelie changeling who helped the Dark Lady attack the Weaver's home last year."

Cassandra drew a sharp breath. She had not forgotten that terrible storm full of voices preying on her deepest fears. She still had nightmares of it.

Jane's face instantly went from pouting to cheerful. "You're the Seelie Tempestarius!"

Her gaze slid over Henry in a possessive way that made Cassandra uncomfortable.

Henry took a step back from Jane. "The what?"

She giggled. "The Tempestarius. The weather mage."

"I suppose."

"Oh, there's no need to be modest about it. We are special. Powerful. Your parents were royal, too, weren't they?"

"Yes," Henry said reluctantly.

"My father was King Henry the Eighth," Jane went on. "And my mother was Jane Seymour. She knew she had to have a son or she would end up beheaded like Anne Boleyn. So, she made a deal. A trade. She gave my disgusting father a boy child cast off from the Fay, and she sent me to be a princess among them. And then she died anyway," Jane finished cheerfully.

"Then Edward VI was a changeling," Henry said.

Cassandra stared. It explained his poor health and short life, dying as a boy king. The royal family certainly had many dealings with the Fay.

"Yes, poor weak little thing." Jane smirked and adjusted her tiara, the beads of water catching the sunlight. "He's long gone now, along with my half-sisters, Mary and Elizabeth. Ha! What were they? Mortal monarchs, struggling with mortal bodies and mortal men to cling to their power. What I have is so much better. Someday I will be more than they ever were."

"But you're trapped with the Unseelie Fay," Henry said.

Jane's eyes glittered as she studied him. "I'm glad that you think like a mortal. It makes you weak. You are no competition for me."

A chilly wind stirred in the garden, and Henry narrowed his eyes. "If you plan to hurt people, you will see what the strength of my human emotions can do."

She laughed, a sharp sound like glass breaking. "You amuse me. Perhaps I won't destroy you."

Henry's lips pressed into a thin line, but he didn't bother responding, just folded his arms and watched her warily.

Fitzhugh smirked. "You see, we are already having fun."

He turned to Cassandra, something hard glittering in his eyes. She touched the small knife she kept hidden under her skirts and wished for her crossbow. Fitzhugh would not soon forgive her for stabbing the Dark Lady with her iron pin. She expected some threat—perhaps even an attack—but he smiled at her. Even more frightening.

"How is your lovely family, Miss Weaver?" Fitzhugh asked.

She took a deep breath of the air perfumed with Amy's roses. "They're well, no thanks to you."

He laughed. "Oh, I did my part to protect them. You ought

to be grateful. But how are you faring now, after your little adventure?"

"I am well, too, as you see."

"I wasn't inquiring about your health, though of course your leg never will be well. Not unless you let one of the Faerie Courts help you."

Cassandra flushed. "No, thank you."

Henry stepped closer, putting himself between her and the Unseelie elf.

Fitzhugh ignored him. "Regardless, I imagine it's a heavy burden to carry, everything you know. It sets you even more apart from the others, doesn't it? From your sisters, your neighbors."

Cassandra only shrugged. Her leg already set her apart, and at least it was easier to hide being Sabbath-born.

"Do you sleep well, by-the-by? You do look a little peaked."

Cassandra distrusted the way his eyes gleamed when he asked that. "Quite well," she lied.

He grinned. "Oh, my little pet. Your defiance is endearing. I am glad my queen chose the vengeance she did for you."

Cassandra tensed, and her weak hand spasmed. She was certain Fitzhugh saw it.

Henry put a protective hand on Cassandra's back and turned on Fitzhugh. "What do you mean?"

Fitzhugh grabbed her right hand—the one with the demon mark. He traced his fingers over it like a spider creeping across her palm. She pulled away from him, leaning into Henry.

Fitzhugh smirked. "A demon mark makes you so easy to find. Did you know that all suffering belongs to my queen? That's why she's so powerful—there is so much of it in this world. And she can share it back. Her incubi do not only whisper seductions; they can also tell secrets. Secret pain. Secret suffering."

Cassandra refused to meet his eyes. Was this the meaning of her nightmares? "No Fay can enter my home."

"But some can walk in your dreams. They don't need to touch you. They only need to whisper things that you do not wish to know. And, of course, as Fay, they cannot lie. They share with you the truth."

Cassandra didn't want it to be the truth—all the terrible things she had seen about her friends in her dreams. It was a terrible vengeance indeed. She didn't dare glance at Henry, but she felt his questioning gaze on her face. She didn't want to confirm that everything Fitzhugh said was true.

Chapter Twelve

Amy heard Fitzhugh's words to Cassandra with sinking dread. The Dark Lady was revealing secrets to Cassandra? She didn't want Cassandra to suffer with knowledge that was painful, and she suspected the Dark Lady was telling Cassandra things about the past that would hurt her. Maybe even things about her friends. With the probable exception of Mary, they all had shadows in their histories. Shadows Amy was constantly trying to outrun.

A shuffling inside the house broke the uncomfortable silence, and Amy grabbed the double doors and opened them wide so Domin, Jairus, and—to her surprise—Telesm could carry the table with its map down the steps and into the garden.

Fitzhugh's eyebrows rose at seeing Telesm, but he didn't comment. They hadn't known he was there, and she was surprised Telesm had been willing to reveal his presence. In fact, he almost seemed to have done it on purpose. As if he cared more about what happened with the Faerie Courts than he let on.

The three men lowered the table onto the swath of grass, and Domin righted the tumbled chess pieces.

"Pawns, are they?" Fitzhugh said with a smile. "How fitting."

Amy knew it was the only type of piece they had enough of to represent the dead, but Fitzhugh wasn't wrong. The pieces did mark pawns in the schemes of the Grigori and the Fay.

Domin leveled a quelling look at Fitzhugh. "We are marking the locations of the bodies to determine a pattern. Trying to trace the Grigori back to their lair."

Fitzhugh studied the map through his quizzing glass with a bored expression. He glanced at the pile of extra chess pieces and picked up a bishop, lifting it to Jairus like a toast, and followed it with a knight and a rook. "We have our priest, our white knight, and our guardian. Where have you been hunting?"

"The East End," Henry said tersely. "Where most of the victims likely originated."

Fitzhugh plunked the pieces down on the East End, far from where most of the bodies had been found. "I would expect Domin, at least, to understand more of the way of predators. They have a territory. No bodies from South London. How interesting. A few found in the East End, but many near Drury Lane and Covent Garden." He tapped the map with his long fingers. "Covent Garden has its share of street urchins. It would make excellent hunting grounds."

"Predators also don't like to dirty their own lairs," Domin said.

"True," Fitzhugh conceded. "The Grigori wouldn't dump the bodies in their own back garden. But I know Rushford better than you. He is fastidious. He wouldn't care for the East End."

Amy brightened. "Even if they sometimes hunt in the East End, they wouldn't be living there."

Domin frowned but nodded his agreement. "Instead of stalking their hunting grounds, you want us to trace them to their lair."

"They were doing their experiments far outside of London," Henry said, "but they'll need a new place for that now."

"They must have headquarters in London, too, if they're hunting here," Jairus said, staring off at the tall houses visible beyond Amy's garden well.

Amy followed his gaze with a shiver that raised goose bumps down her spine. Was Rushford somewhere close? Stalking her and her friends even as they hunted him?

Jairus turned his attention back to the map. "And what about the Dark Muse? The creature they're sacrificing these Faerie children to? She must be close, but she doesn't sound like an ideal house guest."

Fitzhugh fixed his gaze on Jairus, all mocking gone. "What are you talking about?"

"Oh, didn't you know?" Jairus asked with false casualness. "The Grigori aren't just killing those with Fay blood. They're offering them to someone they call their Dark Muse."

"In fact, I did not know," Fitzhugh said. "This is more serious than I believed. Come, Domin, you must have some guesses about this Dark Muse. One of the actual Grigori—the fallen angels?"

Amy looked to Domin as well. She knew many of the Seelie Fay, and some were horrid, but there were other, more terrible creatures she had heard of only in whispered rumors.

Domin shook his head. "Unlikely. Those Grigori are primarily male, and Rushford's Dark Muse is female."

Fitzhugh frowned and picked up a queen chess piece.

"Also," Henry said, "the bodies we found weren't just killed. They were drained of life and substance."

"Perhaps a ghoul or vampire, then." Fitzhugh set the queen carefully in the center of Covent Garden. "But why would one work with Rushford? He's still the key."

He added a king to the West End, near Amy's home. The faint click sent a shudder through Amy's core.

She drew a deep breath. "Well, if we're looking for someone in Mayfair, I can be helpful after all." She studied her friends through a critical lens and shook her head. "I will have to order appropriate clothing for Henry, Telesm, and Mr. Hale, as well as for Cassandra and Mary."

Jairus looked down at his battered waistcoat and jacket. "That bad, is it?"

Amy laughed. "For going to a ball, it is."

"Why are we going to a ball?" Henry asked.

Amy gave him an arch look. She liked the idea better the more she thought about it. "Where better to hear all the latest gossip? The theater, too, perhaps. We should attend there as well. But it comes back to the same thing: you need information, and to get that, you need new clothes."

Henry groaned, but Jairus laughed. No matter what either thought, Amy would stand her ground: they could not blend into Society looking as they did. This was one area where she was useful. And she would enjoy buying dresses for Cassandra and Mary.

"I will not be attending any festivities," Telesm said. "I don't deign to be stared at by riff-raff."

Amy rolled her eyes, but Cassandra gaped at him.

"Riff-raff?" Cassandra said. "But even the prince and princesses sometimes attend the balls and theater."

Telesm flicked his fingers dismissively, as though shooing away a fly. "New blood. Practically peasants."

Jane seethed at that—no doubt taking it to include herself—and Cassandra looked horrified, but Jairus laughed again.

"I'm surprised you're not objecting, brother," Telesm said with a speculative look at Domin.

Domin shrugged one shoulder. "I think it's a good idea."

"You do?" Henry asked.

"Amy is right. It's an approach we haven't tried, and we do know the Grigori move in Society."

Amy fought to keep from grinning too widely. Domin liked her idea. If he liked it, it couldn't be terrible. Maybe this was finally her chance to turn things around.

Chapter Thirteen

Mary hung back in the corridor while the others stood in the garden making plans. She didn't want to be anywhere near Fitzhugh, and she didn't have anything to add to their discussion. She would do what her friends thought best.

Lucien came up beside her, staying in the shadows so no one outside could see him.

"Watch out for her," Lucien said under his breath, glaring at the blonde girl who had come through the portal with Fitzhugh. "Jane. She's mad. A human changeling, but one that the Dark Lady likes. Has plans for."

Mary shivered. Anyone the Dark Lady liked couldn't be good. "What kind of plans?"

Lucien gave her an exasperated look. "You think the Fay tell changelings what they're planning? All I know is that the Dark Lady has something big in motion. Something that will hurt everyone. It probably would have been better if you'd let the Grigori take me."

Mary looked away from the group in the garden, blinking

to adjust to the dimmer light in the corridor. "Don't say that! My friends will stop whatever the Fay are planning."

He sneered and gestured toward the back door. "Your friends are working with the Unseelie Fay. Probably playing right into their hands."

Lucien slunk off.

Amy hurried back up the shallow stairs from the garden, a huge smile brightening her face.

"Excellent news!" Amy said, stepping inside. "We're going to a ball."

Mary gawked at her. That didn't sound like excellent news. But at least it also didn't sound like any kind of scheme from the Dark Lady.

~

Mary had never owned a ball gown before—not a real one that she hadn't made herself. When Amy presented her with the dress from her modiste, Mary didn't dare touch the soft folds of airy fabric.

"Go on," Amy said with a smile. "It's yours. And just in time. We're going out tonight."

"Thank you," Mary whispered, taking the bundle and petting it like a kitten.

The dress was blush pink trimmed with white. It was thin on fabric around the top but more than made up for the lack with the full, bustled skirt. Enough extra fabric, in fact, for Mary to conceal her small crossbow beneath the folds.

Mary and Cassandra dressed in their room, Cassandra taking naturally to the rich blue dress Amy had gifted to her. Amy brought her lady's maid back just for the evening—the scandal of poorly styled hair being a greater risk, apparently, than the scandal of Amy's male guests. The maid helped Cassandra with her hair, then Cassandra hurried downstairs, no doubt to find Henry, who would no doubt be appreciative.

Mary stood in front of the mirror in her dress, shy of how low it was cut, yet surprised how well it looked on her. She had always told herself that it didn't matter what she wore. She was a plain, pale girl with no figure and no real hope of attracting a suitor, though she was only seventeen, so not in much need of one yet. But she had always secretly longed to look pretty and wear fine things, even if she scolded herself for thinking it silly.

"Don't you look lovely!" the maid said, grinning at her in the reflection. "My lady was right to put you in pink. It brings out the color in your cheeks."

Mary flushed, putting even more color in them.

Mary hardly knew what to do as the maid adjusted her dress and fussed over her hair. Her father hired a charwoman to help with the heavy cleaning around the house, but otherwise, Mary had never been waited on before. The maid finished buttoning the back of the bodice then studied Mary critically.

"Your face isn't bad. You're pale, but some men like that look. Let's see what we can do with your hair."

Mary had never been able to do much of anything with it, and she could fix almost anything. But she was not a lady's maid. When the woman stepped away, Mary's breath caught. The girl in the mirror looked fashionable and even confident.

"I look...pretty."

"Of course you do. There's nothing wrong with your looks to start with, and the rest is just knowing how to arrange things. You have sad eyes, but that adds some mystery to you."

Mary touched the long curl hanging over her shoulder. It felt odd. Not like her hair at all.

"It's false," the maid said. "An Alexandra Curl, after the

Princess of Wales. She's the most fashionable woman in the kingdom, and it's a look very suited to you. Now, chin up, smile a little, and you'll do just fine."

Mary walked out of the room, dazed. She had always thought she must be ugly because people treated her so unkindly. She had never realized that looking pretty was something obtainable. Yet, she was disappointed to find that it didn't change how she felt: small and easily forgotten. Like she was hiding behind the hair style and fancy dress.

She walked down the stairs, holding the skirts so she didn't trip. She found Lucien in the drawing room, studying a cylinder that spun and created electricity.

He glanced up and then looked again, raising his eyebrows. Mary flushed. Lucien quickly turned back to the cylinder.

"You're all dressed up." He said it like an accusation.

"I'm going to the ball."

"Does that mean they're leaving me alone?"

Mary wasn't sure if he was excited or nervous at the prospect.

"Telesm is staying. Apparently, he doesn't care for being stared at by common people."

"Hmph. I don't like Telesm. Too much Fay in him."

"I don't see why that should matter." Mary was probably too much Fay as well.

"It matters a great deal when you have creatures deciding who lives and who dies based on how much Fay blood is in their veins. And I don't mean those Grigori."

Mary clenched her fists. "Fay changelings are thrown out, too, and no one cares if we live or die."

Lucien narrowed his eyes at her. "That's right. I almost forgot you were one of them."

"I'm not one of anyone. I'm just me."

"No, you're one of them even if you don't like them. You're like Telesm. Enough Faerie blood to have your own magic and be free."

That caught Mary off guard. "You're free now, too."

"I'll never be free. Like Henry Stewart, except they want to keep him alive. When the Dark Lady remembers me, she'll probably kill me herself." He twirled the cylinder. "I'm just some failed experiment—part Fay and part human, but with too much human blood to have my own magic and no noble bloodline to make me important. Since I disappointed them, they threw me away."

"I'm sorry," Mary whispered. It was all she could think to say, weak words that didn't fix anything. "No one should be thrown away."

Lucien looked at her, and something vulnerable flickered in his eyes. Then it was gone. "You look like one of them, all dressed up in that costume. But watch your back or your Faerie-blooded friends will throw you away, too."

Mary drew a sharp breath, going cold at the thought. The Fay had already thrown her away once—Fitzhugh had been very clear about that. Even before she knew the truth about what she was, it had gnawed at her, that feeling that no one wanted her, that at any moment, even those who were kind would abandon her.

Cassandra's voice echoed down the corridor.

Mary slowly let out her breath and shook her head. Cassandra had not deserted her yet, even after seeing her behave like a coward. Neither had Amy. But Lucien couldn't understand that because he'd never had a real friend. Mary could try to be a friend to him, but she couldn't fix his broken heart or soul—that was beyond her magic.

"My friends wouldn't toss me aside," Mary said quietly.

Lucien sniffed derisively but didn't say anything.

She backed out of the room and found herself facing a mirror in the corridor. Even the lovely pink dress couldn't bring color to her pale cheeks now. A costume, Lucien had called it. She toyed with the Alexandra Curl, tempted to yank it off. It wasn't really her—not a part of her. But she glanced down the corridor where her friends were making plans for the night. She didn't want to seem ungrateful. So, she smoothed the curl back into place and hurried to join them.

Chapter Fourteen

Cassandra had trouble focusing on the conversation as Jairus and Domin discussed strategy with Amy. Henry stood close to her, and he kept glancing her way, clearly not paying any more attention than Cassandra was. After a year of not seeing him, she just wanted to drink in being close to him again, to talk to him about everything. Almost everything. She wasn't ready yet to speak about her nightmares.

"Let's be off, then," Amy said with a decisive nod.

Cassandra gave a guilty start and hoped she hadn't missed anything important.

Henry helped Cassandra into her cloak and handed over her cane as if it were the most normal thing and not something she should hide. She smiled at him, and he offered her an arm, his eyes never leaving her face. She flushed and tucked her hand against his elbow. It felt right. Safe, even though Fitzhugh would be catching up with them outside. Jane had declared she would not make an entrance into Society until she could do so under her own name and title, when everyone would know and admire her.

Their party stepped out of the house, hoods pulled up to protect their faces from a warm wind—Jane's work. The Unseelie changeling had loudly announced that the stink of London was unacceptable. Cassandra agreed with Jane for once. She hadn't realized how much she appreciated country air until she had to breathe the thick fumes of the city again, a mix of smoke and the stench of river sludge.

Jairus took the lead, escorting Mary, and Amy took Domin's arm cautiously, as though afraid he would shake her off. They left Henry and Cassandra in the rear.

"At least the breeze cleared out the fog," Amy said.

Cassandra took a deep breath. "And the smell."

Henry gestured and the breeze picked up, carrying cool, fresh air over them.

But something still felt wrong to Cassandra, an itch like someone watched them. Perhaps Fitzhugh?

Someone grabbed her by the shoulder and spun her around. She found herself facing an abnormally tall man in a white suit. His eyes glinted orange and he grinned—his mouth too wide to be human. He pursed his lips and breathed a wisp of blue flame at her face.

Cassandra ducked and grabbed the iron knife hidden in her bustle. She jabbed it up, catching the man in the arm.

He yelped and let go of Cassandra. Then Henry was between her and the strange man, the air around him crackling with cold.

Cassandra raised the blade at the stranger. "Who are you? What do you want?"

The man straightened his white waistcoat. "I'm

Spring-'eeled Jack, I am, and all I wanted was a little kiss. Look 'ow you've mistreated me, lovey."

"Stay away from me." Cassandra brandished the iron knife, her thoughts reeling. She had heard stories about the mysterious Spring-heeled Jack who terrified women in London. She'd thought they were just legends, but perhaps she should have known better.

"Laurik," Domin said from behind Cassandra.

Spring-heeled Jack grinned. "Domin! You old troublemaker. Laurik ain't my name no more. They call me Jack now. They even wrote some stories about me in the papers."

Domin grimaced. "Jack, then. Leave us alone."

"I can't do that, old friend. 'Aven't you 'eard? There's something 'unting the streets for Faerie blood, and thanks to you, I can't do much to defend myself."

"Thanks to you?" Amy asked Domin.

Jack grinned. "Oh, didn't 'e brag about 'ow he wounded old Jack?"

"I don't consider it a significant accomplishment," Domin said.

"Now that just 'urts my feelings." Jack turned back to the ladies. "'E used a cursed blade on me, 'e did—iron laced with a touch of silver. One that devours magic."

Amy tilted her head. "Then how are you still alive?"

"The blade is 'ungry for *Faerie* magic," Jack said. "I was 'alf Fay and 'alf fire elemental, and now the fire elemental is all what's left. I could change shapes almost as pretty as Domin can, before he stuck me."

"You're a shape shifter?" Cassandra asked. They were very rare.

Jack flashed a grin, showing off sharp teeth. "I can't change much anymore. Just do little tricks with fire. You see, that's why Domin owes me some 'elp."

Domin grimaced. "You were a murderer."

"I 'aven't murdered anyone in ages, though. I'm reformed."

Cassandra tightened her grip on her iron knife.

Amy shook her head and turned to Domin. "You have a blade that destroys magic?"

"Had. One of Telesm's creations."

"Whatever 'appened to that blade?" Jack asked, his eyes glittering orange. "It broke when you stuck me in the ribs, but what a useful thing the rest of it would be."

A hot swell of sickness washed over Cassandra. She had seen that in a dream: Domin jabbing a knife into a man's side, the blade breaking under the force.

"It's gone," Domin said to Amy, ignoring Jack. "It was too dangerous."

Jack grinned. "Ain't that a shame."

"How do you expect us to help you?" Domin asked.

"Keep me safe from the 'unters, of course."

"We're trying to catch them," Domin said. "What can you tell us about them?"

Jack lifted his chin, looking down on all of them. "They're taking people off the streets. Poor souls what don't even know they 'ave traces of Faerie blood."

"You must know these streets well," Domin said. "You can't sense more?"

"Well, thanks to some old friend of mine, I can't sense much of anything. I just know that things are wrong. The wind smells too cold for this time of year, and it gives me the willies, it does. Something bad's coming."

"Do you know where the Grigori like to hunt?" Jairus asked.

Jack's eyes widened. "Grigori? Why you going on about them?"

"The humans who kill Fay. That's what they call themselves," Amy said. "They're looking for more knowledge about magic so they can use it. Or destroy it."

Jack shuddered. "Well, we can't have that, can we? I've already lost all the magic I can afford. I can tell you I've never seen 'ide nor 'air of them in my domains in South London. And I feel safer on the East End than the West right now."

Cassandra and her friends exchanged looks. The West End, then.

Jairus's eyes narrowed. "If your domain is South London, what are you doing here?"

Jack leaned in like he had a secret to tell. "There are Unseelie Fay about."

"You thought they might be connected to the Grigori?" Amy asked.

"I thought they might 'elp poor Jack, since you lot 'aven't been easy to find."

"The Unseelie are working with us," Domin said, "and you will not find them sympathetic. But we are trying to stop the Grigori. If you have any contacts on the streets, see if anyone knows where the Grigori are hiding or what Faerie creature they're working with."

"A Fay working with them, you say?" He tapped his teeth with a long fingernail, looking thoughtful. "Right! You can count on Jack!"

Jack tipped his hat and leapt from the ground to the roof of the building next to them. Cassandra gawked at the feat.

Amy gasped. "I think he was the one who broke into your boarding rooms. Is he bound by Faerie law to stay out of dwellings?"

Domin shook his head. "He's not. He's part fire elemental as I am part daemon, so he can follow their laws. Which don't restrict him much."

Cassandra huddled closer to Henry as she realized what that meant. Spring-heeled Jack might claim to be helping them, but there was nothing trustworthy about him, and he could get into Amy's house if he wished. The Grigori weren't the only enemies they had to be wary of in London.

Chapter Fifteen

"What on earth was that?" Fitzhugh asked, stepping up to them from a side alley and raising his quizzing glass to study Jack's aerial path.

Amy sighed. "Apparently, it was Spring-heeled Jack."

Fitzhugh raised an eyebrow. "Really? One of us, is he?"

"He is his own creature," Domin said. "Part fire elemental."

Fitzhugh accepted that with a distracted nod, which roused Amy's suspicions. He was always scheming something, playing a double game. Who would it hurt this time?

Amy stuck by Domin's side as they walked the short distance to the residence where the ball was being held. Domin paused before they ascended the stairs, shifting his features. He took on a face he had worn many years ago—at the time of the Gunpowder Plot, when Amy had betrayed him. Her heart turned heavy, and she looked straight ahead. Why did Domin choose that guise over any other? He said he had forgiven Amy, but this seemed a cruel reminder.

They entered the house. A staircase wrapped around the

foyer, and both were crowded with women in low-cut ballgowns and men in black suits and white gloves. It wasn't the Season, but that might work in their favor. Since London was thin of entertainment in the autumn, everyone would come to the ball.

Domin guided Amy up the stairs. A carpet softened their steps as they reached the height of the candle-lit chandelier. The vantage allowed them to scan the foyer below as well as the ballroom ahead. Amy squeezed Domin's arm.

Apparently, "everyone" included the Ashbys. Amy hadn't seen them since Sir Walter Ashby had joined Rushford's Grigori and tried to trade Cassandra's baby sister to the Unseelie Queen. The Unseelie Queen had killed Sir Walter instead. Now, his son Robert stood in the entrance to the gilded ballroom, a handsome young man who fidgeted with his cravat. The Ashbys had not been very sociable over the last year—an appropriate period of mourning for Sir Walter's death—but it appeared they were making their reentrance into Society. They couldn't hide forever.

Cassandra, behind Amy, gave a little gasp of recognition.

Amy hesitated over the best way to approach Robert. He had been a reluctant participant in his father's plans, but he *had* helped the Grigori.

Fitzhugh brushed past Amy and strode down the corridor to Robert. Domin tensed and followed, taking Amy along with him.

Robert saw Fitzhugh coming, and his eyes widened. He looked around as though seeking a place to hide, but of course, he couldn't escape in that crowded corridor in front of everyone. Cornered, he straightened his shoulders and awaited their approach.

"Mr. Ashby," Fitzhugh said. "Or, should I say Sir Robert?"

Robert swallowed, his gaze darting between Fitzhugh and Amy. Amy almost laughed to realize that Robert didn't understand how much she knew, and he wouldn't recognize Domin.

"Uh, yes," Robert said. "My father passed...passed suddenly last year."

"And you have taken up his place," Fitzhugh said. "In all of his business matters?"

Robert's Adam's apple bobbed. "I have...limited myself to those I felt were more worthy of my attention."

"I see," Fitzhugh said, his voice like silk. "But you maintain connections with his associates, of course?"

Robert's chin jutted defiantly. "I do not. I have had other, more pressing pursuits, and I do not share my father's interests."

"Fascinating," Fitzhugh purred.

Amy studied Robert. It didn't take a Fay to know he was nervous, but she didn't sense deception in him. Lucien's silver tongue would be useful in finding what Robert knew, but it wasn't safe to bring the changeling out of the house with both Unseelie elves and Grigori about.

Robert made an awkward bow and scurried away. Fitzhugh watched him with a smirk.

"Unfortunately, I think he's telling the truth," Fitzhugh said. "I doubt he knows where the Grigori are currently."

"But someone in here must know Rushford or one of his associates," Amy said, keeping her voice low. "Where they can be found."

"Indeed." Fitzhugh smiled. "Time for me to go to work."

Fitzhugh walked through the bright ballroom, past the alcove where the musicians played, stopping to flirt with a pretty girl. Finally, he went through an entrance on the other side toward the card room. Amy breathed out a sigh. He would do less damage and hear more gossip there than on the dance floor.

Amy glanced back. Cassandra and Henry walked through the crowd, probably more focused on each other than the people around them. Mary sat along the wall with a cup of lemonade, nearly invisible to the gossiping ladies around her, and Jairus had managed to vanish after he left Mary there. He would not have gone to play cards given his aversion to gambling, so he might have headed back downstairs or to the garden.

She looked to Domin. "And what do we do?"

"Eavesdrop," Domin said. "You can encourage the people around us to talk freely."

Amy nodded. With Robert a useless lead, she feared the night would be wasted, but at least there was still something she could do.

Domin offered his arm again, and she took it, letting him lead as she focused on her desire to hear more gossip. The people around them talked freely, though most of it was babble about marriages, the royal family, and the latest actor to conquer the stage. Domin's foreboding expression and lack of connection in the room discouraged anyone from talking with him. He didn't know anyone in modern London Society. And he hadn't worn that face for over a century. Then, he had been connected with everyone. More social. Happier. How much of the change was Amy's fault?

The guise he chose nagged at her conscience.

"Red hair is not as popular now as it was when the Tudors had the throne," Amy said. "Why choose to appear like that?"

He looked surprised and ran his free hand over his face, as if checking which one he wore. "I'm not certain. I suppose, walking into a dance with you, I lost track of time." Sadness edged his words, and he glanced at one of the mirrors catching the candlelight and the colorful dancing couples, their reflections skipping off into eternity.

Amy flushed. "I'm sorry to have reminded you."

He shook his head. "No need to be. It's pleasant to remember. To think of those who have gone on."

Amy smiled at her own memories—those before the bad times. "Do you recall John Byre singing for the queen?"

Domin chuckled, a low rumble in his chest. "I had forgotten. He's fortunate she didn't execute him for damaging her ears."

"It will always haunt me," Amy said with a mock shudder. "Oh, but his wife had the voice of an angel."

"Indeed. Fortunate man."

Amy studied his face. He was a novelty. Even with Jairus and Cassandra's immunity to magic, Amy could sense a little of their emotions, but Domin was able to close himself off completely. It was peaceful, being around him. Until she remembered why she didn't deserve that peace. Still, she saw the sadness in his eyes. He met her gaze as if allowing her to see more. When he had last worn that face, they had been friends. Close. And she had betrayed him. But for a moment, it was easy to forget the years in between.

"You should ask me to dance," Amy said, hardly thinking what she was doing.

He looked at her, his eyebrows raised. She felt foolish and wished she hadn't spoken. They were allies now, but she wasn't sure they would ever be friends again.

She shook her head. "Never mind, I—"

"Would you like to dance?"

He held out a gloved hand. She nodded, blushing, and took

his hand. He pulled her close and twirled her out onto the dance floor. Dancing with Domin wasn't like dancing with anyone else. It wouldn't be, because he wasn't like anyone else. He moved with the grace of...of a panther, an apex predator stalking the room, all that power and control contained in muscles she could feel through the sleeve of his coat, in the hand that held hers. He led her firmly but gently, his hand guiding her but not constraining.

She glanced up and met his green eyes watching her but impossible to read.

"When did you learn to waltz?" she blurted out.

It seemed she turned into a fool when talking to Domin— more of a fool than usual. She had to trust that Domin's shield keeping others from feeling his emotions also kept him from always knowing hers.

He smiled faintly. "I keep up with whatever fashions will help me to mingle where I need to. You assumed I do not dance?"

"Oh, I remember you dancing very well, but the fashions were so different back then."

"They were."

"Did you prefer the old style?"

He tilted his head. "It can be uncomfortable to be forced into close proximity with a dance partner, but it's also useful for detecting more about a subject."

Amy chuckled.

"Why is that humorous?"

"You are so accomplished a dancer. Don't you ever do it for enjoyment?"

He looked surprised. His hand tensed on her waist, then relaxed. "I used to. I suppose it has been a while. I'm enjoying it now. Perhaps dancing with someone I know makes the difference."

Amy flushed, pleased with herself. Domin didn't hate her. Could even enjoy dancing with her.

"And you dance well, too," he said.

"I have practiced enough, thanks to my mother forcing me to be accomplished, and I believe I do it well. At least it's *something* I can do."

Domin's brow furrowed. "You're capable of a great many things."

She laughed humorlessly. "And maybe someday one of those things will be valuable."

"Your value doesn't lie in what you do."

"And yet, you're the one who could only remember the value of dance as a way to gain information from someone."

He frowned at that, worry flitting over his expression for a moment. "I wonder if both of us have let the years weigh on us too much."

Domin hadn't spoken his thoughts that openly for ages. Amy suddenly felt it was only her and him in the room, spinning through glittering candlelight. As if, for a moment, all the things that were so fleeting fell away, and they were standing alone in a timeless universe, sharing the burden of carrying too many years without resorting to the callousness of the immortal Fay. They locked eyes, and Amy felt it, that shared understanding between them, the loneliness of watching loved ones age and die, the worry that striding against the river of time was a journey that would someday wear them away. Domin tightened his grip, and she did the same, not sure if he was reacting to her sudden dizzy sense of helplessness, or if they were truly sharing it.

And then, they were not alone. A new feeling intruded on

Amy, hungry and sharp and tasting of blood and fury. Domin inhaled sharply, dug his fingers into Amy's back. And to Amy, the lights in the room faded as if a shadow crossed over them. The wail of a winter wind sounded in her ears.

She blinked hard, and the room was back to normal—bright, hot, she and Domin two figures among many. But the sense of danger still hung over the room like a storm cloud ready to burst.

Chapter Sixteen

Cassandra was supposed to be gathering information, but her attention kept drifting to Henry. He had kept a reassuring grip on Cassandra's arm when Amy and Fitzhugh interrogated Robert Ashby, no doubt knowing the Ashby's betrayal of her family still stung. She and Henry didn't dance, but it was enough to stroll together, pretending for a moment that they could be like any normal man and woman, with whatever gossip they were supposed to be gleaning rolling past unnoticed.

Cassandra sighed, hating to interrupt the precious time they had together. But the Grigori were out there, and all of them were still in danger. "Perhaps you should fetch me some lemonade so you have a chance to see and hear more. I will find an inconspicuous place to eavesdrop."

Henry smiled ruefully. "Yes. We're not here for our own amusement, are we?"

He pulled his hand away, his fingers brushing her bare arm.

A pleasant shiver raced over her skin, and she longed to call Henry back to her side, but they had work to do.

She leaned on her cane, making her way to the side of the room where ladies stood and chattered. One of the other young ladies also had a cane. Cassandra caught the girl's eye and gave her a friendly nod.

She smiled to herself as she found a place to stand and listen. She wasn't such an oddity after all. She was torn between compassion for the other girl's injury and a desire to ask her how she came to have it. Other than Georgina, she had never had anyone who understood about her illness, and Georgina had a different set of challenges instead of worries about braces or canes.

She forced herself to focus on the conversations around her, people gossiping about the newest plays and Princess Alexandra.

Then, Cassandra noticed two young ladies walking together, both limping. Her skin flushed hot. Were they mocking her or the other girl with the cane? Yet they didn't appear to be paying attention to anyone else.

Another lady walked by with a limp so exaggerated it could not be real. Cassandra glanced down at the woman's feet. She wore one boot with a heel and the other without. Had she had an accident and broken her shoe?

Amy walked by with Domin, and she caught Cassandra's confused stare. "Oh!"

"What is it?" Cassandra asked. "Is it some sort of illness?"

Amy shook her head. "I'm sorry. I should have thought to warn you. You see, Princess Alexandra had a bout of fever and developed a limp. She is the height of fashion, so..."

Cassandra dropped her voice. "Do you mean people are limping on purpose to copy her?"

"It's horrendous, isn't it? She cannot like having her injury mimicked all over town."

Cassandra stared at the limping young ladies. "They'll hurt themselves, too. It isn't pleasant to limp or to have a cane." She suddenly felt like crying, though she couldn't quite say why. It almost let her blend in with Society. Yet, they were all pretending. Cassandra couldn't simply put on a matching pair of boots and be healed.

"It's not easy," Domin said in a low voice, "but you'll do best to ignore them and know that the fashion will pass."

Cassandra huffed to herself and nodded. Someone who had to put on a different face to attend a ball would know what it was like to be misunderstood by Society.

Domin and Amy moved on, both scanning the room as though searching for some hidden threat. Cassandra tried to go back to listening for hints about Rushford, but her eyes kept tracking all the girls who used canes or wore mismatched shoes to limp.

A serious-looking young man strolled past Cassandra and rolled his eyes at her cane. Her flush returned even brighter. She wanted to hobble after him and protest that she wasn't pretending. But what was the use? It was only more proof that she didn't fit in Society without pretending—even when Society was pretending as well.

A gentle pressure on her arm brought her back to herself. Henry looked after the man with disgust.

"I could dump this lemonade over his head," Henry whispered, a mischievous smile quirking his lips.

Cassandra giggled at the mental image.

"Then I could freeze it," he added, a dangerous glint in his eyes.

Cassandra sobered at that. It brought back memories of her terrible dreams. Of Henry freezing a village's crops.

"You mustn't actually hurt anyone," Cassandra whispered.

The strange gleam faded from his eyes, and he looked confused. "No, of course I wouldn't."

"Besides, why should he enjoy an ice when the rest of us have lukewarm lemonade?" Cassandra said, trying to lighten the mood.

Henry smiled and placed the glass of lemonade in her hand, rested his fingers next to hers. A chill moved over her fingers and into her drink.

"Now you'll be the only one to enjoy it," he whispered.

She met his gaze. "Then I am the luckiest young lady here."

He leaned closer, his lips parted with a response, and her heartbeat picked up pace.

A jolt brought Cassandra back to herself. One of the limping girls had tangled her cane with Cassandra's and tripped.

"Oh, I'm sorry," Cassandra said.

The young lady glared at her. "You ought to be! Stay out of my way."

Cassandra shared a confused glance with Henry over the rude reply. Behind him, two men had broken into a loud argument over who was to have the next dance with a frightened-looking girl. Outrageous behavior.

"Is this Fitzhugh's doing?" Cassandra asked.

"I don't—"

A sound rang over the music—the long, low cry of a hunter's horn. It stabbed deep in Cassandra's core and filled her with a crippling ache. She grabbed Henry's arm to keep from bending double. He had gone very still, his eyes wide.

"What was that?" Cassandra gasped.

"I don't know," he whispered. "Something terrible approaches."

The air in the room changed. Despite the press of bodies, it smelled sharp and cold, like a winter storm. A group of men on the dance floor had descended into a brawl, angry words and fists flying. Women shrieked and scolded, and one pulled a pin from her hair and jabbed at the fighting men.

Henry's posture froze, and his eyes went wide. He put an arm around Cassandra's shoulder and drew her closer. Much too close for this company, but Henry clearly wasn't thinking. His fingers dug into her arm, and they weren't pleasantly chilly, but icy cold.

Cassandra turned to look over her shoulder.

A tall woman strode toward them, epaulets adorning her shoulders and a double row of golden buttons glinting on the front of her bodice like a military uniform. Her black bustle swept the floor behind her, a stark contrast to the cheerful colors of the ballroom. Her red hair was piled artfully on her head, and a jewel in the shape of a crow glittered at her throat. Men and women paused their dancing and arguing to stare as she passed. She smiled as if she were a queen and it was her due.

The Morrigan had come to London.

The musicians started their next song, one with a decidedly military air.

Cassandra backed into the protection of Henry's grip, waiting for the woman to summon her sword and slash them down.

The Morrigan paused in front of them and dipped an elegant curtsey. Her gaze traveled past Henry, and she smiled.

"Domin. I can't tell you how delighted I am to see you here." She smiled, showing off perfect white teeth.

Cassandra glanced back at Domin, who had come to stand beside Henry. Domin still wore the guise of a red-headed man.

"Leave this place," Domin said.

The Morrigan laughed. "I'd forgotten how much I like this look on you. Red hair is not so popular now as it once was, but I've always fancied you were flattering me with your choice. Though you would say that Queen Elizabeth had a soft spot for fellow redheads."

"You have no business in London," Domin said.

"There is always blood in London, and soon there will be so much more. Those Grigori are getting quite out of hand, and I smell the delicious scent of war on the wind. The Lord of Annwn rides tonight at the head of the Wild Hunt."

Cassandra cast a confused look at Henry, who had gone pale.

The Morrigan's smile broadened. "You're not going to fire that pistol in here, priest."

"I'll do what I have to, to stop you," Jairus said from behind her. "There's nothing delicious about war."

"Oh, but there is: the love in the tears of the fallen and those they left behind, the nobility of those who sacrifice themselves for a cause, the bloodlust of those who learn to hate and revel in destruction. It lingers, you know; it soaks into the ground of battlefields and makes them hallowed places. Such rich emotions for me to feed on."

Cassandra glanced around the room. One man held another in a choke hold. When the second man wrestled his way free, he knocked over the girl they had been fighting over. She shrieked and tumbled to the ground, tripping up two ladies with uneven shoes. They all collapsed into a pile and fell to shouting and slapping at each other, and the whole time, the music played faster.

The Morrigan wasn't just drawn to conflict: she caused it wherever she went.

The sounds of a brawl came from the card room: yelling, fists thumping, the crash of something glass shattering. Pandemonium. Cassandra shrank into Henry's protective embrace. If any of those men had a gun—

The music suddenly stopped. Then it started again, but this time a soft, peaceful song. Amy had taken over the harpsichord and led the musicians in a gentle melody.

The shouts and shrieking cooled. People dabbed at bloodied noses and lips and picked themselves up from the floor. Some scrambled out of the room, others looked shame-faced and mumbled apologies. Couples resumed dancing, pretending nothing had been amiss.

The Morrigan laughed. "The elfling is clever. But a little music will not be enough to stop what's coming for London."

She turned and walked away, the train of her dress trailing behind her. The threads caught the light, and deep red shimmered among the black.

Fitzhugh hurried from the card room in time to see the Morrigan exit. "That explains a great deal."

Domin turned on Fitzhugh. "She said the Lord of Annwn rides tonight. Did you know of this?"

Fitzhugh's eyebrows rose. "I did not. I wonder if the Lords and Ladies convinced Annwn to hunt the Grigori."

"What is Ah-noon?" Jairus asked.

"Annwn is another part of the otherworld, similar to Elfland," Domin said, "except it's a waiting place for departed souls. The Lord of Annwn is a guide of the dead."

"So, this fellow is a grim reaper!" Jairus looked interested. "And he's our ally?"

Domin shook his head. "He owes allegiance to no one in

this world. His horn summons the Wild Hunt to chase lost souls. But the Hunt also calls to the darker, wilder side of humans. The Morrigan fed the chaos here tonight, but if the Wild Hunt continues to haunt London, it will bring madness to the city."

Cassandra clutched her cane. "Can we stop him?"

"Perhaps by stopping the Grigori," Fitzhugh said. "If he's hunting them. We may be too late tonight, though."

"Too late for what?" Domin asked.

"Before that entertaining scuffle broke out, I learned that a group of men didn't attend the ball tonight because they had a meeting of their 'scientific club.' It sounds like the Grigori."

"Where are they meeting?" Henry asked.

"That, I don't know," Fitzhugh admitted.

Jairus holstered his pistol, looking thoughtful. "I might. I also heard some men talking about a club meeting tonight down by the Strand."

"Near Covent Garden," Domin said grimly.

Henry took Cassandra's arm. "Then we need to hurry."

Chapter Seventeen

Amy found Mary deathly white and staring wide-eyed at the Morrigan's retreating back. Amy's heart still hammered, and her fingers had almost been too shaky to play the harpsichord, but at least the Morrigan was leaving for now.

Amy grabbed Mary's arm and gave her a gentle shake. "Come, she's gone, and our friends are leaving."

Not waiting for Amy and Mary. Amy was tempted to take umbrage at them running off and leaving her and Mary, but it meant they'd learned something important.

"I have my crossbow," Mary whispered. "But I could not draw it."

"Probably for the best, dear, since we're in a crowded ballroom. Come."

She half-dragged Mary through the crush of people who were just beginning to shake off the Morrigan's poisonous effects. None of the confused dancers paid any heed to two young ladies trying to escape the house.

Amy didn't bother stopping for her cloak, though the evening was chilly, instead hurrying Mary down the front steps.

"Now, which way did they go?" Amy muttered.

Mary pointed, and Amy caught a glimpse of Henry and Cassandra, Cassandra's limp slowing her down and giving Amy and Mary a chance to catch up. They rushed after their friends. Rushed toward the Thames. Toward the Strand district in particular, Amy realized.

The shops and coffeehouses were closed, but the district bustled even at night with people coming and going from the theaters. The excitement in the air was so thick, Amy imagined even humans could feel it. And in the alleyways, thieves and criminals lurked. She saw the reason in her friends' direction. It would be an ideal place for conspirators to gather. In fact, Amy had once been among them, when she'd met to help plan the Gunpowder Plot. Her stomach tightened, but she led Mary onward, catching up with the others just as Henry and Cassandra stopped.

Fitzhugh caught sight of Amy and grinned. "It's good to be back here, isn't it? What times we had."

Domin's forehead creased at the reminder, and Amy glared at Fitzhugh. "Terrible times. Where are the Grigori?"

"Excellent question." Fitzhugh looked to Jairus. "Where are they meeting?"

"No one mentioned an address." Jairus scanned the adjacent buildings, a mix of shops and houses.

"They could be anywhere, then," Amy said, her hope falling. There were so many little coffee shops where conspirators could meet.

"No." Domin lifted his face to the breeze blowing off the Thames. "No, let's reason it through. They will want somewhere comfortable. Somewhere they can come and go unobserved. Probably their own space and not a public one."

"One of the houses above the stores," Jairus suggested.

"You're thinking like an American," Henry said. "Too practical. Rushford would not like the taint of the shops."

"There used to be grand houses along here," Amy said, trying not to sound nostalgic.

"Now the best buildings may be the theaters and the hotels near Charing Cross Station," Domin said.

"A hotel might serve their purposes," Henry said.

Fitzhugh nodded. "Luxurious but anonymous."

They started for Charing Cross when a series of screams rang out over the street.

Amy's chest tightened. Any number of crimes might happen along the Strand, but somehow, she knew it was the Grigori.

A flock of crows streamed overhead.

Amy pointed the direction they had come from. "That way."

Domin nodded, and they all hurried south toward the newly-opened park of the Embankment. Amy remembered the girl she had found in Covent Garden, the last of her life bleeding away. She would not see another scene like that. Not if anything in her limited abilities could stop it. She hiked up her silk skirts and ran. Only Domin kept pace with her.

The crowd gathering along the pathway told her where to go. With that many people, the Grigori were either scared off, or Amy and her friends were too late.

Her speed carried her right through the onlookers to the body sprawled out on the turf. A body long past her help. A young man, fully dressed, but his skin sunken and dry. Amy's pulse thudded in her ears, and she could only stare and gasp for breath.

Domin gently took her shoulders to turn her away. "You don't have to see that."

"No, I need to. I need to know what they're doing. The price of...of my failure."

"Amy," Domin said. "This is the work of the Grigori, not you."

She met his eyes and winced away from the sympathy and understanding she saw there. How foolish Domin must think her. How helpless she felt.

Fitzhugh led the others through the crowd. Amy felt the glamour rolling off of him, likely making the bystanders passive and forgetful. They wouldn't interfere or call for a constable until Fitzhugh wanted them to.

Henry knelt beside the young man and shook his head. "He's long dead."

"No, he's not," Cassandra said. "I mean, yes, he is dead. But he can't have been dead that long. Look at his fingers. Georgina's fingers look like that when she's just finished painting."

Cassandra's face was bright red when she finished talking, but Henry examined the poor lad's fingers.

"Yes," Henry said. "This paint does look fresh."

Fitzhugh crouched beside Henry, prodding the body with his cane. "Interesting. An artist, recently killed but drained of substance. Were the other bodies also artists?"

Henry rubbed his head. "Not that I noticed. Young, poor, and with Faerie blood. That was the pattern we found."

"But we could have missed it," Jairus admitted. "This fellow had Faerie blood, too?"

"Yes," Domin said. "A great deal, in fact. He may have been

a Faerie changeling. Perhaps his magic found an outlet in his painting."

Mary made a little squeaking noise and took another step back.

Fitzhugh gave her a derisive look and turned to Amy. "How did he feel when he died?"

Amy wrapped her arms around herself and glared at Fitzhugh. "How did he feel? Terrified, no doubt. Helpless and alone."

"I'm not asking you to guess. I'm asking you to try to sense it. I don't feel any extraordinary suffering from him."

Amy raised an eyebrow. "He's past all suffering now."

Domin sighed. "If he died recently, some trace of his emotions might linger."

"Oh." Amy did not want to know how the young man felt while he died. But if it might help... She drew a deep breath and held it, stepping closer. Still nothing. She released her breath and took another, then placed her hand on the dead man's hand.

Emotions didn't swarm her as they would with a living person, but Domin was right: traces lingered. Amy looked up at the others, confused.

"He was...happy. How could someone be happy when this was done to them?"

"He wasn't thinking clearly, perhaps," Henry said.

"Or it caught him unexpected," Jairus added quietly. "If he was painting—doing what he loved—and then he was gone."

Fitzhugh pushed himself up with his cane and stared off toward the Thames flowing like a dark thread through London. "I don't like this."

Jairus snorted. "For once we agree on something."

Fitzhugh gave him a cutting look. "We need to know what

creature did this. The Grigori may have helped, but they could not have caused this death."

"Rushford's Dark Muse then?" Henry asked.

"If only you hadn't bungled your early searches and had noticed if the others were artists, too," Fitzhugh said.

Amy thought of the girl she had seen die. The one who had fought off the Grigori. "I think...I think the one I saw was a singer or an actress. She had that feel about her. Creative."

Domin frowned at that, his green eyes troubled. He looked to Fitzhugh. "The Grigori were trying to summon a Leannan."

"A demon," Jairus said, glancing at the brand in his palm.

"Of a sort," Fitzhugh said. "She's a Fay who was banished from this world. But Rushford didn't finish the ritual," Fitzhugh said. "They didn't make a sacrifice. And even if they had, she should have been contained in the circle."

Cassandra gasped. "No! They broke the circle in the fighting. The lines were smudged away."

"And," Henry said to Fitzhugh, "your queen spilled Sir Walter's blood in the circle."

Fitzhugh paled, then his color came back, and he laughed. "So, they succeeded after all. They turned a Leannan loose on England."

"What does a Leannan do?" Cassandra asked.

"Dark Muse is an apt description," Fitzhugh said. "They're drawn to creative people, and they make a trade: a short but brilliant creative career in exchange for the person's energy and life. The more she feeds, the more powerful she becomes."

"And they like those with Faerie blood?" Jairus asked.

Fitzhugh shrugged one shoulder. "Not necessarily, but the Grigori do."

"So, perhaps we know what we're fighting," Jairus said. "That will make it easier."

Domin shook his head. "No. The Leannan, like the Morrigan, can be banished, but not killed. Now that she's free, she will not go easily back into the dark."

Mary sagged. Amy caught her arm but felt like swooning herself. How were they supposed to stop a creature so powerful? One that couldn't die?

Chapter Eighteen

Amy's gas lamps burned bright in the foggy London night, giving Henry the eerie feeling that they were sending up a beacon for the Leannan and the Grigori. Amy still refused to invite Fitzhugh inside, but he seemed content enough with his quarters in the garden. The Unseelie elf had looked thoughtful on the walk back from the Strand, which made Henry even more uneasy. He stayed close to Cassandra as if he could shield her, but he didn't have any idea how to fight a Leannan.

"If we stop the Grigori, won't that stop the Leannan?" Amy asked once they'd gathered in the drawing room and closed the curtains on the view of the street.

"Or it might cut her tether and set her free to prey on even more people," Domin said. "We don't know if the Grigori have any control over her."

Lucien shrugged. "So, let her continue consuming the Fay. I don't understand why you're trying to stop them."

Amy bristled at that, but Henry cut in, "I swore I would try to stop the Grigori, and you know as well as the rest of us that a Faerie oath is binding."

Lucien gave Henry a grudging nod, then fell into a brooding silence. The changeling didn't like any of them—though he tolerated Mary—but he seemed willing to listen to Henry. Perhaps because they were both human changelings or because Henry had a form of freedom from the Fay. Even that level of trust made Henry uneasy, uncertain he deserved it, but he hoped he might help Lucien find some measure of peace, if not freedom.

"So, we have to stop the Leannan and Grigori both," Jairus said. "We should banish the Leannan first. Take away their most powerful ally."

"But how?" Cassandra asked quietly.

That brought them to silence again.

Jairus sighed. "We should sleep on it. We ain't going to accomplish anything tonight."

Everyone mumbled their agreement. Henry knew he wouldn't be able to sleep, but they did need rest. Mary was practically asleep standing up, Amy had dark smudges beneath her eyes, and even Domin looked weary.

Henry smiled at Cassandra as she turned for her room, and she returned a tired half-smile, still lovely in her ballgown despite her tired eyes. Henry strode to the window, peeking past the curtains to watch the empty street. He would protect Cassandra. And everyone else.

"You're not going to sleep?" Domin asked behind him.

Henry sighed and turned. "I don't think I can. The Leannan is out there, And the Grigori. And Spring-heeled Jack."

"He is no threat, at least," Domin said.

"I don't know. If Amy's correct, he broke into our old lodgings. I don't trust him."

"You shouldn't. But I find it unlikely that he would harm any of us while he wants our protection from the Grigori."

Henry took small comfort from that. "The Morrigan is out there, too. And the Wild Hunt may ride again. I don't want to see a war in London. Between her and the Leannan..." One brought widespread destruction, the other personal devastation. Both were terrible. "Last time, we thought we were safe at the Weaver's house because we forgot about the dangers of the Dark Lady's human allies posed. I don't want to make that mistake again."

Domin's tense posture softened. "You're correct. But you don't have to guard them alone. I need less sleep. You should rest."

Henry wanted to argue, but Domin was right. "Thank you."

The room Henry shared with Jairus and Lucien was more comfortable than any place he had slept since leaving Elfland, but still he didn't rest well, worrying about everyone in London. Worrying about Cassandra. By dawn, he didn't have a solution for London, but he did have an idea that might protect Cassandra and his other friends.

He snuck downstairs at dawn without waking Jairus or Lucien and sought out Telesm. Luckily, the Faerie changeling seemed to need as little sleep as his brother, and he was already in the dining room, frowning at a cup of tea as if it had offended him.

The table was still outside, but Amy had arranged a sideboard for them to place their food on and several chairs scattered about the room.

Henry pulled a chair up to sit across from Telesm. "You

made your cottage a sanctuary—a place where no other creature can enter unbidden or uninvited."

"Yes," Telesm said, raising an eyebrow. He said it in the same cool, confident manner that Domin used, but with a bit more arrogance.

"How did you manage it? Could you do it here? I think it would be wise to keep our enemies away if we can."

Telesm's cool arrogance softened, replaced with a spark of interest. "I created warding spells to animate my guardians. I am a Faerie changeling, recall—and a rather powerful one—and I can infuse things with magic. Like your little friend Mary Leland, though I am much more proficient than her. You could not do it, because you are a human changeling. Though..." he tilted his head and studied Henry. "You are different. You can manipulate Faerie energy, too. That is strange."

"That's the work of the Dark Lady. She pushed so much magic through me that it... it broke something inside of me."

Telesm laughed. "You are giving her too much credit. What she was doing could have killed you, but it could not have unlocked an ability that you didn't have. You are a royal changeling, are you not?"

Henry had to resist the urge to roll his eyes after listening to Jane's boasting about royal blood. Instead, he only sighed. "Yes, I am."

"I don't know as much about your cold, bleak little island —such an out of the way place in the grand scheme of the world—but I know in Persia, our kings had some Faerie blood. That is why I am a Faerie changeling and not a human one—my mother was pure Fay, and my father part human and part Fay."

"Both of my parents are—were—human," Henry said.

"Mostly human, but I sense a trickle of Faerie blood in you as well. Your royal ancestors knowingly or unknowingly mingled with Fay in the past. I suspect the Fay's tinkering with bloodlines may have backfired on them in your case. Eh, Domin?"

Henry turned to find Domin listening to their conversation with evident interest.

"You have been a guardian of this bloodline, Brother." Telesm gestured to Henry like he was a pedigree chart on the wall. "Has it intermixed with the Fay?"

"Not directly," Domin said. "No human-Fay alliances. But yes, some of Henry's ancestors married people with Faerie blood."

"There you have it." Telesm dunked a thin slice of the sugar loaf into his tea. "With some Faerie blood in your veins, and the foolish Faerie Queens actually giving you magic, they unwittingly bestowed on you the ability to use that magic against them as well." Telesm grinned like it was the best joke he'd heard in ages.

"Does that mean Jane can do so as well?" Henry asked, thinking of the manic gleam in her eyes. "She and I would be distant cousins."

"Oh, she probably could, if she was determined enough to reach that deeply. But she's not very stable. You must have been very motivated and willful to learn to do it."

Henry remembered watching his friends—watching Cassandra—ready to fall to the Dark Lady. "I was."

"Let us hope that Jane never learns this," Domin said. "And that she never finds the will to bend that magic in different ways."

"Does this mean that I can set up a protection, then?" Henry asked.

Telesm sniffed. "Of course not. You're still not a Faerie changeling."

Domin gave his brother a stern look. "The Lords and Ladies are not changelings, either, and they establish the boundaries of the realms."

"Your little charge here is not a Faerie Lord."

"Thank goodness!" Henry said. "I only want to protect this place—or someplace—more securely against the solitary Faerie and our human enemies. The Dark Lady and the Seelie Queens can't come in without an invitation, but their influence still might, especially with some of her servants here."

"Don't want Fitzhugh spying on us, eh?" Telesm sipped his tea. "I do agree with that idea."

"Then you can protect this place?" Henry asked.

He set down his cup. "Not entirely, because it is not mine. It belongs to the pretty traitor."

"She's not a traitor," Domin snapped.

"Well." Telesm raised an eyebrow. "When did you start defending her?"

Domin shrugged one shoulder. "We've all made mistakes. She's paid for hers and is trying to move past it. We should as well."

Henry echoed Telesm's surprise. He knew Amy had betrayed Domin—hurt him—but before that moment, he had forgotten that to be wounded deeply, one also had to care deeply.

"Hmph." Telesm smirked. "Regardless, Amy does not have a strong will."

"You underestimate her," Domin said. "She does not have a great deal of confidence, but her will is surprisingly resilient."

"Really?" Telesm gave his brother a speculative look. "If you think she's up to it, then we could try to protect this house."

~

Amy set down her toasted roll as she listened to Henry and Telesm's plan, not certain she understood. "You think I could create a sanctuary? Against powerful Faerie creatures?"

Telesm shrugged. "Personally, I don't think you're up to the task, but Domin does. He says you are remarkably willful."

Amy flushed and mumbled, "Yes, I suppose he would think that."

"He didn't mean it that way," Henry said, casting Telesm a withering look. "He said you were resilient."

"Oh." Amy thought that over—all the times her mother had pushed her down, and Amy continued to get back up. To hope for something better of herself even when no one else did. Was that resilience, or only stubbornness? She *had* chosen not to associate with the Faerie courts. She was not truly as independent as a solitary Fay—not strong enough to completely break free from them—but she supposed that it did take some willpower even to step back. The idea filled her with warmth. "Well, then I think it's an excellent idea."

"I want the Faerie changeling for this, too," Telesm said. "I might as well teach her something useful. She's not exceptional, but she has some raw talent."

"I'm sure she'll be delighted to hear herself described that way," Henry said.

Amy snorted. "We won't pass on Telesm's exact words."

Telesm shrugged. "Whatever you think best. I don't deal in people. Magic is my interest, and you do pose some interesting magical theories for me to test. In fact, I'd love to experiment on you later, Henry."

"No, thank you!" Henry said.

Amy laughed.

"Bring me some objects that are yours—that have personal

meaning to you," Telesm said. "And bring me the changeling girl."

Amy summoned Mary to the dining room, and then she went to her room to pick out a few favorite pieces of jewelry. She chose things that were distinctly hers—not her mother's, and definitely not her late husband's: a pearl necklace, an emerald pendant set in gold, a delicate ring with a piece of shell carved into a rose, and an enameled brooch with a harp.

Amy brought the jewelry downstairs and laid the objects on the sideboard.

Telesm pulled Mary up beside him and gestured to the objects. "You are going to learn to infuse these things with magic.

"I really only know how to fix things," Mary said quietly. "Mechanical things."

Telesm ran his hands over the jewelry and frowned at Amy. "I'm not certain any of these have a strong enough emotional connection, anyway. You might think they're pretty, but there's no depth to your feelings about them."

Amy pursed her lips. She liked wearing those things, but Telesm was right: she didn't have any strong memories associated with them. Many of her memories were unpleasant, and she tried not to dwell on them. She glanced at Mary, who stared at the jewelry with a despondent expression. None of the jewelry needed to be repaired or even cleaned. Amy took excellent care of her possessions.

Amy brightened. "Wait! I have an old clock. The first one I purchased for myself. It doesn't work anymore."

"Ideal!" Telesm said. "Mary will repair it, but with the idea that the sound will keep unwelcome guests away. Then, as long as it runs, it will help protect those within these walls—those that Amy invites within."

Mary looked skeptical, but Amy left her to discuss the idea with Telesm, hurrying up the stairs to the attic. She hated revisiting the memories there—memories of her many past failures. She had regretted putting the clock there when it stopped working, but it had fallen out of fashion, and the clock maker had convinced her to buy a newer one.

The clock face was not very large, but it was built into a delicate pedestal of carved wood that looked like flowering vines, which made it almost as tall as Amy. She took out a white handkerchief and dusted off the oak case and the gilding that adorned the carved roses on the pedestal and the tiny dryads supporting the clock's face. Her late, so-called husband would have hated it—he had insisted on everything in his home being stark and masculine. This was one of the first things Amy had purchased when she was free of him. One of her first steps toward declaring her own mind and will.

She lifted the clock and smiled to herself. Domin was right. She was willful. And resilient.

Chapter Nineteen

Mary stood alone with the broken clock in an unused sitting room. Telesm had insisted not only that she could enchant this clock, but also that she was better suited for it than he because she was more personally involved.

She touched the clock face, her fingers trembling. Repairing it was simple. She could already sense what was wrong with it. And sometimes she was able to convince mechanical things to work better for her. That, as far as she knew, was the extent of her magic. Not imposing her will on the moving parts of machines.

The craftsmanship of the clock was exquisite. She ran her fingers over the gilded flowers and the delicate, carved vines on the case. Amy said the clock made her feel more independent, but Mary sensed nothing of that from it. Just that it was lovely. Whoever had created it had put love into it, though.

Her father would admire this clock, too. Her throat tightened at the thought. She was angry with him for keeping her origins a secret, but she still loved him. She missed him. He hadn't objected to her coming to London when she announced she was going with Cassandra, but he had looked worried and sad. He let her go, perhaps sensing that she needed to do this. To find herself. Now was her chance to do just that.

She took the clock apart, carefully lifting the mechanical workings from the beautiful case. Even the brass gears of the escapement, which rocked back and forth to tick away the time, were delicate. Luckily, the clock was old enough that it didn't use iron to offset changes in temperature or weather. It might be slightly less accurate, but probably more amenable to magic. Mary smiled as she ran her fingers over the brass pieces.

Amy cleared her throat and walked up beside Mary. "I'm sorry to interrupt, but Telesm said I should assist."

"Oh." Mary didn't know how to have Amy help. "Well, it's good that none of the pieces need to be replaced. The escapement had been knocked out of alignment, but when I put the pieces back together, they'll work again."

"I'm glad. I like this clock." Amy stroked the case.

Mary cleaned and oiled the parts, and her thin fingers worked easily with the small pieces. The gears wanted to work, to tick away the minutes and hours. She encouraged them, and as she placed each in its place, she told them to do more—to frighten enemies away with every swing of the pendulum, with every tick.

All that was left was to set the clock in motion. She checked her own pocket watch to adjust the hands on the white enamel face, then made certain the pendulum was attached correctly.

"You can set the weights," Mary said.

Amy nodded and pulled them into place with obvious familiarity.

The satisfying tick of the clock filled the room, and Mary grinned.

"Hmph."

Mary gave a start and turned to see Telesm watching them.

"I repaired it," Mary said, her voice shaking under Telesm's critical stare.

He sighed and walked over to the clock. "Yes. I expect it will keep perfect time now. But that's all it will do. You haven't taught it to keep the unwelcome away."

"I tried," Mary said, her eyes stinging. "I don't know how to do anything different."

"You're not trying hard enough." Telesm yanked out the mechanism, silencing the clock. He set the pieces on the table. "Do it again."

Mary fisted her hands against her skirt. Her father was a much better teacher.

"Maybe if you helped us," Amy said.

"You simply have to put your will into the device," Telesm said.

"I don't know how!" Mary snapped.

"You'd better learn how—and find a way for the elf to help —or you and your friends may die."

With that, Telesm strolled out of the room.

Mary was tempted to throw her tools at the back of his head. Pompous, arrogant, petty. She gritted her teeth. How was she supposed to learn if he wouldn't teach her?

Blinking back stinging tears, she turned to the pieces. Luckily, Telesm hadn't damaged anything when he ripped the heart from the clock. She touched each piece gently as if she could reassure them that she would set them right again.

"He's impossible!" Amy said. "But we'll work it out."

If only Mary had Amy's stubbornness. Maybe then she would be able to do more impressive magic.

"What are you trying to do?" asked a voice from the doorway.

Mary looked up to find Lucien watching them warily.

"I'm fixing Amy's clock," Mary said.

Lucien wandered into the room and flopped down on the sofa. "I thought you were supposed to be good at fixing things."

"I am," Mary said quietly. "But I don't know how to make things do more than they were intended to do."

Lucien perked up at that. "Like what?"

Mary and Amy exchanged uncertain looks. How much should they share?

Mary realized Lucien would have some interest in deterring unwelcome guests, and he had his own kind of magic. "Keeping the Leannan and other enemies away."

She shuddered at the memory of the Morrigan gliding through the ballroom, sending belligerence through the crowd like a drop of oil spreading over water.

"With a clock?" Lucien asked.

"I know, it seems silly," Amy said, "but you haven't seen what Telesm's magic can do."

Mary sighed. "That's Telesm's magic, not mine." She looked up at Lucien. "Even you were able to put your anger into that electrical machine."

Amy looked surprised. "He did?"

"I don't know," Lucien said. "That's not how my magic usually works. I only have Mary's word that it happened."

"No, I felt it, too, now that you mention it." Amy studied Lucien. "The same anger you're radiating now, it was part of the machine."

"But my only magic is my voice, and it does me no good in a house full of people immune to Faerie magic." He tilted his head. "I did talk to the machine, though. When I was working on it, I complained to it about how the Fay treated me."

"Your voice might work on more than humans," Amy said. "The Fay sometimes make changelings more powerful than they intended."

Lucien's eyes brightened. "Like Henry Stewart. I've heard he can fight back against them."

"Yes," Amy said. "And this is our chance to fight back against the people who want to hurt us or use us. We just have to find a way to make it work. Telesm can do it."

"He's so powerful," Mary said.

"Well, I'm sure he wasn't always powerful," Amy countered. "And there are three of us."

Mary looked down at the clock pieces. It was hard to believe she could ever be more than the sad creature she was now.

"You don't think you can do this?" Amy asked her gently. "You've let the Fay convince you that you have no power, but you have to silence those voices. Fay like my mother don't lie, but they deceive."

"I don't have much power, but I want to help you and my other friends." Mary slid one of the gears into place.

Lucien scrutinized Mary. "How do you know they're not just using you for your magic? That's what the Fay do."

Amy gasped in indignation.

Mary adjusted the gear, remembering how kind Cassandra and Amy and Jairus had been to her, even when they didn't benefit from anything she did. No, she did not have the type of magic that people sought. More often than not, she was in the way, and she knew it. But her friends didn't turn her away. They worked together like the pieces of the clock. She added the next gear, and it hummed in satisfaction, ready to work—more than that, ready to obey.

She glanced at Lucien. "You don't know what it means to have real friends."

"No, I don't. The Dark Lady wants us to suffer. It feeds her. If we did make friends, she would only use them to hurt us more." Lucien shifted forward, a heavy sadness weighing down his shoulders.

"I'm sorry," Mary said, grateful once again that she had been spared from life with the Fay. "The people in my village are cruel to me, but my father is good, and my mother before she died. I know it's hard to believe that people can be caring when you've only seen them be heartless, but my friends are kind." She thought of Henry. "Most of the time."

"Then the Fay will destroy them." Lucien glanced again at Amy. "You know it's true."

Amy glared back. "My mother and her sister queens may try, but I will stand against them. I may not be as powerful, but I will die before I let them control me—or my friends."

The heat of Amy's emotions flooded the room—even warmed the gears under Mary's fingers.

"Then you probably *will* die," Lucien said.

Mary pinched her lips together and set the last gear into place with a firm click. "I won't let that happen."

Lucien folded his arms. "I don't see how you have any hope of standing against the Dark Lady. Someone who wins more with every setback you suffer."

Mary's hands froze, and they were all silent for a moment. It did seem like an impossible task.

"I suppose we can't let our setbacks cause us misery," Amy said. "If suffering helps her, then hope must keep her away."

Mary glanced up at Amy's stubborn pout, and she did feel hope. She didn't know why. Maybe because she'd seen the others successful at hurting the Dark Lady and fending off the

Seelie Fay. They'd done it once, so why couldn't they stop the Grigori as well? After all, the Grigori were only human.

She set the pendulum and felt her stubbornness twine with Amy's hope, both flowing into the clock. But would it really be strong enough?

"I don't know how to find hope," Lucien said quietly. "I'm not even sure what it feels like. When I think about it, I..." He screwed his face up and shook his head. "No, it's not worth trying."

Amy's face softened, and she edged closer to Lucien. "It can be frightening to hope. If we hope for something and it fails, it hurts. But if we don't try—if we don't keep trying—then they win."

Lucien's eyes flashed. "I don't know about that. But I don't want *her* to win. She always wins. Always. And I'm so tired of losing. I just want to be free." He jumped to his feet and pointed at the clock. "That has to work. It has to keep us safe."

His words reverberated in the room, all the way down into the brass pieces of the device. The bells chimed, their silvery tones filling the room.

Amy gasped, and they all stared at the clock.

Mary's fingers trembled as she set the weight, and the clock began its steady tick, each beat echoing through the silent room, a new power pulsing with each click of the gears.

"Much better," Telesm said from the doorway, wearing a smug smile.

"You made us angry on purpose," Amy said.

"Of course. It was the easiest way to rouse your emotions and your wills. And it's working." He tilted his head. "Using the human changeling's silver tongue was an interesting addition. I'll have to study how it affects the magic. But as long as the mechanism ticks, it will deter anyone who intends you harm from approaching the house. I'll add my own touches to the wards, but this is an excellent start."

Lucien glowered, and Amy huffed and put her hands on her hips, but Mary grinned to herself and rested a hand on the clock case. She might not be powerful enough to do magic like Telesm's on her own, but with her friends, she felt strong. And who knew what else she could accomplish?

Chapter Twenty

Amy placed the clock exactly where she wanted it in the front drawing room, moving it carefully as if she could disrupt the magic by jostling it. The clock struck the hour, the bells resounding through the house, and she could feel their protective influence swirling through the corners of the room.

The rest of her friends gathered around, staring at the clock. Mary grinned with pride.

"It worked, then?" Henry asked.

Domin nodded. "It did. Miss Leland did this?"

Amy smiled at Mary. "She did. Though, Lucien and I helped."

"Telesm said he was going to do more," Mary said quickly, as if distrusting her contribution.

Domin returned his attention to the clock. "He will probably set a guardian, but this will be very efficient. It's impressive."

Mary flushed and glanced around as though she didn't know where to look.

"It will keep our enemies away, then?" Jairus asked.

"It will turn away anyone who means us harm," Domin said. "What it lacks is a means to deal with those who try to fight their way past it. Telesm's lions serve that purpose for him. I imagine that will be his contribution."

Amy's eyebrows rose at that. She wasn't sure she wanted stone lions in front of her house—especially not ones that might come to life and terrify passersby. She would have to talk to Telesm about what he had in mind.

A knock sounded—at the back door. She had almost forgotten Fitzhugh. The clock hadn't driven him away, which meant that either he didn't mean them harm, or that he would soon be a victim of whatever beast Telesm was crafting. Amy swept past her friends to see what Fitzhugh wanted.

She opened the door to find him glaring at the roses climbing the sides of the house. "Yes?"

"You have been busy in there," Fitzhugh said. "Telesm's work?"

"Miss Leland's, in fact," Amy said, proud of her friend. But when Fitzhugh looked up with sharp curiosity, Amy worried that she should not have mentioned Mary. She quickly tried to divert his attention. "Does it bother you?"

"Not particularly, but Jane is extremely uncomfortable now. Whom is it supposed to affect?"

Amy didn't answer him, just glanced over his shoulder at where Jane paced in the back of the garden like a caged animal. Interesting. Fitzhugh didn't mean them harm—at least not in any direct way—but Jane did.

Fitzhugh looked past Amy into the house. "You might as well call your friends out here. I have an idea about the Leannan."

That drew Amy's attention. "Really?"

He raised an eyebrow. "You know I cannot lie."

He could deceive. Still, it was worth hearing his idea. She left the door open, since he could not cross the threshold, and called her friends to the garden. She didn't know where Telesm was, and Lucien refused to go anywhere near the Unseelie Fay, but the others came out, all looking wary.

Jane watched Cassandra with a deep interest that worried Amy, especially if Jane meant someone in the house harm. Cassandra had a demon mark. It drew the attention of dark things.

Jane bounced over to Cassandra. "What kind of magic do you have?"

Cassandra stepped closer to the roses along the house. "I don't have magic."

"Fitzhugh!" Jane called sharply. "Fitzhugh, tell me what kind of magic this mortal has. She is lying to me."

Fitzhugh smirked. "She didn't lie. She has no magic. She is Sabbath-born and can resist Faerie magic. That is all."

Jane's gaze sharpened, and she grinned at Cassandra. "Really? Fitzhugh can't enchant you? How annoying that must make you."

Cassandra colored. "I hope to annoy any Fay who tries to trifle with me."

"But being Sabbath-born doesn't make you immune to weather magic, does it? I could still freeze your blood or burn your bones."

Henry stepped up beside Cassandra, glaring dangerously at Jane.

Cassandra whisked out her iron knife. "Not so quickly as I could stab you with this."

Jane laughed. "Oh, you are the one who stabbed my Dark Lady? How droll. I'm sure someday she will let me play with you, then. But for now, I believe she had a reason for keeping you alive."

Jane met Henry's eyes and smirked, then she flounced back toward the small gazebo in the rear of the garden.

Amy let out a slow breath. Yes, she was glad Jane could not enter the house.

Jairus turned to Fitzhugh. "Lady St. Clair said you had an idea to stop the Leannan."

"I do." Fitzhugh walked to the table on the lawn with the map and the chess pieces. He picked up the queen. "There is a weapon we can use to defeat her."

"And what would that be?" Amy asked. "If it's something of Telesm's..." she glanced at Domin, who looked skeptical.

"You think he would allow us to use one of his toys?" Fitzhugh asked.

Amy smirked. "Probably not. He doesn't like you for some reason."

Fitzhugh grinned. "Foolish of him. It shows poor taste, don't you think?"

"I don't trust you."

"*That* is wise, my dear."

"Are you trying to manipulate us into stealing something from Telesm?" Henry asked.

"Not at all. In fact, even if he does have something that would work against the Leannan, we don't need him."

"What do you have in mind?" Domin asked.

Fitzhugh held up the queen. "She escaped from the world of spirits, correct?"

Domin nodded.

"Then we send her back."

"So, kill her?" Jairus asked, putting his hand on his pistol.

"No, it's not that simple," Fitzhugh said with exaggerated

patience. He looked to Domin. "But the Wild Hunt gave me an idea. What if the Hounds of Annwn chased her down? They could bring her to heel, don't you think?"

"Hell hounds?" Cassandra asked.

"No," Henry said. "Hell hounds are Faerie beasts commanded by the Lords and Ladies. The Hounds of Annwn hunt lost souls, like those escaped from the Otherworld."

The garden grew quiet except for the chirp of birds. In the distance, a crow cawed, and Amy spotted a flash of black feathers.

She wrinkled her forehead. "The Wild Hunt has already ridden through London. It didn't stop the Leannan or the Grigori."

Fitzhugh shrugged. "Not this time. I believe now that the Hunt is seeking the Leannan and not the Grigori, since she is the lost soul, but the Wild Hunt is a blunt weapon, not a precise tool. It's riding without direction."

"Do you plan to tell the Lord of Annwn to search the Strand?" Amy asked skeptically.

"Do you want to see him tear through the Strand?" Fitzhugh asked. "Do you want the Wild Hunt to ride through any part of London again and drive all those people mad?"

Amy lowered her gaze and shook her head. No, she did not want to see what the Wild Hunt would do to London before it found the Leannan.

"That sounds like something you would enjoy, though," Henry said, watching Fitzhugh suspiciously. "Why would you want to stop it?"

Fitzhugh took out his quizzing glass and spun in on its chain. "Oh, humans would suffer, and we would draw strength from it, but it would take so long, and then we would still have to find the Grigori."

Amy exchanged glances with her friends. They could not trust Fitzhugh or any of the Fay—especially the Unseelie Fay—but Fitzhugh and Jane were sworn to stopping the Grigori, too. A Faerie oath was one thing they could count on.

"What do you have in mind, then?" Amy asked.

"We find our way to Annwn and borrow one of the hounds. If we set a single hound to coursing in the Strand, it could lead us to the Leannan and the Grigori without the chaos you all dislike."

"You want to walk into the land of the dead?" Henry asked.

Mary let out a small groan, and Amy found herself in sympathy with her. That sounded like madness.

"Only to the gates," Fitzhugh said, as though that were reasonable. "One of its aspects is a castle on an island off our shores. It's shrouded in storms, but the Tempestarii can guide us through." He gestured to Henry and Jane.

"It can't be that easy to reach the lands of the dead," Jairus said.

"It won't be easy," Fitzhugh said. "Though I can offer you a faster—but permanent—way to journey there."

Jairus smirked. "Ha. After you."

"You wish us to journey the Twilight Vale and return," Domin said. "That's only possible..."

"Yes," Fitzhugh said, "twice a year. On May Day and on All Hallow's Eve, which is just a few days away."

"You're also suggesting we steal from the...the grim reaper," Henry said.

"Borrow. And he's not permitted to hunt souls out of vengeance. The Hounds of Annwn are among the few creatures that could return the Leannan to the otherworld where we would all prefer her to stay."

Amy looked to Domin. "Could this work?"

He sighed. "It's possible, yes. Once set loose in this world, one of Annwn's hounds would chase down a spirit that doesn't belong here and take it back to the otherworld. The Wild Hunt is a turbulent force without inhibitions, but a single hound would be more manageable."

"I still don't trust any plan that comes from you," Henry said. "How would you make sure the hound chased the Leannan and not another lost soul?"

"You think there are that many?" Fitzhugh asked.

"I think there are," Jairus said.

Fitzhugh shrugged. "Then we give it the Leannan's scent. Guide the hound to the site of her latest victim."

"Is this really the least...risky way to stop the Leannan?" Amy asked, looking to her friends and not Fitzhugh.

"Turning one of Annwn's hounds loose in London is only risky to wandering spirits," Domin said. "It's the Wild Hunt that's dangerous to the living, not the hounds alone."

"And the Lord of Annwn won't seek revenge?" Henry asked.

"I doubt he'll be happy with us, but Fitzhugh is correct that he does not seek souls out of vengeance. The hound would return to him. No, the riskiest part is walking the Twilight Vale. It's true that it should be possible to walk it and return on All Hallow's Eve, but if anyone lost their way, they would not be able to return to the mortal world. Or if the Lord of Annwn caught us, he might force us to join the Wild Hunt. There is also a danger of us leading angry souls back into the mortal world."

"If we don't stray from the path, we would be safe," Fitzhugh said.

"Have you ever journeyed through the vale?" Henry asked, looking at Fitzhugh and Domin.

Fitzhugh shrugged. "No, but I know it can be done."

"I have not traveled it, either," Domin said. "Usually, those who do so are trying to find a lost soul and restore it to the mortal world before the person passes fully to death. They rarely succeed."

"And there's not a less...mystical way of capturing the Leannan?" Jairus asked.

"She must serve those who are able to resist her... temptations," Domin said, "but even if we were willing to risk facing her, that would only subjugate her, not banish her. What Fitzhugh suggests might be the surest way to rid London of her feeding and deter the Wild Hunt's devastation."

They all grew quiet, thinking, Amy guessed, as she did of the deaths the Leannan had already caused. Faint voices from the street reached them, reminding her of the naive world out there, unaware of the danger.

"I'm willing to try," Amy said.

"That's good," Fitzhugh said, "because you should be able to help us find the entrance to the Twilight Vale."

"Me? Why?"

"Because it is marked by the dreams and hopes of those that are lost there, in the world between the living and the dead. Your sensitivity to emotion would make it easier for you to find."

"You can sense emotion, too," Amy said.

Fitzhugh frowned. "It seems I can only trace negative emotions."

Amy stared at him in horror. "Only negative?"

Fitzhugh snapped the chess piece back down on the board. "Yes, all feeling is now suffering to me."

Amy gasped, and Cassandra covered her mouth in horror.

"Save your pity for someone who needs it," he said, his eyes troubled.

Amy did pity him. He had chosen the Unseelie Court thinking it would make it stronger. And perhaps it had. But it had cost him his ability to feel any joy in the accomplishment.

"I'm also willing to try Fitzhugh's plan," Henry said quietly, "since Domin thinks it's reasonable."

The rest of them nodded. They would continue trying to track down the Grigori, and in a few days' time, they would journey the path through the Twilight Vale.

Chapter Twenty-One

All Hallow's Eve. Cassandra's birthday. They were leaving that night for the realm of the dead, but Henry wanted Cassandra to know that he was thinking of her. That he thought of her all the time.

He snuck out early to find exactly what he wanted to give her. That wasn't true. What he wanted to give her was himself. The chance to find out if what he felt was real. If she felt it, too. He didn't know much about love. How could he, when he had known so little of it? What he did know was that Cassandra made him want to be better. To be worthy of the way she looked at him. And he wanted to make her happy in return.

He returned just after breakfast time with a rose in a pot. A new statue by the front door caught his eye. A carved dog. He eyed it warily.

"Telesm has been adding his own touches to the house," Fitzhugh said behind him.

Henry turned, and Fitzhugh flinched away from the rose.

"Ah, yes." Fitzhugh studied the rose through his quizzing

glass. "It's Miss Cassandra's birthday, is it not? You should stop toying with her."

"I don't know what you mean," Henry said.

Fitzhugh snorted. "Liar. I don't need to be an elf to know that you desire her, and she you. It is not a subtle emotion."

"It's not that simple," Henry said.

"It's very simple. You're thinking too much like a human." Fitzhugh pocketed his quizzing glass. "You cannot marry her—your Lady would be far too jealous and use it against the both of you—but our kind often take human lovers."

It was only the flower pot in his hands that kept Henry from lashing out at Fitzhugh—not as much at his suggestion but at the reminder of what Henry couldn't have. "I'm not your kind, and neither is she. Even if she wouldn't be insulted by the idea, I would never put her in a situation that would risk leaving her vulnerable—cast off by Society."

"Oh, no real harm would come of it." A bitter note entered his voice. "Seize your happiness where you can."

Henry scoffed. "Unseelie Fay know nothing about happiness. Neither do most of the Seelie Court. But I've seen glimpses of it, and I won't settle for the Faerie substitute."

With another glance at Telesm's dog, which remained motionless, Henry pushed open the door.

Domin met him in the foyer. "It's not safe to wander about alone, not with the Grigori out there. And especially not on All Hallow's Eve."

"I waited until daybreak," Henry said. "I doubt the Grigori are even awake this early. And it's Miss Weaver's birthday. So, before you tell me that was a foolish reason to sneak out—"

Domin's expression softened. "I only said it was foolish to go alone. You think I would have stopped you?"

Henry sighed. "I don't know. I guess I assume everything I do is reckless, and you won't approve."

"Love is always risky," Domin said. "That doesn't mean it's wrong."

Henry gave a start at that. He had been talking about going to the flower market early, not his feelings for Cassandra. But maybe that's what all of this was about. He set down the potted rose. "You loved someone once. A mortal woman." It wasn't a question. He'd already gleaned the answer.

Domin nodded once, and Henry thought that was the end of it. Domin didn't discuss the past if he could help it. But Henry waited.

Domin sighed and rubbed his eyes. "Maybe I still love her, in a way. It's been so long, and even my memory fades over time. I think I only cling to the ideal that she represented. She was brave and full of vitality and faith. They were things I didn't have at the time. Maybe things I've started to lose again. I was drawn to her like the rivers are drawn to the sea. I needed to be worthy of her."

Henry shifted, uncomfortably aware that this woman Domin loved was an ancestor of his—the founder of the bloodline Domin swore to protect. Yet it sounded like Domin had once felt for her what Henry felt for Cassandra. "She must have been remarkable."

"I thought so. She taught me to be better. But, though we were friends, she chose a mortal love."

Henry flinched at those words. Was this his destiny as well? To love from a distance and lose his own mortal love to time?

"Do you regret it?" Henry asked.

Domin shook his head slowly. "It has been painful, but it also helped me to be who I wanted to be. I will never regret loving, even if I might have wished it ended differently."

Henry didn't want to think of such an ending for himself. He looked down at the thorns adorning the stems of the rose, touching the sharp edge of one of them. What a long, lonely life it would be after the one you loved was gone. If Cassandra would agree to be with him, even knowing that she would age and he would not, he would someday lose her and be alone. "Such love must only come once in a lifetime."

Domin looked struck by the question, and his expression grew distant. "Not necessarily. It is something I thought of at one time...in the past. I believe a first love will always dwell in a corner of your heart, but to love again is not necessarily disloyal. It could honor the first love by showing that you remember that love is something worth taking the risk for."

It seemed so strange to hear Domin speak of taking risks. Of course, he was talking about Henry. Wasn't he?

Domin picked up the potted rose and studied it thoughtfully. He handed it to Henry, then walked away.

Henry took a deep breath. Well, he was reckless.

He found Cassandra in the library. She looked up from the letter in her hands, a frown creasing her brow.

"What's worrying you?" he asked.

She sighed. "My sisters are unhappy not to be in London. I wish I could warn them how dangerous things truly are here."

"We'll soon have London safe for everyone again," Henry said. He held out the potted rose. "In the meantime, happy birthday."

"You remembered!" She limped over to take the plant.

"I thought you would like a live plant better than cut flowers. It's an apothecary's rose. Not as flashy as some roses, but beautiful."

She flushed. "And I suppose it will keep the Fay away."

"Quite effectively." He grinned and gave in to the temptation to brush his thumb over her freckles.

Her flush deepened, her skin warm beneath his thumb. He ran his fingers down the smooth curve of her jawline. Her lips parted, and her eyes fluttered shut. He ached to kiss her—deeply—to run his fingers through the tangled auburn curls of her hair, to pull her close to him. They were walking into the land of the dead that night. Who knew what might happen?

He leaned closer, and the rose she held pricked him, its thorns pressing against his chest. A kiss was like a promise, and what could he promise her?

He took a steadying breath and settled for a gentle kiss on her forehead.

"How do you want to celebrate your birthday?" he asked, his voice low.

She opened her eyes and gazed at him, her expression a little sad. "I've been reading up on the stories about Annwn..."

Henry shook his head. "No. I think if we're going to face death, we should do it full of life. What do you actually want to do?"

"Actually?" She smiled and gazed down at the rose. "I would like to walk in Hyde Park and eat ices and not worry about any of this."

"Done," Henry said. "I can even provide the ices."

"Isn't that a silly way to use your abilities?"

"Not if it makes you happy. I'd much rather use it for this than something dangerous."

Henry wondered if he'd said too much, referring to his past. But Cassandra just nodded, her eyes full of understanding. He offered his arm, and she set the rose aside to take it, leaning slightly on him to offset her limp.

"Do you want your cane?" he asked at the door.

"I don't think I need it, if you're escorting me."

He smiled and led her outside to the square in front of the house. The morning sun was warm, smiling down on them. Would it be their last morning under the sun? No, they would return from the Twilight Vale. They had to—not just for themselves, but for all these strangers chatting with friends or gazing in shop windows. The Grigori and the Leannan couldn't be allowed free access to the innocent, or even the not-so-innocent.

They walked past an ice shop, and Henry bought one for Cassandra. He could have produced the ice himself, but this attracted less attention. They strolled on to the park, Cassandra leaning on him, and he happy to help her keep her balance. She helped him keep his in a whole different way—reminding him of all that was good in the world despite the Fay and Grigori and the rest of his troubles.

They found their way to the Serpentine Lake in Hyde Park. Cassandra smiled at the sight of a mother swan guiding her nearly-grown cygnets into the water. A heavy feeling grew in Henry's chest. Cassandra probably wanted children, but his magic might make him unable to give them to her. As much as he cared about her, and he believed she cared for him, he saw no way to offer her the happy life she deserved. Like Domin, he might have to watch the person he loved share her life with another in order for her to be happy—be a protector instead of a lover.

Cassandra looked up at him, and he forced a smile. "We could take a boat out on the lake. Or, if you prefer, I could freeze it, and we could skate."

A flash of unease flickered in her eyes, just as it had when he'd joked about freezing the lemonade at the ball. Did she hate the reminders of his magic? Or was it something else?

"Miss Weaver?" He touched her arm, and she tensed. Like she was afraid of him again. He quickly drew his hand back. "Please, tell me what's wrong."

She frowned and stared out at the lake. "I... I don't know. I mean, I'm not sure if I can ask because I think I know the answer, but I don't want to."

A hollow, sick feeling opened in Henry's stomach. She was realizing what he already knew—that their relationship was doomed. "I will tell you anything you want...*need* to know."

She sighed and closed her eyes. "It's... the Dark Lady."

"Did Fitzhugh hurt you?" Anger crackled through Henry at the idea. He would kill Fitzhugh whatever the consequences.

"No, but the Dark Lady found a bitter revenge." She met his eyes. "Mr. Stewart...I see things in my dreams. Terrible things. And I'm afraid they may be real."

"I'll protect you—"

"No." She shook her head. "I see you. And Domin. Amy. Even Mr. Hale. In the past. There's so much violence and pain."

"Oh." Henry sat heavily on a bench facing the lake and took off his hat to run his hand through his hair. His past was always there, waiting to ruin his hopes of happiness. "I've told you that I did things I regret. I didn't mean to hide anything from you."

"I know. But it was much easier when that was an abstract idea. When I hadn't seen it for myself. I'm not saying... I know that's not who you are now. That the Fay made you do things. But it can be hard to separate."

Henry crushed the brim of his hat. "I'm sorry. That's not a burden I would wish you to carry. It's one I have to carry for the rest of my life."

Cassandra stood silent for a few moments. Then she sat next to him. She placed a tentative hand on his arm, and he resisted the urge to grasp it for reassurance.

"I don't want to throw the past in your face," she said. "I only want you to understand why sometimes it alarms me to be reminded—"

"I won't use my magic anymore," Henry said quickly. "Not if it frightens you."

Her hand trailed down his arm to his fingers, and she stroked his hand in a way that was dangerously distracting. "No, that would be wrong. Your magic is a part of you. It doesn't frighten me anymore."

"I don't want it to stand between us," he whispered.

She squeezed his hand. "It's not your magic between us. It's the Fay."

"I will find a way to break free of them."

He met her hazel stare and raised her hand to his lips, pressing a kiss on her gloved knuckles. Then he turned her hand over, baring her wrist, and kissed the warm skin where her pulse beat fast beneath his lips. She sighed and closed her eyes. He pulled her closer. He could not kiss her there in the park, in front of everyone. He should not kiss her at all. But his gaze traveled down to the soft fullness of her lips, and he leaned near enough to feel her breath on his cheek.

Someone shouted.

Cassandra jumped back, her eyes wide and guilty. Henry flinched. He was being reckless—reckless with Cassandra, and he could not forgive himself if he hurt her.

More shouts drew him back to his surroundings.

"What happened?" Cassandra asked a little breathlessly.

"I think we should go see." He helped her to her feet.

They followed the sound of alarmed voices. Henry tightened his grip on Cassandra and kept her close as they pushed their way through the gathering crowd. They found people clustered around a woman lying in the grass next to an easel, her eyes staring at nothing.

"Let me through," Henry called. "I'm a surgeon."

Not entirely true yet, but he was more helpful than the people standing about gawking.

The crowd moved for him, and he knelt beside the young lady. Based on her clothing, she was relatively well-off. And she was dead, her neck broken.

"She was an artist," Cassandra said, her voice tight. "Look at her painting."

Henry barely took in the faithful representation of the park. He looked around at the bystanders.

"What happened here?" he demanded.

"A man attacked her," one woman said breathlessly. "Tried to drag her off—a respectable girl in the middle of the day!"

"She fought him," a young man said, swallowing several times, "and she fell. I should have chased the man, but I stopped to see if she needed help and...and..."

"There's nothing you could have done for her," Henry said. "But you were right to try to help."

He should have been the one to chase the man down. One of the Grigori, no doubt, becoming bold or desperate to abduct a middle-class girl in front of a crowd. And if he hadn't let himself be distracted, wishing for things he could never have, he might have been able to do something about it. To catch the man. To save the poor girl.

A constable approached, and Henry backed away. There was nothing more he could do there. He took Cassandra's arm again in a protective grip and led her away.

Her eyes were rimmed red, her lips pressed together in pain. "She reminded me of Georgina." Her voice caught. "We have to stop them."

Henry nodded. "Tonight we raid Annwn."

Chapter Twenty-Two

Amy found her way outside well before the sun went down. The others weren't ready to leave yet for the Twilight Vale, but she was too restless to stay in the house, so she decided to be the first to their rendezvous point in the garden.

Well, except for the Unseelie Fay.

Fitzhugh paced around the table with the map and chess pieces, his expression as close to worried as Amy had ever seen it. Jane had made herself at home in the small gazebo near the back wall—as far from the roses as possible. She had a large mirror hung inside to assist in arranging her hair, pillows to rest on, and colorful fabric festooning the wooden supports.

"You're being short-sighted," Jane called out to Fitzhugh, not knowing or not caring that Amy was present. "There is much more to be had in Annwn than a stupid dog."

Fitzhugh sighed, looking as weary as a parent with an over-energetic toddler, and rubbed his eyes. "Our lady ordered us to stop the Grigori. Nothing more."

"She always wants more," Jane snapped. "And the treasures in Annwn's Keep—"

"Are in the keep," Fitzhugh said. "Mortals cannot tread there and return unchanged—including Fay."

"Change is not always bad," Jane said, fastening up another braid.

"Our lady has a distinct lack of appreciation for change that she didn't initiate."

Jane hmphed and went back to her hair.

Jairus soon joined them. He kept a hand on his pistol and jumped at every sound. "We're being watched. Not all the eyes are friendly."

"It's the dead," Domin said, coming down the stairs. "They are restless tonight."

"Do they know we're coming?" Jairus asked.

Henry and Cassandra walked into the garden together, and Mary snuck behind them as though hoping to be overlooked.

Domin squinted like he was trying to pierce the veil between worlds. "They might know our intent and hope that we will offer them a way back to this world. But we cannot begin our journey here. The path to the Twilight Vale starts along the old corpse roads, though it diverges from them— body and soul parting ways."

"So, are we going to be tromping through people's fields and houses?" Henry asked.

Domin shook his head. "Crops won't grow along the paths of the dead, and people would feel an aversion to building homes there. It's not a place for the living."

Even Jane looked a little uncomfortable in the silence that followed.

Amy shook off her unease. "I have ordered us a carriage for

the first part of the journey. Domin, you will have to tell it where to go."

He nodded, and when they went around front and crammed into the carriage, he instructed the driver to a small village outside London.

"Will you need a ride back, then?" asked the driver, eyeing them curiously.

"No," Domin said.

Amy shivered at the finality of his words.

When they settled into their seats, she was squished between Cassandra and Domin. Cassandra's emotions were muted, as always, but little flares of alarm sparked from her, and she leaned against Henry on her other side.

Domin was completely blank to Amy, and she wished for once she could sense something from him. Some hint that he thought they would survive this. His forehead creased and his green eyes focused on some far-off worry.

He glanced down, perhaps sensing her eyes on him, and he caught her nervous gaze. One corner of his mouth lifted in a half smile, and he squeezed her hand, his strong fingers reassuring against hers. Then, he was back in his own thoughts. But as Amy rested her head against the carriage seat, she was no longer as frightened. If she had to walk to the gates of death, at least she was doing it with the strongest person she knew.

The driver left them at a lonely little village comprised of a few stone cottages.

Jairus drew his gun, his eyes alert.

"Sense something, priest?" Fitzhugh chuckled.

"If you don't, you're more dead than them," Jairus said, looking around like the veil had already parted for him.

Amy swallowed hard. She thought Jairus was right. She

sensed the whispers of many old emotions: grief, pain, regret, relief.

Domin pointed. "The corpse road starts there. We'll have to tread carefully to find where the Twilight Path splits from it."

They walked forward, falling into a single file line. Domin took the lead, Amy behind him, and Jairus behind her. Jane and Fitzhugh fell to the back.

They reached a sharp turn in the corpse road where a little stone bridge went over a stream. The dead did not cross moving waters. Domin looked back at her. The road had to split here, and they expected Amy to sense it.

Amy tried to focus on the emotions around her. She opened herself to them, and they spilled around her like water flowing to a drain. She had to separate out the threads. Domin was a stalwart form before her that gave away nothing. Fitzhugh was...pain and frustration. Jane was burning with determination. Henry radiated determination too, but his was more like an ember, not as bright, but likely to burn hotter and longer. Mary was afraid. Cassandra was as well, but hers was a deeper fear, a gnawing worry. And Jairus exuded curiosity.

Now, Amy had to dig deeper. Feel more. There was no one else around. No one else she could see. But if the dead traveled this path, she should be able to sense them.

And it was there, like the tracks of an ancient road, faint but deeply worn. She had almost missed it because it wasn't what she had expected—fear or despair. There was some confusion, and yet also a deep sense of peace. An inevitability. The knowledge that, at some point, all must follow this path.

The feeling caught hold of her. It drew her in, and she walked forward, leaving the marked road. If she could find rest by following it, why should she not walk in the steps of the path that someday all would walk? Part of her mind screamed at her to hold on to the smell of the grass and the wild tang of the breeze whipping through her hair, but that part seemed so distant, so long ago and far away that it no longer mattered, and even though everything was in darkness, she sensed that there was a light out there, beyond the horizon, a new hope and meaning that she had not yet dreamt of and would not understand until she had gazed on it for a while.

"Amy."

She knew that voice. Or, she had once. It had been important to her. Domin.

"Amy, it's not your time to listen to that call." Domin's voice tickled her ear, his breath warm and close. A very physical sensation that pulled her back through the darkness until she could smell the earth and the night air again.

Her eyes fluttered open, and she found that Domin was holding her arm to keep her from stepping off a sheer drop. He looked down at her, his gaze heavy with concern.

"Domin?" she whispered. "I'm not sure where I am."

"You're back where you belong." He stroked a strand of hair from her face.

Domin looked back to Fitzhugh. Oh yes, Fitzhugh was there. Weren't they trying to do something? It had been so very important, but she couldn't focus on it anymore.

"This is too dangerous," Domin said.

"You have another way to trap a Leannan?" Fitzhugh asked, his tone mocking.

Amy's memory clicked back together as if she had finally awakened from a deep and confusing dream. Domin didn't think she could do this.

"It's not too dangerous," she said. "I could sense which way the path goes. Down there, through that ravine."

"Excellent." Fitzhugh smiled. "Then let us away. We must make the trip while the sun is setting."

They found a place to climb down the steep walls of the ravine. Cassandra and Mary struggled with the narrow footholds, but Henry helped them both down. The bottom was narrow and too close and made Amy feel confused again, though there was only one way for them to go.

And then the ravine stopped, a huge boulder blocking their way.

"I suppose this would be no trouble for spirits," Henry said, "but we can't go through it. Or over."

Jairus scooted his way forward, studying the stone.

Fitzhugh looked back at Amy. "See if you can sense a way around."

Amy was afraid to try again. Afraid to lose herself to a path that was not yet hers to tread. But the desperate need to prove she could be of some use after all made her close her eyes.

"Fitzhugh, this is unwise," Domin said.

"We need her," Fitzhugh replied.

"No," Jairus called before anyone could argue about it further. "I found a cave. It's this way."

Fitzhugh narrowed his eyes. "How can you be certain? We cannot afford mistakes."

Jairus smirked. "God shows me the way. 'Yea though I walk through the valley of death—' Even you should know that one. One of these days, someone will be reciting it for you."

Fitzhugh looked shaken for a moment, but then he grinned. "Long, long after they have said it over your grave, human."

"We'll all be fortunate to escape this unscathed," Domin said.

The entrance to the cave was narrow and dark, barely wide enough for someone to squeeze through. Amy couldn't see anything beyond the gaping mouth. She sensed nothing from it. She was not nearly as useful as Jairus had been—just a silly girl almost getting herself lost or killed.

Jairus stepped toward the cave.

"Wait," Domin said.

Everyone turned to look at him.

"You have some sage advice for us, shape-shifter?" Fitzhugh said. "Even you haven't faced death."

"Not personally," Domin said, and he hesitated, pain in his eyes.

Amy remembered what he had once told her: that every time one of his charges died, he tasted a portion of their death. Centuries and centuries worth of loss.

"I've been on the edge of death," Domin went on quietly, "and I know something of it. Especially this: everyone walks the Twilight Path alone."

They all looked at each other.

"I mean," Domin said. "That we may find ourselves alone on the path. Or with companions who aren't among the living. Don't wander off course. Remember, the path will remain straight."

"What will we find through there?" Henry asked.

"I don't know for certain," Domin said. "But I believe at the end of the path, we will have to cross a lake or sea—not one of this world. Annwn's Keep is an island."

Jairus closed his eyes. "I smell salt water through the cave."

"Excellent." Fitzhugh said. "We stay on the path and find the sea. I imagine there will be a boat?"

Domin shrugged. "Perhaps."

Jairus holstered his pistol and stepped into the darkness. Fitzhugh and Jane followed, then Henry and Cassandra. Mary crept behind them.

Domin looked to Amy. "You don't have to follow. You are sensitive to the kinds of emotions that spirits cling to."

Amy shook her head. She would not be left behind again. "No, we all go together. But, I'm frightened. How will we find our way back?"

"I'm not entirely sure," he said. "But I think something in us will draw us back where we belong, as long as we return before dawn."

Amy wasn't sure where she belonged, except that it was with her friends.

Domin held out a hand to help Amy down to the cave entrance—to the liminal place between the worlds of the living and the dead. She allowed him to guide her forward, keeping a tight grip on his hand. But when she stepped into the darkness of the cave, all sense of him vanished. She was alone in the Twilight Vale.

Chapter Twenty-Three

A bullet whizzed past Jairus's ear, buzzing like a wasp. He threw himself to the ground. In the dim light, cannon boomed, shaking the earth and echoing in his chest. Nothing solid to hold onto.

Not again. His mind chose the worst moment to throw him into the past. He just had to hold to something in the present. But where was he?

A dying horse shrieked in the darkness.

"It's not real," he whispered.

"Oh, but it is," a female voice said. "Some poor souls are trapped in the past, reliving it every moment. Never able to find peace."

Jairus scrambled back, reaching for his pistol, but it was gone. The Morrigan stood above him, smiling with feline glee.

"You're not real," he said.

But he wasn't sure. The spirit of battle had never featured in his bad moments before.

She shrugged one shoulder. "What is real? I am here, but I

am not. I am one of the few who cross between life and death, after all, and tonight it is easy to walk through both at once."

"And I suppose you enjoy this," Jairus snarled.

"Ah, little mortal. You truly do see through a glass, darkly. I am not Unseelie. There is only suffering here—no striving for glory or for a cause—and suffering alone does not benefit me or bring me pleasure."

"Then why are you here?"

She swept her sword toward the struggle. "You think me one of your monsters, and perhaps I am, but I also bring an end to suffering for some. If any will look up, I will lead them onward to the Twilight Path so they can continue their journey."

"You mean I ain't on the path?" Jairus asked, looking around. And there, just beyond the fighting, he saw the road leading onward.

"You were distracted," the Morrigan said. "Unless you came to join the comrades you left behind? You're never far away from them, are you?"

Jairus straightened. If only the gunshots in the background would stop their ceaseless hammering, or his ears would stop ringing with screams. "I'll join them when it's my time. But I don't think that time's tonight."

"Then you had best find the path. But be warned: one of those who sets out on your journey tonight will never set foot in the living world again."

He narrowed his eyes. "Are you a prophet now?"

"I am the chief among the banshees; I can sometimes read the fates of men."

A chill took Jairus at her words. He would not see anyone killed. "Who, then?"

"That is not for me to say. You each must make your own choices."

"Then why bother telling me?"

"Consider it a warning from one warrior to another. There is a shadow over you, but you may yet escape it."

"I won't let someone else die in my place."

"That may not be your decision to make."

A whisper in the back of his mind, able to reach him even through the hellscape of war, affirmed that what she said was true.

He nodded in acknowledgment and turned his back on the Morrigan to face the road. He flinched as soldiers fought past him and guns blasted nearby. What happened if someone were shot in this twilight world? *I shall fear no evil.* They were only echoes from the past, and he had new battles to fight. *Thou art with me.* His heart hammered a fast tattoo, his pulse thrumming in his ears to the quick beat. His fingers twitched to draw a weapon, to join the fight. But that wasn't why he was here. He took a deep, uncertain breath. *Teach me thy paths.*

Henry reached back, searching for Cassandra's hand, but she was gone. He shook off his frustration. Domin had said they each had to walk alone. Cassandra was brave. She would find her way through. He had to hope he could do the same. He stepped deeper into the darkness, and the cave entrance widened into a path through a dimly lit forest.

Henry stopped. No. This was wrong. He knew this place. It was Titania's kingdom, though fallen under an endless dusk. Had they somehow walked through the wrong passage? He looked back. Only darkness waited behind him.

"Miss Weaver?" he called quietly into the gloom. "Domin?"

Nothing. He turned to face the road.

A dozen pale figures stood before him, staring with empty eyes. Henry stumbled back, instinctively drawing on the energies around him.

But there was nothing there. No energy. No magic. As if everything was dead.

This *was* the Twilight Vale, then.

And these were the dead.

He straightened to face them. More had gathered behind the first group, a wall of gray bodies blocking in his way. What was he supposed to do?

Domin had said the path must run straight, but he hadn't said anything about not talking to the dead.

"What do you want?" Henry asked.

They only stared, accusation in their hollow eyes. A shiver crept down Henry's back. There was something familiar about many of the faces, and he began to remember. The starving farmer with the wind-blasted crops. The shivering girl watching as her home burned. The woman drowned trying to save her cow from a flood. These were the humans the Fay had required him to punish for chopping down a favorite tree or speaking contemptuously of Titania. And he had done it: used his magic against them. Directly or indirectly, he had caused their deaths. And now, he had to face them. His stomach tightened into a heavy knot.

He was tempted to turn back or go around. But the path was straight. Directly through the crowd of angry spirits. Spirits who had every right to be angry. He ran a shaky hand through his hair. Perhaps this was where his journey ended. An ending he deserved.

But he had to help his friends. And the people the Grigori

and the Fay would harm or kill in their ongoing feud. He had to keep going for their sake, if not for his own. That meant he had to find a way forward.

"I'm sorry," Henry said, looking at each of the spirits in turn, as far as he could meet their eyes. A prick of pain struck his chest for each life he had ruined. So many. How could he ever make amends? "The Fay tortured me if I did not hurt you. But that did not make it right."

The bodies shifted as if swaying to a wind that did not blow for him, but they did not part, and he did not think it wise to try to push his way past.

"You wish to keep me here with you?" Henry asked, looking around the gray replica of the Faerie kingdom. He rubbed the thick scars on his wrists from Titania's tortures. "I acknowledge the justice in it. But I have always hoped to make amends for the wrongs I did. That's why I'm here tonight. I'm seeking to protect the innocent from another Faerie creature. One that harms others the way the Lady of the Woods harmed you. And harmed me. Let me cross, and I vow to keep fighting the Fay to protect the innocent."

Silence met his words, the strange, dusky gloom swallowing them so no echo returned. Henry awaited his fate. If this was his punishment, he would accept it. He would regret losing his friends. Most especially, he would regret losing Cassandra.

Another wind brushed through the spirits, a sound like a conference of whispers. One by one, the spirits stepped back, opening the way for Henry to continue.

"Thank you," he said. "I will not fail you again."

Cassandra ventured hesitantly onto the path that ran through swirls of shadows. She limped, but it felt awkward. Wrong. She tried another step. Her foot no longer twisted when she put weight on it. She gasped and held up her right hand, now as whole and nimble as the left, its only flaw the demon mark. She laughed, tears clouding her eyes. It had to be a trick, like when Fitzhugh had tried to tempt her to come to the Unseelie Court, but she ran a few steps and twirled just to remember what it felt like. Glorious and free, something she could only do in her dreams.

"Cassandra!" Henry called.

She smiled and spun to face him as he stepped from the shadows.

"Mr. Stewart!" She extended her hands. "Look!"

He took her right hand. "That's amazing. This place is amazing, don't you think? Like a dream?"

"It is," Cassandra said, a troubling thought wriggling through her happiness, though she could not quite make sense of it.

Henry grinned. "If it is a dream, then we can do anything we like."

He drew her closer, and her breath caught, her heartbeat pounding at the thought of being close to him. Of kissing him again. He met her gaze, something wild and hungry in his eyes. Eyes that were dark. Not Henry's eyes.

She pushed him away, scrambling for her iron knife, but it had vanished. "Get away from me. You're not Henry."

The man smiled, and his features shimmered into something else. A handsome, boyish face with an innocent smile but dangerous eyes.

"I can be him, though," the man said. "I can be anything you want. You can be anything you want while you're here."

"No, it's not real."

"Does that matter, as long as it makes you happy? I could make you forget what's real and what's not, you know. You could live out eternity here, with me, in dreams we spin together."

She clenched her fists, and her fingers brushed the scar on her hand, the wound stinging as though it were fresh. She gasped. "I know what you are: incubus."

He grinned. "But I wager you don't imagine what pleasure I can offer you. I don't only produce nightmares, but also dreams beyond any fantasy your innocent mind has conjured. Dreams where you are always whole, nothing holding you back. Where you forget all the sorrows of the past."

His fingers brushed her hand, and a shiver of longing ran through her. A hunger. She wanted to feel more of what he promised. To be free. To forget her pains in a dream of endless pleasure.

But then she would also forget her sisters, her friends, Henry. Even herself.

"No," she managed, yanking her hand away. "No! Being trapped here would always hold me back."

She hurried past him, but he followed her.

"This may be illusion," he called, "but everything in your dreams is real. Your friends have done terrible things. What makes them any better than I am, when I can offer you so much, and they can offer you nothing?"

"They want to be better," she said, more to herself than the incubus.

The shadows around her swirled into misty forms from her nightmares: her friends deceiving, fighting, killing.

"The past will always be there," the incubus called. "It is what it is, and no power of human or Fay can purge it."

"But I can let go of it," Cassandra said through clenched teeth. "I can leave it behind."

She kept her eyes firmly on the road, putting her temporary healing to good use and rushing forward. She could still hear their voices whispering terrible things, so she gritted her teeth, covered her ears, and ran, the incubus close on her heels.

Mary had never seen a place so dark. There was no road and only a faint haze of light like the moon behind thick clouds. With every step she took, her feet sunk deeper into the muck around her. She was alone and had no idea where to go, and the ground was sucking her in. Was she so small and insignificant that the Twilight Path was closed to her? Perhaps because she was not human or Fay, she was now lost forever. It might be peaceful to just be forgotten. Not be a burden on anyone again.

She sunk further into the mire. Stopped fighting it.

A soft gray glow made her look up. A form hovered several yards in front of her. It did not beckon but hovered, waiting to be noticed. Mary could never forget those familiar features, even obscured as they were by the hazy light. She straightened slowly, shaking all over.

"Mother?" she called.

The form seemed to consider her.

"Mother, I know what I am now. And I'm sorry. I want to bring my sister back to Father. To make up for what you lost."

Her mother's figure continued to float in place as if waiting for something.

"I don't know what else to say." Hot tears traced down Mary's cheeks, and her voice caught on a sob. "I'm sorry. I wish I wasn't what I am, but I can't fix it."

Mary.

The voice washed over her like an embrace. The hard knot of shame in her stomach melted and she relaxed into the feeling of being wrapped in safe and loving arms. Rocked against a chest where echoed a steady heartbeat that didn't care where she had come from, but only accepted and cherished her. She was not forgotten, not alone.

The tears flowed freely now, a dam breaking, relief and longing all mingled into one. She crumpled to the soft ground, her body shaking with the sobs that welled from the constant ache inside of her. The place that craved unquestioning love.

Mary.

The voice was gentle but urgent.

Mary wiped her eyes and looked up. She saw it now. Her mother stood on the Twilight Path—only a small patch of it illuminated by the spirit's gentle glow. And Mary was sinking deeper into the ground with every moment. She had to follow or risk being trapped there forever. She swallowed several times and pushed to her feet, then slogged forward, trailing behind her mother's ghostly form into the gloom.

The Twilight Path lay straight and clear before Domin—a pale road against a dark, featureless landscape. He frowned. He had expected more from the vale of the dead. He had buried many friends and enemies over the years, and he had thought— hoped?—he might see some of the friends that night. Perhaps death was not as far from him as it had once been, and therefore it waited in patient silence.

He started forward, and a figure strode up beside him: a tall woman in leather armor, her eyes bright as they fixed on him.

Domin stopped, his throat tight with disbelief. "Bradamante."

He hadn't spoken that name for decades. Centuries perhaps. He hadn't been lying when he told Henry he could hardly remember what she'd looked like, but there she was, as clear and bright as when she had lived and breathed.

Yet, his reaction was not what he would have expected. He was happy to see her, flooded with long-buried memories, but he felt the distance between them as well. So much had happened since he last saw her, experiences they could not share, and he was not the same person he had been centuries before. He felt fondness, but not the intense devotion she had once kindled in him.

"You have forgotten me," she said. She didn't sound angry or hurt.

"I haven't," he protested. "I guard your line, as I promised."

She took off her helmet, revealing plaited blonde hair, and studied him. "Yes, but I sense you don't do it for me as much anymore. I think you now do it for yourself."

"Have I become selfish, then?" he asked.

"Is it selfish to spend your life serving others?"

That had been the way with her: asking questions that made him question himself. "Perhaps," he admitted. "Because I do it to give my life meaning, so I am not tempted to become what I once was."

"Selfish?" Bradamante asked, smiling.

Domin answered with a wry half-smile. "It is a deep flaw with me. But I did not like who I was when I was a prince among the Fay. Cruel, without mercy or softer feelings. You helped me see that. You saved me."

"One person cannot save another in the way you mean, though," she said. "You had to do that yourself."

"What are you saying?"

"I'm not certain." She frowned. "I think I've been gone a very long time, and much of what passed then does not seem to matter anymore. It's all a dream, and this is now what's real." She gestured to something in the distance that Domin couldn't see.

"Is that what you came here to tell me?" Domin asked.

She laughed. "I didn't come here to tell you anything. No, I think you called me here by remembering. But if you want a message from the dead, I will tell you this: while you are among the living, you should live."

Domin wrinkled his forehead at that. "You think I am not living?"

"I think you are still holding back. Punishing yourself for things that are long faded from any memory but your own. You were once fierce in battle. Now, you have turned that fierceness against yourself. And perhaps those around you as well?"

Domin sighed. "I would hope that over a thousand years, I might become something better."

Bradamante smiled sadly. "Ah, Domin, I didn't say you're not better. Just that your journey is not over. And you don't have to walk it alone."

"You would not walk it with me," he said, and, centuries later, that still hurt a little, though the pain was dull, a wound mostly healed.

"That was not my fate, dear friend. You have chosen a heavy burden for yourself—a noble burden—and one that you often had to shoulder alone, but that does not always have to be the case. While you are alive, there is yet time and hope."

He frowned at that, wondering what she meant, but before he could ask, she put her helmet back on.

"I must be off. There are other battles to fight after the

mortal one ends, and this night is lively. I hope, when we meet
again, that you will have remembered how to smile again."

And then Bradamante was gone, and Domin was alone
again. He thought of what she said. It had been long since he
had been able to talk with anyone about who he really was.
Before Amy had betrayed him, she had known and understood.
He had felt closer to her than to anyone since Bradamante. Amy
had brimmed with life and hope—and even now she clung to
them despite the difficulties she had faced. He had nearly
forgotten how comfortable it felt to have a like mind to pour
out one's hopes and worries to, and who in return trusted you
with their own, even now that he had several friends he did not
have to hide from. But he had not forgotten the pain of
betrayal. The cost of trust. The danger was great, but wasn't the
reward great as well?

He thought of what he had told Henry about the risks of
caring. He had meant it, and now his words bit. Because, in that
way, he had forgotten Bradamante. He'd forgotten what he
learned from her about living, and he wasn't sure how to find
that again.

Amy could barely make out the pale shimmer of the path in the
dimness. Twilight Vale indeed. A liminal place, not light or
dark, not life or death. She shivered and carried on, her steps
hesitant. Worry pecked at her mind like a crow. What if she
never found her way out? What if she found her way out, but
the others did not, and she ended up alone in this in-between
place? She wrapped her arms around herself, pushing forward.

Lights bobbed here and there to the side of the road. Will o'
the wisps. Lost spirits. She almost thought that here she could

make out their voices. Sad, faint whispers of souls confused and angry. She was careful not to listen too closely. She didn't look too closely, either, afraid of what she would see.

The road veered away to her right, and she paused. Domin had said she must go straight. But he also admitted that he had never walked this path. What if he was wrong? What if she had to follow the road or she would be lost forever in this dim wilderness? She stood at the bend in the way, agonizing. And the trip had to be made on All Hallow's Eve. How much longer would that last? If she couldn't decide, she would be trapped there forever anyway. And she always chose wrong.

She stared straight ahead. If she went that way, how would she be sure that she didn't veer from the path? She needed a lodestone. Something to keep her on track. A steady light or a star. But the will o' the wisps bobbed all around, confusing her sense of direction and giving her nothing sure to fix her sights on.

A rumbling noise made her start, and she looked back, wondering if she had hesitated too long and some terrible fate now came for her. It was a carriage all in black, pulled by four huge black horses, its curtains like a velvet night and its wheels gleaming onyx.

She pulled back, not wanting to leave the path but not wanting to be run down, either—for surely a mortal could die in the Twilight Vale. The horses pulled to a stop in front of her, their breath billowing in white clouds from their nostrils. They pranced in place and tossed their heads impatiently. Amy shivered and shrank from their huge hooves cloaked in a great profusion of feathery black hair.

The coachman stared down at Amy, a black hood blocking his face from her view. Nevertheless, Amy could feel his eyes boring into her.

A pale woman looked out of the carriage. "What is happening out there?"

The hooded figure said nothing that Amy could hear, but the lady looked down at Amy, seeming to see her for the first time.

"Oh, poor elfling! Are you lost?"

Amy found her voice. "I think I am."

"I cannot let you wander out here alone. There are crows about, and the night is strange. Come, join me in the carriage." The woman smiled, her face pleasant and inviting.

Amy took a step toward the carriage. Then she remembered what Domin had said, that everyone traveled the Twilight Path alone.

"Where are you journeying, my lady?" Amy asked.

The woman's pretty, pale forehead wrinkled. "I think it was somewhere I did not want to go. And I became a little...turned around. But I'm certain we'll find our way out soon. I don't want to be alone. Please, won't you join me?"

Amy didn't want to be alone either, and she didn't know what to do. Her instincts were so often wrong. Clouded by emotion. "I'm not certain."

The woman pouted. "It's dangerous out there. Death will find you. Come into the carriage, and we will travel together. It's safer. Wiser."

Amy's stomach jumbled into knots. Was she being foolish? Maybe she was supposed to ride in the carriage. What if that was the only right way to go?

She stepped up to the carriage. The woman watched her with glittering eyes. She opened the door, revealing a soft black interior that seemed to absorb any light that filtered in. The woman extended a hand. A thin, pale hand. A hand made of nothing but bone.

Amy gasped. The pale woman grabbed her wrist, cold finger bones pressing into Amy's skin.

"Come!" the woman said, her eyes burning with feverish glee. "We will return to the land of the living together."

Amy yanked her hand free, rubbing her bruised wrist. "No. You are not going where I need to go."

The woman howled in fury. The horses tossed their heads, and the coachman lashed the air with his whip. Amy cringed but didn't relent.

The door slammed shut, and the carriage rumbled on down the road like a thunderstorm retreating to the horizon. That confirmed Amy's decision. She would not follow the road. She had to go straight, cross the open field. But how to keep her bearings?

She stared ahead, squinting into the gloom. Something seemed to flash in the distance. Not a will o' the wisp. A more rhythmic flash. Like light on water. Was there any light here? She wasn't sure, but the path was supposed to reach the water. The light flickered but didn't move. She would fix her eyes on that glint of light in the distance and let it guide her.

She headed out into a wide landscape like a wheat field bathed in purplish hues. The ground was uneven, and she often stumbled, but she kept going, keeping her eyes fixed on that distant light, hardly daring even to look down and make sure she didn't trip for fear that she would lose her way.

The vale grew darker, the light so faint she might have been imagining it. She had chosen wrong again. Naturally. She always did. She would wander forever, lost in the twilight world between life and death. She wanted to stop. To sit down and rest just for a moment.

You are resilient.

The words bubbled up from deep under her memories and

fears and pulled her out of her stupor. She had to keep moving, one step into the darkness at a time. One uncertain foot in front of the other. Even the smallest shuffle brought her closer to that faint glimmer in the distance and the hope that she might still have a future.

Chapter Twenty-Four

Henry stepped from the woods onto a beach, and his vision shifted as though someone had lifted gauze from his eyes. Fitzhugh and Jane waited by the edge of a lake as calm as a mirror reflecting the starless night. A large coracle made of glass instead of wicker and hide floated on the still water like a giant crystal bowl. In the distance, storm clouds churned over the water.

"I see you had no difficulties in the Twilight Vale," Henry said.

Fitzhugh lifted one shoulder. "Of course not. Suffering makes us stronger."

"But the dead are pests," Jane said.

Fitzhugh laughed, but Henry only felt sympathy for those he had seen on the path.

A scuffle behind Henry made him turn, and Jairus ran down onto the beach, watching behind him. He stumbled to a stop, panting, and looked up at Henry.

"I hope they can't get through," Jairus said.

"The dead?" Henry asked, wondering what Jairus had seen.

Cassandra dashed out of the trees, fixed her eyes on Henry, and flung herself into his arms. "It's really you, isn't it?"

"It's me," Henry held her tight, wishing he could protect her from whatever nightmares had haunted her path. He had never seen her run before. Here in the liminal world, her physical afflictions had less hold, but still she clung to him for support.

Domin strode down across the sand, his expression serious and thoughtful. He looked over the group gathered there. "Not everyone is here?"

They all turned to look back at the dim passage to the shore. Something moved in the shadows, and Mary shuffled out of the gloom. Her boots and dress were stained with mud, but her thin face was set in determination.

Then where was Amy?

Domin stepped forward as if he might be able to retrace the path, but then Amy appeared, her steps tired but her face triumphant.

"I did it," she said, grinning at them.

"All's well for now," Jairus said, looking uneasy. He pointed at the boat. "And I suppose this is our next step?"

"We don't have to be alone anymore?" Mary asked. "Or is this some type of..."

"We are all here," Domin said. "That was the Twilight Vale. Now, we must travel to the Western Isle."

They all turned to stare at the thunderous clouds in the distance.

"Shouldn't there be a ferryman?" Jairus asked.

"For the dead, there probably is," Domin said. "We don't belong here."

"So, do we have to row?" Amy asked.

Jane snorted. "I do not row."

Fitzhugh grinned. "This is why we have the Tempestarii. They will summon wind to direct us. Time to prove your worth."

Henry frowned and reached out, trying to sense the energies of that place, but they were foreign to him and did not answer his call. He shook his head.

"I have no connection to the powers here."

Jane pursed her lips. "I can feel something. I think I can reach it. I am the older Tempestarius, after all. My powers run deeper than yours."

Domin shook his head. "It's wiser not to reach too deeply here."

Jane looked like she was going to object, but Jairus climbed into the boat and grabbed a silver oar. "We're low on time, so let's start rowing."

Henry and the others followed. The glass boat was slick, but a flat ledge around the rim gave them places to sit. Only Fitzhugh and Jane remained on shore and empty-handed.

Henry motioned to the last two oars and smirked at Fitzhugh. "Well, I suppose it's time for the Unseelie Fay to prove their worth."

Jairus laughed. Fitzhugh cast Henry a cutting look, but he strode to the boat and snatched up an oar.

"I am a princess," Jane said. "I don't—"

"Take an oar," Fitzhugh commanded. "We have a task, and everyone works to accomplish it, royal blood or none."

Jane glowered at him, but she grabbed an oar and held it with an expression of extreme disgust.

"You'll regret this," she hissed, climbing into the boat.

Henry wasn't sure if she was talking to Fitzhugh or to all of them.

They dug into the smooth waters. Henry's oar encountered little resistance. The boat glided easily over the strange sea. Soon, a fog rolled around them, and they were lost in the cloudy haze. Thunder shook the air, though the waters remained smooth. Answering lightning flashed, showing them nothing but the faces of their companions and the gray walls of the fog. They had nothing to guide them.

Henry instinctively reached for the reassurance of the natural energies around him, but nothing here responded. The boat slipped along the surface of the sea, but where were they headed? If they didn't find Annwn's Keep, they might drift on those cold, still waters forever.

"This feels wrong," Amy whispered, her voice muffled in the fog.

"We keep going west," Jane said.

Henry stopped rowing for a moment, listening to the storm. He couldn't touch its energy, but he could certainly feel it—a brooding power hovering above them. But this was only the outer edge of its fury.

"No," he said. "We need to turn."

"It's called the Western Isles," Jane snapped. "We continue west."

Henry shook his head. "Are you certain that's truly west? Listen to the storm. Feel it. It's pushing us away because we don't belong. If Annwn's Keep is in its heart, we need to go that way." He pointed into the storm.

Jane huffed and looked to Fitzhugh. Fitzhugh pursed his lips, looking between Henry and Jane.

"Turn the boat!" he ordered.

Jane threw her hands up in exasperation. Henry didn't meet her eyes or Fitzhugh's. He didn't want to be involved in a power struggle, but they had to find their way to the island and bring a

hound back with them to track the Leannan Sidhe, and they
had to do it before dawn.

The rowing turned difficult. The water was still as smooth
as glass, but it felt thick, like rowing through treacle. Henry's
arms ached, and he was sure the women, unused to any such
exercise, felt the strain. But they continued rowing without
complaint—even Jane, who worked her oar with a dangerous
gleam in her eyes.

The rumbling overhead grew more intense, shaking Henry
to the core, but the fog began to thin.

Silence broke over them, almost painful after the roar of the
storm.

Cassandra gasped. Henry looked up, and his grip slackened
on the oar. He didn't know what he had expected from the land
of the dead, but it was not this.

Annwn's Keep was a massive, four-sided castle with high
walls and a tower at each corner. The storm surrounded it, a
revolution of clouds, with the castle in its eye. The edifice
appeared to be made of smoky crystal or glass. The walls shone
like polished obsidian, reflecting back the storm so Henry could
not see through them. The flashes of lightning redoubled along
the walls of the fortress like a spark flashing off a thousand
mirrors.

"It's...beautiful," Amy said.

"Death is frightening for the living," Domin said, "and the
legends say that this is a prison for some. But those who have
lived well are said to find feasting, music, and rest within while
they await whatever comes at the end of times when all things
will be destroyed and reborn."

"And it holds great treasures," Jane said, casting her oar
aside. "The treasures of the ages."

Fitzhugh rolled his eyes. "Regardless, we aren't here for the feasting or cursed treasure. We need to draw out one of the hounds." He looked to Domin. "Perhaps you can pose as prey."

Domin scowled. "Let's get to land and examine the fortress. I have no interest in being caught by the hounds."

Fitzhugh grinned. "That's the beauty of my plan: I win either way."

They steered the boat into a harbor, and Domin tied it to the pier. They stepped onto the shore. Henry didn't feel the sensation of the ground rising and falling beneath him that usually followed a voyage by boat. Even in the storm, the water had been too smooth. Only the rotating of the clouds overhead gave him any sense of motion.

Above, on the walls of the castle, silent guards looked down on them, shadowy figures holding spears. Henry couldn't decide if they were there to keep people out or to keep them in. Huge gates stood in the wall of the castle of glass.

Fitzhugh gestured to the gates. "No one should approach those if they wish to return to the land of the living. We won't rescue anyone who steps inside."

Jane rolled her eyes at Fitzhugh.

Domin shifted. "I can turn into a stag and try to draw the hounds out, but how are you going to catch one?"

Fitzhugh smiled and pulled something shiny from his coat. He unfurled a silver net. "With this." He produced two more. "I'll take the priest to help me with mine. The rest of you can divide up and take a net. Snare a hound if it comes to you, but you'll do best to drive it to me."

Henry took one net and motioned Cassandra to join him. That way, he could make sure the hound didn't grab her as it hunted. Mary and Amy took the other net uncertainly. Jane looked between them and then joined Henry and Cassandra, holding one end of the silver net.

"Very well." Domin glanced at the others, then transformed into a white stag with great horns reaching skyward.

He raced past the gates. For a long moment, Henry didn't think the hounds would pursue, but the gate slowly swung open, and a pack of white hounds with red ears ran, baying, from the bright light within.

Henry held the net up on one end, with Cassandra in the middle and Jane on the other side. The hounds were huge—almost as tall as a person—and he did not want them to simply rush over the group. He wished he could use magic, but the silver net would have to do.

Domin ran along the shore, dodging the teeth of the hounds and luring them closer to Fitzhugh.

Cassandra yelled something, and Henry looked over to see Jane dashing for the open gate.

"Don't be a fool," Henry shouted, but the hounds were coming their way again, so he yanked the net up and drove them toward Fitzhugh.

Amy and Mary did the same on the other side of the beach, and the hounds broke apart to go around them and come back for Domin.

Domin turned and lowered his horns at the hounds. They paused, trying to circle him, but Domin charged and scattered them apart. He chased one hound away from the others, directly toward Fitzhugh's waiting net.

Fitzhugh and Jairus sprang forward, bringing the net down on the hound. They lifted it like a hammock with the struggling beast inside.

"Go!" Jairus shouted.

Henry tugged the silver net from Cassandra and whipped it toward the nearest hounds while Cassandra ran for the boat.

Amy and Mary side-stepped their way to the dock, using the net as a shield.

Henry scrambled aboard the boat after the women. Fitzhugh and Jairus managed their bundle onto the boat as well, while Domin kept the hounds at bay. Then, Domin leaped from the shore, changing shapes to land in the boat on two feet.

Everyone kept their distance from the trapped hound panting in the center of the boat. It eyed them and growled.

"Jane went inside," Domin said.

"We cannot wait," Fitzhugh said. "She stays behind."

"That's monstrous!" Cassandra said.

Fitzhugh shrugged. "She knew the risks. And we are the Unseelie Court. Always practical."

The other hounds howled in fury.

"Unfortunately," Domin said, "We do have to leave."

Henry felt some pity for Jane since he'd made his own share of rash choices, but they couldn't stay or none of them would make it back.

Grabbing an oar, Domin paused and looked at Fitzhugh. "In the old ballads, it said only seven returned from the land of the dead. And there are seven of us."

"Yes, I did consider it likely that one of us would fall."

"Never to set foot in the land of the living again," Jairus said quietly.

Fitzhugh shrugged and grinned at Domin. "If anything, I thought the hounds would catch *you*."

Domin gave Fitzhugh a disgusted look and pushed off from the dock.

Chapter Twenty-Five

The boat sailed onward in the dark, and a deep chill settled into Cassandra, seeping through her dress and making her fingers icy where she clutched the oar. She'd never liked Jane, but she felt sick thinking of abandoning any living soul in that place. They'd left Jane to her death.

Henry guided them onward by something he sensed in the air, occasionally instructing them to push their oars in a different direction. The hound in the center of the bowl-shaped boat grew still as they put distance between themselves and the land of the dead. Cassandra kept as far from the creature as possible. It was not a hell hound, but it reminded her of the creatures sent to destroy herself and her sisters.

The hound made a grumbling noise in its chest.

"Will it turn on us when we release it?" Cassandra asked.

Domin paused his rowing to study the creature. "No. Its purpose is to return lost spirits to the otherworld. Once it's in the land of the living, it won't concern itself with us."

Cassandra looked again at the creature trapped in the silver net and felt a stab of pity. It probably would rather be with its pack. But their plan wouldn't hurt it.

The hound fixed large, black eyes on Cassandra and whimpered.

She hesitantly reached a hand close enough for the dog to sniff. Its tail thumped against the side of the boat. She very cautiously moved her hand closer, and the hound lowered its head. She poked her fingers through the silver net to scratch behind the hound's red-tipped ears, and its tongue lolled out.

Fitzhugh laughed. "Miss Weaver is charming the hunter of the dead. You can't keep it as a lapdog, you know."

She glared at him. "At least I can show it kindness. Not something you would understand."

He rolled his eyes. "Are you still upset about Jane, pet? She understood her choice. There are treasures in Annwn that surpass even Telesm's toys."

"But she's lost to the world of the living," Amy said. "What good do the treasures do her?"

Fitzhugh shrugged.

Cassandra scratched the hound again and looked at Fitzhugh with suspicion. He was selfish, but he seemed remarkably unconcerned about the loss of his companion. Wouldn't the Dark Lady be angry? She had plans for Jane. A chill went over Cassandra's skin.

"Jane *can't* return, can she?" Cassandra asked. "With whatever treasure she finds in that castle?"

Domin sighed. "Not as she was before. But like the Leannan, some souls find a way back from the lands of the dead."

Cassandra shivered and leaned against Henry.

A thick fog rolled around them, and the boat pitched as the

waters turned choppy. Henry put a steadying arm around Cassandra's shoulders.

"Where are we?" Jairus asked.

"As long as we've returned before dawn, we should come back to the land of the living," Domin said. "Beyond that, I don't know where the boat will bring us."

Amy wrinkled her nose. "It smells like London."

The fog parted before them. Henry smiled. "I can use magic again."

Cassandra looked over at the dark water around them. It was dark, but not the strange black mirror of the land of the dead.

"I think it's the Thames!" Amy said.

"That would be convenient," Domin said. "The hound will not have far to go to find the Leannan."

"How will it bring her back?" Cassandra asked.

"It has its own way of returning to the land of the dead once it captures its prey."

"Good boy," Cassandra told the dog, smiling in relief. Soon, the Leannan would stop her killing. They would still have to find the Grigori, but Rushford's men would be less powerful without their supernatural ally.

The boat bumped up against a dock, and they pulled their oars out of the water. Jairus tied the boat up, and they climbed out, Fitzhugh and Domin pulling the hound with them onto the shore.

Jairus stopped and held up a warning hand.

Cassandra tried to peer through the fog to know what he saw. She couldn't make anything out, but she felt something. Something wrong in the air.

"Is this our world?" she whispered to Henry.

"This energy feels like ours." He gestured, and the fog

cleared again. The false twilight before dawn gave the air an eerie glow, and the streets around them were empty.

"There's something wrong," Jairus said.

"What do you sense?" Domin asked.

Jairus cleared his throat. "Well, you know how God talks to me?"

"Uh—" Henry said, sounding skeptical.

Jairus didn't wait for Henry's response. "Since the Grigori branded me, I've been seeing things, too."

"What kind of things?" Fitzhugh asked, his gaze bright with interest.

"Ghosts, I would say."

"You can see the dead?" Domin asked.

"I think that's who they are. They're generally in the background, like shadows of the past that haven't faded. Or maybe the veil is a bit thinner in some places, and I can see through it now."

"It's not impossible," Domin said. "The demon mark would make you attractive to restless spirits."

Jairus sighed. "It's always been hard to keep the ladies away."

Amy laughed, but Henry shook his head. "You're just telling us this now?"

"I thought you would have noticed how the women pine after me." Jairus grinned.

"Hale!"

"All right." Jairus held up his hands. "Normally the shades I see are just...there. But now, they're moving. Not like they're going anywhere, but like when you run a stick through a pond of still water. They're drifting, but I can't understand the current that's pushing them. They don't look happy, though."

Domin furrowed his forehead. "I can't see them, but I can

sense their presence. You're right. Something has disturbed the dead."

"Oh, delightful," Henry said. "What could do that? The hound?"

"The dead should be used to the hounds of Annwn. It must be something else." Domin pressed his fingers to his forehead. "Some deep and powerful magic."

"Is it the Fay or the Grigori?" Amy asked, peering across the empty street.

"It could be either who summoned it," Domin said. "We will have to investigate."

The hound whimpered in its silver net.

"Can the hound help us?" Henry asked. "Or will it just chase after the spirits of the dead?"

Domin knelt on the street to study the creature. "The shades Hale sees are probably echoes of those in the process of letting go of this world and moving on. The hound should be more interested in hunting a creature escaped from the land of the dead like the Leannan. We can turn it loose and see where it goes."

Fitzhugh pulled the net loose. The hound staggered to its feet and shook out its short, white coat. It lifted its head, sniffing the wind, and let out a piercing howl. With that, it dashed off.

"Follow it!" Domin said.

He dropped into wolf form, and the rest, confined to two feet, trailed behind. Cassandra found herself at the back, her foot once again twisting beneath her. Henry slowed and took her hand, helping her along. The hound's call guided them through London's thick fog.

They came to a stop in Hyde Park. It was dark and wreathed in swirls of mist, a strange contrast to the bright place where she and Henry walked there that morning. As if they still stood in the lands of the dead.

A figure approached from the fog: a person mounted on a black stag.

They all stopped, Cassandra struggling to catch her breath. The hound paced, panting and whining.

The black stag approached. It wasn't solid black, but covered in cracks that throbbed an angry red like the heart of a dying ember.

Cassandra instinctively shrank from it. From the darkness emanating from it. Not the peaceful darkness of a restful night, but the confusion of thick, smothering smoke. A heavy, creeping dread that she couldn't flee because it had already wrapped around everything, choking her.

The stag paused before them, and the rider's blonde hair flowed free in the wind.

"It's Jane!" Amy gasped.

Cassandra struggled to breathe.

"So," Fitzhugh called, "you found it."

"I told you I would," Jane said, grinning down from her mount.

Jane held up a horn. It was silver and curved in a long half-circle. The hound of Annwn whimpered and tucked its tail.

"No!" Domin shouted and rushed up to the black stag. "What have you done?"

The stag tossed its head, its great antlers dark against the approaching dawn.

Jane turned the creature from Domin. "I have stolen something my queen long desired."

"What is that?" Jairus asked, his voice strained.

"It's the horn of Annwn," Fitzhugh said, his tone flat.

"Whoever holds the horn directs the Wild Hunt," Henry whispered.

Jane raised the horn to her lips.

"Don't do this!" Domin called.

"I agree," Fitzhugh said. "Jane is too untested for such power."

"You are jealous that I was the one brave enough to take it," Jane said with a sneer.

"Jealous?" Fitzhugh asked. "You cannot dismount from that stag in the mortal world. If this plan goes awry, you have sacrificed much."

Jane glared at him, her cheeks red and her eyes flashing anger. "I will not fail. I will bring the Wild Hunt under my control and destroy our enemies."

Domin transformed into a panther and leaped for Jane. The stag knocked him aside, its horns burning long gashes into his side. Henry gestured, and a blast of icy wind smashed against Jane, but she smiled grimly and motioned it away.

Jairus scrambled for his pistol, but Jane raised the horn and blew.

The note sounded long and low. Cassandra groaned. It was a cry of such mourning, the sound of heartbreak and loneliness and sorrow. The secret ache of her heart when she was ill and alone at night and wondered if she would die and if anyone would miss her. And yet, it echoed aloud for all to hear, calling to every lonely, aching soul.

A long stillness settled over the park, like all of nature listened.

Then a horrible baying broke over the trees. Cassandra flinched and covered her ears, but the sound grew quieter as the figures approached: a pack of white hounds with red ears. The rest of Annwn's hounds. Behind them rolled a great mass of churning fog.

Jairus went pale and raised his gun, jerking back and forth as if he didn't know where to aim. Cassandra couldn't see what he saw, but she felt it—angry and hurting souls all around them. She fumbled to grasp Henry's arm. The hound they had kidnapped quelled at her side.

"Lost souls," Henry whispered to her. "The Wild Hunt gathers lost souls. Once you join it, you stay with it until the end of time."

"How do we fight them?" Jairus called.

"They cannot withstand the dawn," Domin said, rising again in his human form.

Even as he spoke, the sun broke over the horizon, and Jane and her horde vanished like scattered mist.

Cassandra gasped in relief. "They're gone, then?"

Fitzhugh's lip curled up. "Only until nightfall. Then Jane will return. She may find the Leannan and the Grigori, but she will leave chaos in her wake."

Chapter Twenty-Six

Amy stared in horror at where Jane had disappeared, her heartbeat still thundering. The Wild Hunt had been so close, and she had felt its call. The others stood with pale faces, as if unsure the threat had vanished. And it hadn't, of course. It would return with the darkness and devastate London. A sour taste bubbled in Amy's throat.

A single hound remained: the one they had stolen. It alone of its fellows didn't recognize Jane as the Lord of the Hunt.

Fitzhugh looked disgusted but not frightened or even surprised by this turn.

Amy turned on him. "This was your queen's plan all along! How—how could you allow it?"

Fitzhugh's eyes narrowed as he stared at the place where Jane had vanished. "My Lady has long coveted the power of the Wild Hunt. She would approve of any opportunity to control it."

"But you don't," Amy said, surprised.

He grimaced. "It will bring suffering, but not suffering we

can control or foresee the end of. And Jane is half-mad already. She should not have such power, regardless of my Lady's plans."

"What plans are those?" Henry asked.

Fitzhugh smiled grimly. "Likely the same plans your lady has for you."

Henry glanced at Cassandra, his eyes troubled.

"So, now we have to stop Jane, too," Jairus said.

Fitzhugh leveled a speculative look at him and thought a moment before speaking. "Stealing the horn from her would be no easy feat. And impossible at night while she rides, unless you also wanted to join the Hunt forever."

Amy wrinkled her forehead. She had the sense that Fitzhugh was giving them a hint. He was probably under a geas to say no more, but any crumb of information was valuable. If they could trust it.

"What about the Leannan?" Cassandra glanced down at the hound hunkered by her side. "Will our plan still work for her, at least?"

Domin knelt and placed a hand on the quavering hound. "Perhaps. This creature has two missions: to follow the horn and to return lost souls, and while those duties are in conflict, it's confused."

"The Wild Hunt may find the Leannan eventually," Fitzhugh said. "But under Jane's direction, its focus will be creating chaos and suffering."

"Then we will resume our search for the Grigori around Charing Cross today," Domin said. "Tonight, we must face the Wild Hunt. Perhaps we can warn people away or divert the hunt."

"What, by offering yourself as prey?" Fitzhugh scoffed.

"I'll create a terrible storm," Henry said. "It will keep people off the streets."

"Jane will counter it," Fitzhugh said.

"Maybe you can offer a helpful idea then?" Amy snapped.

Fitzhugh stepped closer and ran his thumb along her chin, grinning when she jerked away. "I have said what I can, my dear. For the moment, I will return to my Lady's court. There is sure to be feasting and rejoicing, and I want to tell my share of the adventure."

He tipped his hat and walked away, leaving Amy seething.

"We'd better grab a few hours' sleep," Jairus said. "We have more battles to fight."

Everyone nodded, looking numb. On the walk home, Amy watched the streets, imagining them full of fire and blood when the Wild Hunt rode that night. Her stomach clenched, and she felt a wave of guilty relief when they reached her front door. Telesm was nowhere to be found, though. Lucien looked up from his study of a painting of Paris in the dining room when they stumbled past him. He did a double take at the hound but seemed to sense their low spirits and said nothing.

Amy stopped in the sitting room looking out over the square. Her neighbors were stirring after late nights at parties and plays. They had no idea of the horrors the next night would bring.

Movement behind the shrubbery in the square caught her attention. A tall figure in a white suit. Maybe Spring-heeled Jack had news. She hurried out to meet him.

"Your 'ouse feels unwelcoming," Jack complained when she approached. "And I don't like lingering in the streets like this."

Amy glanced at her home, protected by Mary's magic. It should only keep away those who meant them harm.

She took a step back from Jack. "What news did you bring?"

"Nothing. I came for news, is all. Something changed just before dawn. What 'appened?"

"The Unseelie Court has seized control of the Wild Hunt."

Jack looked shocked, then he grinned, showing his sharp teeth. "You've made quite a bungle of things, 'aven't you, lovey? Well, old Jack's not afraid of the 'unt. Not a lost soul, am I?"

Amy glared at him. "Just a cruel one, it seems. The Grigori are still out there. And they still want your Faerie blood even if you don't have Faerie magic. Don't forget that."

"Don't you forget it, neither," he said with a smirk. "They'd love to 'ave you. You keep 'unting them, and then I'll be safe again."

He blew her a kiss laced with flame and hopped over the shrubbery to dash off. Amy seethed, but the heat of her anger slowly cooled to a lump of dread in her belly. They *had* made a bungle of things. She had.

She trudged back to the house. Domin waited in the entrance hall.

"Was that Jack?" he asked.

She nodded.

"It would be best not to talk to him alone. He's dangerous."

Amy nodded, fighting back tears. "I know. I probably shouldn't try to do anything alone."

Domin stepped closer. "What do you mean?"

She felt hot and sick at the thought of what a spectacular failure she was, but it wasn't as if Domin didn't already know, so she let it spill out. "Everything I touch goes wrong. Fitzhugh knew from the moment he suggested Annwn that this could happen. I let him trick me. Again."

"If so, he misled all of us."

"But I know him better. I should have known better. I always hope there's still some good in him. I'm such a fool."

"It's not foolish to hope," Domin said gently.

"But it is foolish to make rash decisions based on false hope."

Domin was silent for a long moment, and that almost broke Amy. Even he could not help but admit she was a fool.

"Amy," he said. "There is a difference between making a foolish decision and being a fool. We're made up of hope and sorrow, sharp words and soft edges. Everyone makes mistakes, but we are more than those mistakes."

"I'm not." Amy's chin trembled. "I *am* a mistake. A disappointment to my mother—to everyone."

Domin studied her face. Amy wished he would just leave so she could cry in peace.

"You are not a disappointment to me," he said softly.

Amy's heart twinged at his words, and she choked on a sob. "How can I not be? I've probably caused more trouble for you than for anyone else."

His lips curled up at the corners. "Certainly, at times you have kept things...lively for me. But *you* are not trouble. Your resilience and hope are admirable—even the energy that occasionally leads you into unwise decisions—I find it inspiring. After all, it means you still care."

"What use is caring if I never manage to do anyone any good?"

"I wish you could see your worth apart from anything you've done."

"Well, I am trying to do the right thing."

He shook his head. "That's what I mean. Your worth isn't about the good things you've done, either."

Amy huffed and wiped her eyes. "You mean none of it counts for anything?"

"It counts for you trying to be the person you want to be.

But your worth doesn't come from what you do. It doesn't come from your mother or even any of your friends. It's that spark of life in you—it's precious."

Amy stared at him. "I don't think I understand."

"I hope someday you will." He squeezed her hand, and with that touch, warmth flooded through her and settled in her chest, a seed swelling with hope.

She looked to Domin in surprise. He had let her feel that—not forced a false feeling on her, but shared his own. Few Fay had such control, and he almost never tapped into his Faerie abilities.

He released her hand with a sad half-smile and walked away, leaving her warm and confused.

Chapter Twenty-Seven

"Cassandra?"

Amy's voice broke into Cassandra's troubled nap, and she sat up, instantly awake.

"What's happened?" Cassandra asked, clutching her demon-marked hand. Since Mary's spell with the clock, the incubus hadn't troubled her with nightmares, but her mind still produced plenty of their own.

Amy looked apologetic. "Your sisters are here."

"What, all of them?" Cassandra rubbed her eyes, imagining all six of her sister running through Amy's house. This had to be a strange dream.

"Only the eldest two, but it's...not an ideal time for visitors." Amy glanced down at the hound of Annwn stretched out beside the bed.

Cassandra groaned. The Grigori. The Wild Hunt. "Father must have some business in town. I'll encourage them to hurry on their way." She hesitated. "If they are reluctant, they might need your urging."

Amy nodded, her eyes weary. Cassandra hoped Amy had a chance to rest. They all needed it. But Cassandra had to deal with her sisters first. She would enjoy seeing them, but as Amy said, this was not an ideal time.

She quietly straightened her dress and hair, careful to allow Mary to continue sleeping, and hurried down to the drawing room. The hound trotted along after her.

"Cassie!"

Georgina stood and embraced Cassandra. Sophie was more dignified, but she rose with a smile.

"What a strange dog," Georgina added, glancing down at the hound.

It tilted its red-tipped ears at her voice, then wagged its tail. Cassandra wondered if they had somehow damaged it by separating it from its pack, and it would just be an odd pet in the future.

"Oh, yes, it's, err..." Cassandra's imagination failed her, and she quickly changed the subject. "It's good to see you both. I haven't had a letter from Father about a visit. What brought you here?" She settled on the sofa across from her sisters.

"Mother decided that we should come," Sophie said. "After all, you have this opportunity in London, and we might benefit from a similar excursion."

There was an edge to Sophie's words. Cassandra wished she could help her sister understand that the kind of opportunities she had here were not those that Sophie wanted.

"I'm surprised she didn't wait for the Season," Cassandra said.

"I'll be eighteen soon," Georgina said. "And we thought it might be easier to manage my introduction to Society when there are less crowds, because..." She made a vague gesture to her ear, referencing her near-deafness.

"I see," Cassandra said. They were not here for a short trip, then. Her stomach knotted.

"You don't seem happy to see us," Sophie said.

"I'm just not certain it's the best time to be in London. I would hate for it to be a disappointment."

"You've had your chance to make a match. Why shouldn't we?" Sophie asked.

Cassandra's face burned. "I don't know that I've made a match."

Sophie lowered her voice. "We saw Henry Stewart in the other room talking to that young page. Or footman? He looked Spanish, perhaps?"

That would be Lucien. "He's French, I believe. Creole." Cassandra would have no luck convincing her sisters he was also part Fay. "And he's actually a guest."

Sophie wrinkled her forehead. "Lady St Clair keeps an odd household, doesn't she? Regardless, I can't imagine why Mr. Stewart would be here except to court you. Unless you're keeping him dangling while you hope for something better?"

"No! It's not like that."

"So, you do care for him?"

Cassandra sighed in resignation. "I do, but...but there are circumstances." Henry would never age. The Fairy Queen kept him captive. Cassandra and her demon mark might attract danger to him.

"He's not settled in his career?" Sophie made a dismissive gesture. "You should secure him anyway."

"Secure him?" Cassandra said. "He's not a bandbox on the back of a carriage."

Sophie scowled. "It is a tenuous thing to be a proper young lady of marriageable age. We must act while we can."

Cassandra realized with a pang that Sophie was thinking of

her own circumstances, jilted by one young man and then seemingly abandoned by Robert Ashby after he had shown interest in her. "We don't need to be hasty. I'm certain you'll have another opportunity to meet someone."

Sophie stiffened. "How generous of you to think I still have a chance."

Cassandra winced, and Georgina's eyes widened—she read lips and posture well enough to catch the unfortunate turn of the conversation.

Sophie leaned forward. "You think you have so many opportunities now, guided by your fine friend, but before you know it, they'll be gone, and then what will you do if you've thrown away *your* chances? You're fortunate enough that Mr. Stewart shows interest in you despite your infirmities."

Angry spots burned on Cassandra's cheeks, and Georgina waved her fan as though she could distract her sisters from their argument.

"You have it wrong," Henry said from the doorway.

Cassandra jumped and stared at him, wishing she could disappear under the sofa pillows. Why did he have to hear that conversation?

Sophie opened her mouth, closed it, then swallowed. "Mr.... Mr. Stewart. Uh—"

But Henry ignored her, catching Cassandra's eyes. "I'm not interested in Miss Cassandra despite her infirmities. Or because of them. I'm interested in her—all of her. Regardless of infirmity or age or illness. The only thing that would keep me away from her is if I couldn't give her the happy life she deserves."

Cassandra's eyes burned as she met his gaze. She was happy when she was with him, but she was also afraid of what would become of them. She saw the same agony of indecision in his expression.

He gave her a sad half-smile and left.

Sophie stared down at her hands folded in her lap, her face bright red.

Georgina looked at Cassandra, her eyebrows raised. "I like him. You should marry him."

Cassandra sank down in her seat. "He would have to ask, wouldn't he?" And even then, how could she say yes when she might slow him down and put him in danger? What if Titania punished him for taking a mortal wife or used Cassandra to control him?

"It's clear he wants to," Georgina said. "Maybe you just need to show him that you would welcome his offer."

Cassandra nodded dully.

"Why don't we speak of something else?" Sophie mumbled.

Cassandra was more than happy to, but what could she tell them? Nothing that she had been doing since she had arrived. "What plans do you have?"

Sophie perked up at that. "Mother has a few friends in town, and she's secured us several invitations. We will go to musicales and balls."

"And I am to take a lady's drawing class," Georgina said, her eyes bright with excitement.

Cassandra's stomach twisted. Oh, how she wished her sisters could enjoy their time in London. But it was too dangerous now, with Jane controlling the Wild Hunt.

"Mother was speaking to a modiste about the latest fashions," Sophie said. "We're going out for more shopping this afternoon."

"The weather will be dreadful tonight, though," Cassandra

said. "Better to stay in and not become ill. It would ruin the rest of your stay."

Sophie looked out the window skeptically. "But it's sunny today. Quite pleasant."

Cassandra was going to need Amy's help after all. "I think Lady St Clair will support me in this. I'll just fetch her."

Her sisters exchanged a confused glance, but Cassandra popped out into the corridor and found Amy. She motioned her friend to join her, and Amy nodded her understanding and followed her back into the drawing room.

"I was just telling my sisters what terrible weather we're expecting tonight."

Amy smiled, and Cassandra felt her magic seep around them. "Yes, this would be a dreadful night to go out. In fact, this is a terrible season to be in London. Not enjoyable. Not fashionable."

Sophie frowned at that and looked worried.

"I'm enjoying it," Georgina insisted. "We have the art galleries almost to ourselves."

Cassandra caught her breath and glanced at Amy. She had almost forgotten that Domin suspected Georgina to be Sabbath-born. Not born on Hallowe'en like Cassandra, but born on a Sunday and therefore less susceptible to Faerie magic. And Sophie wanted her time in London. Faerie magic couldn't force her to change.

Amy smiled stiffly. "Really, this is a most disagreeable time to be in London. You should leave and come back for the Season."

Cassandra felt the push. It almost made her rise and leave.

Georgina looked confused, and Sophie lowered her head. Cassandra's heart ached for her sisters. They had been excited, ready to enjoy themselves. Cassandra didn't want to take that from either of her sisters. But she had to keep them safe.

Sophie blinked and looked down at her hands. "Perhaps the weather is a little too dreary. And there won't be as many men to dance with." She nodded and faced Cassandra and Amy. "I'll tell Mother that if the next ball isn't a success, we should try again in the spring."

Cassandra winced, but no amount of wheedling from her or Amy would make Sophie agree to leave that very day.

"Sophie?" Cassandra's mother called from the entry hall.

"Mother!" Cassandra said. Despite her tense relationship with her mother, the familiar voice made her feel like she was home again.

Her mother wandered into the room, showing enough good breeding not to gawk at the finery. "That strange man let me in, but then he vanished. I wasn't certain how to find you."

Cassandra wondered which "strange man" had admitted her. Almost all of the men there would seem strange to her mother. Mrs. Weaver caught sight of the hound and wrinkled her nose at its odd appearance. She looked a little dazed to find that the ways of the *haut ton* did not match up to her ideas of what was proper, but when she noticed Amy, she became all smiles.

"Lady St. Clair, thank you again for offering my Cassandra this opportunity to enjoy London."

"Of course," Amy said. "Though I'm sorry that she has to be here for such a dreadfully uncomfortable time of the year. London is usually much more enjoyable, but it has been simply terrible of late."

Cassandra watched as her mother absorbed Amy's message and the magic accompanying it.

"I'm certain you're exhausted after your travels and want to rest safely—comfortably in your lodgings," Amy said. "Thank you for the visit."

The girls stood, and Amy ushered them out. Henry and Jairus stood near the front door, prepared to hunt the Grigori. Georgina made a little sound of surprise at seeing Jairus. He glanced her way and then looked again. Last time he had seen her, she had just been attacked by a hell hound. She had grown up a great deal since then. Jairus tipped his hat to the ladies, and Georgina flushed.

Cassandra felt Henry's gaze on her, but she didn't turn to him until she had seen her family out. Once the door shut behind them, she sagged, and she was grateful for Henry there beside her.

"I'm sorry," she whispered, aware of Jairus lingering nearby. "For...for that."

"Don't be," Henry said, matching her tone. "I meant what I said, and I'm glad I said it. I'm reckless, you know."

She smiled sadly. "Not *so* reckless."

"Not with you. You mean too much to me."

Cassandra couldn't meet his eyes. In a voice closer to normal, she said, "My sisters aren't leaving. At least not tonight."

"We'll keep them safe," Henry said.

Jairus nodded his agreement.

Cassandra hoped they were right.

Chapter Twenty-Eight

Henry trudged back from the Strand beside Jairus and Domin, keeping a wary eye on the sun's descent toward the horizon. The sludgy stench of the river mingling with cigarette smoke and the slightly burnt odor pouring from the coffee houses turned his stomach. It didn't help that he'd hardly had any sleep and their hunt had been entirely fruitless. Pointless. The theaters were especially packed that evening, and the Grigori were the needle in the haystack—impossible to find, but sure to draw blood when they did appear. It might have gone better if they could coax Annwn's hound out of Amy's house, but it refused to leave the refuge.

They passed the crowds milling around the columned portico of the Lyceum theater, and Henry shivered to think of the Wild Hunt tearing through all those people. He had not wanted to hunt in the rain, but it was time to clear away the stink of London and some of its street traffic. He reached out to distant thunderheads and summoned them, and he was rewarded with a fresh, cold wind heralding the coming storm.

Domin gave him an approving nod, and Jairus caught his hat before a violent gust blew it away. Henry should have been too tired to so easily bring a storm, but his worries over the Wild Hunt gave him restless energy. The Wild Hunt and Cassandra. Her sister's words troubled him. And Fitzhugh's, too, though he hated to admit it. Was Henry just toying with her, wasting her time? Was it selfish to be around her, tormenting them both? If they survived the Wild Hunt and the Leannan, he might have to let her go, but the thought crushed his chest, made it hard to breathe.

When they reached Amy's house, they found Cassandra pacing in the foyer.

"Mr. Stewart!" She threw herself into his arms.

He wrapped her in a tight embrace, inhaling the sweet scent of her hair. "What's wrong?"

"Sophie sent me a message. Georgina insisted on going to her art class this evening. She's out there." Cassandra turned terrified eyes to Henry.

"Then we'll bring her home," he said.

She nodded and loosened her grip on him. He reluctantly released her and looked to the other men.

"I'll come along," Jairus said. "There's trouble brewing, and it's itching at me."

"I need to consult with Telesm about the horn," Domin said. "Don't be caught out after dark."

Henry nodded, and Domin headed upstairs. Cassandra traded her cane for an umbrella.

"The art school is on Oxford Street," Cassandra said.

"Just north of here," Henry told Jairus.

The American nodded and checked his shotgun and pistols. The dull click of the revolvers' cylinders filled the quiet as he loaded one pistol with silver and the other with iron.

Preparation for Fay enemies and human ones. When he was ready, he gave them a curt nod.

It was a short walk to Oxford Street, but the low clouds from Henry's storm gave the sky a dusky feel. Gray drizzled down on them. The Hunt would ride soon.

Henry paused outside the school. Something felt off.

"What's wrong?" Cassandra whispered.

"There's...there's someone here," Henry said. Yes, he was sure of it. The energy of the place felt wrong. Too stifling. Too hot. Ah—

"Spring-heeled Jack," Henry said out loud.

Jack jumped down from a window alcove overhead and straightened his white coat.

"'Ello, lovies. Come to watch the pretty ladies?"

"Pretty ladies?" Henry asked.

"This is a lady's art class," Jack said slowly, as though Henry were dense. Then he wiggled his eyebrows.

Henry huffed. "I'm surprised you're willing to be out with the Wild Hunt loose in London."

"It won't be dark for 'alf an 'our yet. By that time, old Jack will be safely 'idden away."

"Not trying to stop the Wild Hunt, then?" Jairus asked.

"Of course not!" Jack looked shocked. "I leave that to you blokes. The best I can do is keep myself safe and let you work."

"Coward," Jairus said.

"Survivor," Jack said with a smirk.

The art class ended, and the female students trickled from the building, escorted by parents, brothers, or servants. Jack leered but didn't approach any of the girls. Henry distanced himself from Jack and scanned the group, looking for Georgina or any of Cassandra's family.

"There's Georgie!" Cassandra said, pointing to one of the last girls.

Her sister emerged cautiously from the building, watching the crowds and then frowning at the rain. Of course, being deaf, she might be more hesitant in the city with its many hazards.

Cassandra waved, and Georgina's face brightened. She rushed down to share Cassandra's umbrella.

"Cassie!" Georgina said, hurried to her sister. "Did Mother send you to fetch me?"

"No, we were just walking in the area and thought we'd stop by." Cassandra gestured to Henry and Jairus.

Georgina's gaze fell on Jairus and lingered there, though the oblivious American was busy scanning the rooftops where Jack had made his escape.

"Uh, was Mother supposed to meet you here?" Cassandra asked.

Georgina blinked rapidly and looked away from Jairus, a faint flush on her cheeks. "Yes. She and Sophie went to do some shopping, then we would go home together. They must have been held up by the rain."

Cassandra frowned, and Henry felt her annoyance. Cassandra's mother might not have understood the dangers of the Wild Hunt, but she at least should have known that the city had other types of dangers, even near Mayfair.

"We'd best wait here with you," Cassandra said. "They shouldn't leave you alone."

"Is London really so dangerous?" Georgina asked.

"It is," Henry said, glancing toward the darkening sky.

Georgina frowned at that, but she didn't try to argue. Rain trickled from the edge of Cassandra's umbrella, keeping Henry from standing closer to the girls.

A middle-aged man emerged from the building, locking the door behind himself.

"That's my teacher," Georgina whispered too loudly.

The man gave them a nod and opened his umbrella. He stepped down the wet front stairs and then hurried along the street.

Something moved in the shadows.

Henry narrowed his eyes. Was Jack playing a trick? No, another form joined the first, closing in on the teacher. On the artist.

"Hale!" Henry shouted.

Jairus spun, pistol raised.

The two men pounced, grabbing the art teacher and keeping him between themselves and Jairus. The teacher gave a muffled shout, and the two men hauled him down an alley.

Jairus hesitated, glancing at Henry.

"Go!" Henry said. He had to stay with Cassandra and her sister, but someone needed to track the Grigori.

Jairus raced down the alley, splashing over the wet cobblestones.

"My teacher!" Georgina cried. "Did those men just attack him? Why would they do that?"

Henry turned to face her so she could read his lips. "He must have had...something they wanted." He must have had Faerie blood. "Mr. Hale is seeing if he can help, but we need to leave. Can you direct us to your lodgings?"

"What about Mother and Sophie?" Georgina's eyes were wide with fear.

Cassandra put an arm around her sister's shoulders. "We'll find them. Which way did they go?"

Georgina pointed.

They hurried down the street, Henry constantly watching

behind them. He hoped to see Jairus come back with the missing teacher, but the street behind them was eerily quiet.

They reached the corner, where the street grew busier with crowds finishing their shopping before heading home for the night. And there were Sophie and Mrs. Weaver, along with Robert Ashby.

Henry gritted his teeth. Ashby should have known better than to distract them and leave Georgina alone. She could have been taken as well, if she had been lingering on her own.

"Mother!" Georgina cried.

"Oh, Georgie! I'm sorry, we lost track of time." Mrs. Weaver looked over Cassandra and gave Henry a speculative glance. "But I'm glad to see you weren't alone after all."

"And it's a good thing," Georgie said. "My teacher was assaulted, right there in the street!"

Georgina shivered and leaned against Cassandra, who held her sister tightly in the shelter of her umbrella.

"Assaulted him?" Mrs. Weaver looked horrified. "In Mayfair?"

"Even Mayfair is not always safe," Henry said, giving Robert a warning look. "Especially after dark."

Robert looked abashed at that. "Yes, I should not have detained you ladies. Perhaps now we can escort you home?"

The women agreed, and Robert set a fast pace, taking his cue from Henry's urgency.

A rush of wings made Henry's hair stand on end, and he turned to see a murder of crows circling. The Morrigan or one of her banshees. Henry pulled out his iron knife, and Cassandra swished her umbrella closed and raised it like a club. Its steel ribs would be worth something against the Morrigan.

Georgina stared at her in confusion, blinking rain from her eyes.

"Cassandra!" her mother said. "What are you doing?"

Henry gestured as subtly as he could manage. A blast of wind and rain knocked the birds against the brick face of a building. The birds screeched in fury and flapped away in a torrent of black wings. Cassandra swung when they came too close.

"Really, Cassie, isn't that a bit over dramatic?" Sophie asked, a fist on her hip.

"She's fending off...threats," Robert said. He looked to Mrs. Weaver. "Young ladies in London have to stay on their toes."

"Against birds?" Sophie asked.

"They're vicious," Henry said.

Mrs. Weaver eyed Robert and Henry warily, then she wiped rain from her face. "I suppose we should get inside."

Robert nodded and hurried them onward. Cassandra did not reopen her umbrella, keeping it on her shoulder and ready to swing. Georgina gave Cassandra a speculative look before following their mother and sister. Henry's stomach knotted. Georgina was going to have questions that Cassandra couldn't answer. Not without putting her in even more danger. Because if Georgina believed her, then she might also be drawn into the deadly world of the Fay.

The Weavers' lodgings weren't much farther, and the Weaver girls were quick to say goodbye and escape the rain.

Cassandra sagged against the stair railing when she saw them safely locked inside.

Robert turned to Henry. "Tell me what's happening. And what I can do to help."

Henry adjusted his hat and scowled at Robert. "The Grigori are still hunting those with Faerie blood. And in retribution, the Dark Lady has taken control of the Wild Hunt and unleashed it on London."

Robert blanched at that. "Can we stop it?"

"You probably cannot," Henry said, a bite in his words. "The best thing you can do is stay inside. Make certain your mother and sister are safe."

Robert narrowed his eyes at that, but then he bowed his head. "Very well."

Robert slunk off for home, presumably. Henry glanced at the gathering gloom and held out a hand for Cassandra. "Come. The Hunt will ride soon."

Chapter Twenty-Nine

Jairus raced along the streets, splashing through puddles as he dodged rich and poor alike. He didn't carry the burden of an unconscious art teacher, but he also didn't know the streets well, and the Grigori led him again to the Strand.

Despite the rain, people still flowed from coffee shops to theaters. Jairus gritted his teeth and pushed his way through the crowd, but the Grigori vanished into the throng. He swore under his breath, earning cutting looks from the people around him. He was losing the Grigori. He was losing the man they had taken. He was losing, and he couldn't afford that with so many lives at stake.

Finally, the traffic forced him to a stop. He bent over, resting his hands on his knees while he caught his breath, a string of curses rolling through his mind. Rainwater dripped down his neck. He took slow breaths and listened, but the voice that sometimes whispered in his mind was silent. Perhaps he had disappointed it.

He rubbed his neck and scanned the streets. The dead were

there, mingled with the oblivious living. The living moved purposefully, though their colors vibrant, while the dead drifted along, lost and gray. With the Unseelie Queen in charge of the Wild Hunt, even the spirits suffered.

A crow flapped by, its wings flashing in the rain. Jairus huffed and followed it. Down an alley, he found the Morrigan waiting, dry despite the drizzle.

"We meet again, warrior-priest," she said with a grin.

"Tell me where the Grigori went." Jairus shifted his shotgun. The iron shot would hurt her, he was certain of that.

"That is not my role." She stepped forward to caress the barrel of the gun with her fingertips.

Jairus shifted the gun away from her. "Make it your role, or you'll be picking shot out of your pretty face."

She laughed. "This is why you are a favorite of mine, priest. You are a creature forged by war, and you never lose that passion. Domin is a great fighter as well, but he has become so cold. Only some great tragedy will shake him awake again, I fear. But something about your mortality keeps you vibrant. Delicious."

She stepped closer.

"You won't feed on me." He pulled the trigger.

The Morrigan dissolved as the shot passed through her. Then she reformed, still grinning.

"Now then, priest, I'm not like the Leannan," the Morrigan said. "She is a parasite, cultivating the emotions she yearns for, then killing the humans who provide them. I have merely learned to gain strength and knowledge from the energies that exist on battlefields."

"You encourage people to fight."

"But I don't force them to. I don't even deceive them like she does."

Jairus huffed. He didn't have time to argue over the relative morality of the Fay. "If the Leannan is that bad, tell me where to find her."

"Her fate isn't mine to read, priest. Why doesn't your God tell you?"

"I don't know." Jairus often wondered that himself, but he wasn't foolish enough to throw away what he knew because of what he didn't. "He sometimes lets us discover things on our own, and I trust his reasons."

"Ah, faith!" The Morrigan's eyes glittered with interest. "That is one of the rarest feasts in any battle. Rare and bittersweet. But one day, your God will let you down, and you will die. That is why I have come to warn you: the Leannan and the Wild Hunt are only the beginning."

Jairus shrugged one shoulder. "I know I'll die one day. I'll be prepared when it comes—I face my reckoning every day. But I wonder about you. You're going to be called to account someday as well."

"How do you know I'm not simply fulfilling my role like you and your friends?"

Something whispered behind Jairus's thoughts, a quote he knew well. "'And there went out another horse that was red, and power was given to him that sat thereon to take peace from the earth, and that they should kill one another, and there was given unto him a great sword.'"

The Morrigan swung her sword around and grinned. "Oh, bravo! But if I serve one of the four great forces of destruction in this world, you should beware of the other three."

Jairus frowned. The Lord of Annwn served death. But what of the other horsemen? Famine? And the rider of the white horse—pestilence, perhaps?

"It doesn't matter who you serve," Jairus said. "I know who I serve."

"You will need that faith when the other horsemen ride." The Morrigan turned her face toward the west. "The sun sets. The Wild Hunt stirs."

With that, she dissolved into a flock of crows and whirled into the sky.

Jairus stared after her. The Morrigan liked to play games, but she had knowledge Jairus didn't, and he believed her warning—not just about the Wild Hunt, but about future dangers he could not see.

Chapter Thirty

Henry clung to Cassandra's hand, guiding her through the rainy streets of Mayfair for the safety of Amy's house. The sun dipped below the gray clouds, flashing light over the city for a few moments before abandoning them to cold and darkness. In the distance, thunder rumbled, and the baying of hounds rose over the clamor. Chills ran over Henry's skin.

"Too late," Cassandra whispered.

"We'd still be safer somewhere inside." Henry wasn't going to let the Wild Hunt overtake them—overtake Cassandra.

"But what about everyone else?" Cassandra gestured to men hailing hansom cabs to visit their clubs and street sweeps lingering in the rain, hoping for an extra coin to bring home. "They don't know they're in danger."

Henry sighed and kissed her hand. He would never be worthy of her. "Of course, we should try to warn them. It would be easier if we had Amy with us, though."

People weren't likely to listen to a bedraggled man and woman telling them to go inside, not without a magical push.

He scanned the street and gave a start. Someone ran toward them. Jairus.

"Did you stop the Grigori?" Henry called over the wind.

Jairus shook his head and came to a stop in front of them. "They slipped away in the Strand. I did have a run in with the Morrigan." He narrowed his eyes at the storm clouds. "How do we stop the Wild Hunt?"

"Stop it?" Henry asked, incredulous. "Oh, simple: we steal the horn back from Jane."

"That might be an idea," Jairus said.

"An insane one," Henry snapped. "The Hunt would tear us apart before we got close to her."

"All right, we'll think on that later." Jairus held up his shotgun. "How do we fight it? Iron or silver?"

"Iron," Cassandra said, swinging her umbrella around. "The Wild Hunt is Fay, correct? And Domin taught me iron works on all of the Fay."

Henry surrendered. "You can't kill the Wild Hunt, but iron might deter it. We could try to steer it away from people."

The cry of the hounds sounded again, and screams echoed from somewhere nearby.

"Let's go!" Jairus shouted.

They hurried at a fast clip toward the noise, trying to catch the Hunt. At each corner they turned, Henry expected to see the Hunt charging toward them, but every street offered nothing but echoes, the Wild Hunt always eluding them. Mocking them. They found themselves in a dead-end alleyway.

Jairus raised his shotgun, gaze darting around the stone facades of the buildings. Water trickled down all of their faces, and everyone shivered at the damp cold.

"This is fruitless," Henry called. "We have to get ahead of it."

Cassandra gasped and grabbed her scarred hand. Jairus called out a warning.

The sound of hooves pounded behind them. The hairs on Henry's scalp prickled, and he whirled to see the Wild Hunt bearing down on them. It was hard to focus on a single rider in the charge, but he had the impression of a huge host wreathed in clouds of pale gray fog, and in the midst of them rode Jane with the horn.

Jairus pulled the trigger on his gun, scattering some of the mist, but the Hunt rolled closer. Cassandra raised her umbrella, ready to swing it. Henry summoned the might of the storm and blasted the Hunt with icy wind.

Perhaps their attacks banished some of the riders, but the Hunt was unstoppable, and they were trapped before it.

Henry grabbed Cassandra and pulled her into the shelter of a doorway.

"Don't look at them," he called to Jairus, and he put himself between Cassandra and the Hunt, his back to the charging riders.

The hounds bayed, and Cassandra jumped, craning to see them.

Henry pulled her against his chest, cradling her head against him. He could feel her breath against his neck, warm and quickened by fear.

"Close your eyes," he whispered.

Cassandra leaned into Henry, and he wrapped his other arm around her, holding her so close that the rise and fall of their chests became one.

Somewhere, in the distance, Henry was aware of the rush of the Wild Hunt—the baying of hounds, the pounding of hooves —but he was far more aware of Cassandra's warmth pressed against him, the soft give of her curves, her arms tight against his back.

The Hunt's horn sounded nearby, distracting him.

Don't listen to the horn.

But the wild echoes flew around them and rolled off the buildings, and in their mournful call, he heard his name.

The song spoke of his story. Loneliness, hopes crumbling to dust, wandering lost forever. His heart ached at the truth of it. He was so weary of the fight against the Fay and against what their magic had done to him. If he joined the Wild Hunt, he would never be alone again, and Titania could not touch him.

"Henry!" Cassandra's whisper brushed his ear.

His arms had slackened, but he tightened his hold again. What had he been thinking? He didn't need to protect Cassandra from the Wild Hunt—she wasn't the lost soul.

He was.

She held him fast, her breath warm against his neck. He looked down and met her gaze. Her eyes were wide with fear, her lips slightly parted. The mad energy of the Hunt crackled around them, beckoning them to forget everything in the mortal world and be free.

Cassandra closed her eyes and leaned into him, her umbrella clattering to the ground as she ran her hands up his back.

He brought his lips to hers, gently at first, but then deeper, hungrier, wishing there was nothing in the world but Cassandra and him. She returned the kiss, her fingers pressed into his back. He stroked her hair and pulled it loose from its knot, letting it tumble free to be caught by the wind whipping down the street.

His fingers felt hot. So hot he had to be careful not to burn her skin as he caressed the back of her neck.

She gasped and stepped back, her pupils wide as she stared

up at him. He reluctantly let his arms slide down to take her hands.

"Cassandra," he whispered, his voice husky.

He should not have kissed her like that, but he would give everything to do it again.

"The Hunt," she said raspily.

It had passed them by. Henry shook his head, trying to focus on something besides the warmth of Cassandra so close to him, her fresh, rosy scent lingering on his skin where he had touched her.

The chill of the storm brushed over him, and he remembered the others. Still keeping a tight grip on Cassandra's hand, he stepped out of the doorway. Jairus was pressed against a building opposite them. At least the Wild Hunt hadn't taken any of them.

Shouts and wails came from a neighboring street. Henry's stomach twisted. They were failing, and London suffered because of it.

They ran out of the alley into a scene of chaos. Brawls spilled out of taverns into the street despite the rain. Men bashed each other into the cobblestones and drew knives. A woman's body stretched out beside the road, her eyes wide in terror and her mouth open in an eternal scream as rain poured over her waxy skin. Cassandra whimpered but kept her hold on Henry.

"Why is this happening?" she asked.

"The Wild Hunt calls to the darker side of people—the lost and broken parts of our souls. It calls us to give up and join the Hunt." Henry pulled her away from a figure lurking in an alley. "And for those who are not wholly overtaken by despair, I suspect the Morrigan is feeding their rage."

A group of men smashed the window of a shop to grab the

contents. Fire licked from the broken window of another building. Henry drew on the rain and sent a waterspout into the fire, extinguishing it in a hiss of smoke.

At a house ahead, women in ball gowns and men in black suits rushed down the front steps. Shouting came from the house.

Jairus caught one of the men by the lapels. "What happened in there?"

"I...I don't know," the man said, his gaze darting from the house to the street. "There was a rushing sound like a storm, and everyone just went mad."

Henry started for the house. A woman sat on the stairs, slumped against the railing with a hopeless expression. Amy appeared from the crowd. She ran up to the girl, trying to coax her to her feet. Henry and Cassandra pushed through a stampede of footmen running off with the silver.

"What are you doing here?" Henry called to Amy.

She gave a start, then sagged with relief. "The same as you: trying to help people overcome by the Hunt. Domin is inside."

Henry scanned the street and saw Mary huddled by the bottom of the steps with her crossbow, her knuckles white where she gripped the weapon. Jairus helped a trembling woman with an injured ankle down the steps. Cassandra sat beside a distraught young lady in a torn gown.

Henry could help those more seriously injured. He headed inside, searching for Domin. Several people were unconscious or dead on the floor, and a trail of blood trickled down the floorboards and soaked a once-fine rug. Henry knelt to check for pulses. Several of the party-goers were beyond his help, but he rendered aid to those who could still be saved, treating broken noses and knife wounds. He wasn't aware anyone else joining him, but he looked up after what felt like hours to find Cassandra applying a bandage to an injured man and Domin helping to move a body from the corridor. Gritting his teeth, Henry went back to work, knowing that elsewhere in the city there were similar scenes and more people he could not help.

Cassandra had never spent a more terrible night, not even when she had been captured by the Grigori. It wasn't just the blood or the suffering: it was the hopelessness of it all. By the time they finished their gruesome work and helped the injured home, the sky promised dawn.

"The Wild Hunt is terrible," Amy said as they trudged home.

Domin shook his head "This is not how the Wild Hunt is meant to be. It's a gathering place for the dead who are lost. The Unseelie Fay are abusing its power."

"Of course they are," Henry growled.

"We can't spend another night like this one," Jairus said. "We have to retrieve the horn."

"We might be able to during the day," Amy said. "It will be in the Unseelie Kingdom. I think Fitzhugh was hinting at that when he mentioned the feasting."

Domin nodded. "A short rest, and then we'll see what ideas Telesm and Lucien have about the Unseelie Kingdom."

Cassandra's eyes felt so heavy, she could barely keep stumbling along on her weak foot. If it wasn't for Henry, she would have fallen over before they made it to Amy's front door.

Even inside, with the gas lights chasing away the last of the night's shadows, Cassandra kept her hold on Henry's arm. The others scattered to their rooms, but she and Henry stood there alone in the entrance hall. She was afraid to let go. Who knew what the next day would bring?

He planted a soft kiss on her forehead.

"You need sleep," he said.

"I know. But I wish I didn't have to be apart from you."

He caught her chin in a gentle grip. "I wish that too. More than I know how to say. I love you."

Her eyes widened, and warmth poured over her. He loved her.

Before she could say anything, he went on. "I want to marry you. I want to spend the rest of my life talking to you and holding you and trying to make you happy. But I can't offer you anything. I don't have a home or a profession to speak of, so there are no comforts I can offer. I probably can't promise you children. I can't even grow old with you. I would give you the world if I could, but I can't even offer you myself. Even I'm not that reckless." He took her hands and squeezed them. "But whatever parts of me belong to myself, they are yours. Forever. No matter what happens."

She squeezed his hands back, tears stinging her eyes.

She wanted children someday, but she knew that wasn't guaranteed even in a marriage where magic wasn't involved. It would be endlessly strange to age while Henry did not, but perhaps their happiness together would erase that.

But she would slow Henry down. If he was running from the Fay and the Grigori, he had to be able to stay ahead of them, and she never could. If anything, the demon mark on her hand might draw the Unseelie Fay closer to him. She looked at the scar, tempted for a moment to hack her hand off and have it done with. But even then, it didn't guarantee the Fay couldn't use her to get to Henry. To hurt him. And she could never do anything that might hurt Henry.

So, she was trapped. She would hurt him by staying away or she hurt him more by staying close. There was no way to win against the Fay.

"I love you, too," she whispered.

Then she tore away from him and fled upstairs to collapse onto her bed. Mary was already asleep, so Cassandra was alone with her misery. The tears ran down her cheeks, hot on her skin, and sank into the fabric. Henry loved her. She loved him. But the Fay would never let him be free.

Chapter Thirty-One

Amy felt like she had barely closed her eyes when a tap on her door woke her.

"Yes?" she called, sitting upright.

The door creaked open, and Domin peered in. He stopped whatever he was going to say and stared at her with a curious expression.

She flushed and tried to smooth her tousled hair. "Well? Not all of us can look as perfect as we choose as soon as we wake up."

He blinked. "No, I... You look...lovely. But tired. Are you doing too much?"

"What? No!" Amy threw off her blankets before she remembered that she was only in her nightgown, but it seemed even less dignified to scramble after the blankets again, so she raised her chin defiantly. "I can do as much as anyone else.

His forehead creased, but he nodded. "We need to speak with Telesm and Lucien. We have to go after the horn while the sun is high."

"Of course," Amy said, and though her eyes ached for more sleep, she forced a smile.

Domin cast her a last, lingering look, then closed the door so she could dress. In a few minutes, she joined the others downstairs. Her hair, she hoped Domin noticed, was now impeccable.

"Sneaking into the Unseelie kingdom is no small task," Telesm was saying.

"And stealing something from it is even worse," Henry added.

Jairus grinned. "Then we create a distraction. Some of us go in like we're attacking, and the others sneak around from behind and take the thing."

"They'll probably know it's the horn we're after," Henry said. "That will make them guard it more carefully."

"Unless we convince them we're after something else," Jairus said.

"Freeing the changelings." Mary's quiet voice made the others jump in surprise. Mary looked away from their expectant stares but went on. "After what they did to Lucien, of course we would be upset."

Amy looked at her with sympathy. "We would think that way, but they would not. They hardly even think of the changelings as existing. We have to go after something that is valuable to them. Something that gives them power."

Mary blanched at that and pinched her lips together in a tight line. Amy agreed with her sentiment. The way the Fay treated the changelings made her ill, but this was not the time to remedy that.

"If Telesm could be persuaded to come with us, we could go after another Unseelie artifact." Henry glanced at Telesm.

Telesm huffed but looked thoughtful. "Other than the

horn... Oh yes, they do have a sword than never dulls and is said to be sharp enough to cut through a beam of light. It's dangerous in their hands. I wouldn't mind bringing it back to my cottage."

"Excellent." Jairus said. "Then that's what we go after."

"Who, though?" Cassandra asked. "Who attacks them and who sneaks in?"

"Telesm and I lead the attack," Domin said.

"Don't forget me," Jairus added, twirling his pistol. "You won't keep me away from that kind of action."

"You had best not enter," Domin said. "Your demon mark may draw their attention." He glanced at Cassandra. "Miss Weaver is doubly in danger because she once injured the Unseelie Queen."

Cassandra bit her lip, her eyes troubled.

"But it's not too dangerous for the rest of you?" Jairus asked with a frown.

"Of course it's dangerous," Domin said. "But they won't harm Henry because they would like to use him, they would consider Miss Leland beneath their notice, and Amy is banished from her mother's court, so nothing prevents her from venturing into the Unseelie Realm. They might even welcome her."

A jolt ran through Amy at the thought. Yes, they might welcome her. Fitzhugh was always trying to entice her to join the Unseelie forces. They wanted to shape her just like her mother did. Like she was only a pretty doll for the Faerie Queens to play with.

Jairus folded his arms. "At least I can cover your escape route."

Domin nodded. "Yes. And as for the rest... Henry can't be seen attacking the Unseelie Queen or it could provoke a war

between the courts, and he also probably shouldn't be the one
to steal the horn. He can help Amy sneak in and take it."

"Me?" Amy asked, her heart giving a leap. "You would trust
me to steal it?"

"Yes," Domin said, meeting her eyes with a reassuring look.
"You'll understand how to make your way around the Faerie
realms. Henry can protect your retreat."

Despite the insane danger of it, Amy felt like she could fly
into the Unseelie Kingdom. Domin trusted her again.

"You want me to help?" Mary asked, her voice small.

"No one will force you to join us," Amy said.

Mary nodded, looking torn.

"We have one advantage in the Unseelie Realm," Domin
said. "They cannot blow the horn there. If they summoned the
Wild Hunt through their own realm, it would wipe out their
forces."

"How do we get in?" Jairus asked. "Can Stewart open the
way again?"

Henry shook his head. "That only worked because the Dark
Lady had filled me with Unseelie magic. No, we'll need
someone with their own Unseelie magic: Lucien."

"You think he'll help us?" Amy asked.

Henry nodded. "He has no desire to help the Dark Lady,
and I can teach him how to use her magic to open the gate."

"I'll get my shotgun ready," Jairus said.

The others wandered off to prepare in whatever way they
could. Cassandra, Amy noticed, avoided Henry's longing stares
and instead hurried to ask Jairus something about a gun.

Amy turned to find herself alone with Domin.

"Thank you for trusting me," she said.

He smiled a little. "You have proven yourself. You are
stronger and wiser than you once were."

"Wise?" Amy wanted to laugh at the idea. "I only hope... Well, I hope I live up to your trust. Perhaps someday you can esteem me as you once did."

His eyes widened slightly at those words, and Amy cursed herself for speaking aloud what she had only thought secretly.

He glanced at her. "The things that I admired in you then have not changed."

Amy flushed. "Oh?"

"You are as full of hope and energy now as you were then. It has been a long time since I've seen someone persevere as you do."

Amy let the words roll inside of her. She suspected that he was comparing Amy to the long-ago woman whose admiration inspired him to break free from the Fay. Amy didn't want to live in anyone's shadow, though. She didn't want to be a reminder of the past. Amy suspected she had one advantage that the nameless lady had not, though: if Domin ever loved her, she could love him in return.

Chapter Thirty-Two

Mary slunk away from the meeting. Her friends accepted her, but they didn't need her. She was an afterthought in their plans, and her hopes of helping the changelings fell apart the moment she tried to put them together. The way the Fay traded, discarded, and abused changeling children was the most broken thing she had ever seen, and she could not fix it. She could never be brave and clever like Cassandra and Amy.

She found her way to the sitting room and looked out over the square below, gray and cold from Henry's storm.

"Mary," Lucien said.

She looked back at him. He, at least, seemed somewhat cheered to see her. Probably just because he was so bored being trapped in the house. He cocked his head and studied her.

"You look bleak. Did your friends give up on their scheme? I knew it was a bad idea."

"They'll steal the horn," Mary said, then her false bravado failed her, and she turned back to the window. "But they don't need me to do it. I'm useless."

"What do you mean? You helped set the guard on the house."

"With your help. And Amy's. Telesm probably could have done it himself, too. Being a changeling is a cursed existence. Even with Mr. Stewart..." She hesitated over that one. "I don't understand why he's so special."

"Royal blood," Lucien said. "It's his bloodline they care about more than him, and he knows it. Hates it."

"I suppose the Fay gave you the gift of reading minds, too?"

"No. I just learned to pay attention. I had to, to survive. And Mr. Stewart is a human changeling, like me, so it's not hard for me to guess."

Mary hmphed. "So, the Fay don't care about any of us. They feel like they can just...just throw us away. Like we're rubbish."

Lucien nodded and sat in a chair next to her. "It's terrible. What could feel worse than knowing that no one cares? That they're just using you?"

"Nothing," Mary mumbled. "Nothing feels worse."

It lingered there, deep in her chest, a horrible ache like an itch she could never scratch. The longing to know she mattered in some way and the fear she didn't.

"So, what are you going to do about it?" Lucien asked.

She looked away from him, rubbing her eyes before the tears could spill. "What do you mean, do about it?"

"You like to repair things, don't you?"

She laughed bitterly. "I can't fix all of Elfland."

"No, you can't. So, you can either mope about it and practically vanish, or you can get angry and do something."

She stared at him.

He sighed. "I've seen it with the changelings in the Unseelie Court. Some curl in on themselves. Practically disappear.

Others get angry. They use that anger to keep feeling. Keep moving. Sometimes, they even lash out. That doesn't end well when the Dark Lady can rip your life out for her own amusement. But that quiet anger sometimes keeps people alive, just to spite the Unseelie elves."

Mary wrinkled her forehead and stared down at the polished wood floor. Maybe she was angry. Maybe she always had been, a little, because part of her knew it wasn't right for so many people to be unkind to her. For her to feel so awkward and different and not know why and not encounter any sympathy or understanding. "I don't want to be angry at my friends, even if I am a little."

"That's good—that little bit of anger. You don't have to turn it against your friends, though. Turn it somewhere where it will do some good."

Mary laughed humorlessly. "Where can I do any good? Does the Dark Lady need a pocket watch fixed?"

Lucien tapped his fingers on his knee, his face turned up in thought. "Maybe there's something bigger than a broken clock you can repair. Who are you really angry at—the most angry?"

"The Unseelie elves."

"Precisely. Do you still have that scrap of cloth?"

Wide-eyed, Mary reached into her pocket and pulled it out. "You can't mean..."

He took the cloth. "I do mean it. I've been angry for so long, I'm not sure I remember what it's like to feel any other way. But I've been thinking over what you asked of me, and the thought makes me feel...triumphant, which may be the closest I can achieve to happiness. To walk into the Unseelie Kingdom and steal one of her enslaved changelings away. That would be glorious. But we'd have to do it while the elves are distracted.

We'd have to do it when they wouldn't notice who was missing and punish the others."

"While they're under attack." Goose bumps prickled Mary's arm. "You think we could?"

"I do. And I'm willing to take the risk to find out if I'm right."

Mary stared at him in awe. If he was wrong, the Dark Lady could pull his life away, and that of Mary's unknown sister, too. And Mary would be lucky if the Dark Lady killed her outright. Even if Mary succeeded, her friends would be angry that she risked interfering with their plans. They thought the changelings could wait, and they were wise. She couldn't disappoint them. She couldn't take the chance that they might turn her away.

Her gaze fixed on the worn little scrap of cloth in Lucien's hand, its tiny white daisies faded and fragile on their blue background. The love her mother had put into her sewing still clung to it. Mary's vision blurred. Her sister was trapped in the Unseelie Kingdom, and no one else cared. No one else would do anything about it. Mary didn't want to be Cassandra or Amy's shadow. She wanted to be brave on her own.

She met Lucien's eyes. "Tell me what we need to do."

Chapter Thirty-Three

The Unseelie Kingdom. A place built on suffering. Amy shuddered at the thought of venturing there—more so because a part of her was still intrigued by the power it might offer. But she couldn't let Domin and her friends down. She couldn't let herself down.

They had many hours of daylight left when they set out, though Henry's storm continued its gray drizzle.

"Where do we find a gate to their kingdom?" Jairus asked.

"Somewhere full of misery," Domin said. "The East End."

They took a carriage, rolling past people visiting and shopping, unaware of how much danger the night would bring. Amy watched the Strand, wondering where in that warren of shops and entertainment the Grigori lurked with the Leannan. If the Dark Lady had truly meant to rid them of Rushford, she would have sent Jane to the Strand. Fitzhugh knew enough to direct her there. The Unseelie Fay cared for nothing but their own power.

When they reached the Tower of London, Domin called for the carriage to stop.

"Whitechapel," Henry said, looking past the Tower to the east. "It's grim enough."

Amy nodded, but her focus drifted to the stone bulk of the Tower of London. The four-sided White Tower reminded her of a pale imitation of Annwn's Keep, stone instead of glass, slowly decaying instead of remaining untouched by time. In her younger years, it had been a royal residence as well as a prison. It was where Guy Fawkes and her other co-conspirators were held and tortured before being executed for the Gunpowder Plot. A sour taste filled her mouth at the memory. It was a plan she was grateful had failed—that she wished she had never become involved in.

Domin gave her a sympathetic glance, and she quickly looked away. She didn't deserve sympathy. Not for that.

Domin led them on through narrow streets crowded with beggars and littered with horse droppings, vomit, and other filth. Amy took shallow breaths, avoiding eye contact with the people who had to live in that place. Cassandra held a handkerchief over her nose, and Mary turned sickly pale. Even the men, who had been hunting the Leannan in these streets, looked ill.

"Not much farther," Domin said through clenched teeth.

They wound through an alley. Jairus had a gun in each hand, but he wasn't aiming at the people they spotted through doors or windows. He had his sights trained on the darkness ahead of them. Something stood in the shadows: the twisted trunk of an ancient hawthorn tree. It grew atop a low, stone arch that may have once led to a cellar of some sort. Amy at first thought the tree must be dead in its tiny patch of dirt shaded by decrepit buildings, but a few tattered leaves clung to its contorted branches.

"There," Domin said.

Amy nodded. The thick, oily feel of Unseelie magic seeped from the opening below the tree.

Lucien stepped warily up to the tree and peered into the dark cellar below. A few gnarled roots broke through the stone lining of the cellar, and a sour stink breathed from its cold depths.

He glanced back at Henry. "And what am I supposed to do?"

"Do you feel the magic that ties you to the Unseelie court?"

Lucien shivered and nodded.

"Push back against it."

Lucien scrunched up his face and concentrated. After a long minute, he shook his head. "I don't know how to do it. Maybe it's different because of your royal blood."

Henry rolled his eyes. "Bloodlines again! No, this time I'm certain they don't matter. Think of it like...like she's pouring magic into you, and you're spitting the magic back at her."

Lucien smiled a little at that, and he turned back to the dying hawthorn tree. His eyes narrowed in concentration, and he reached out to touch the archway of the cellar. The few leaves clinging to the tree shuddered. Lucien huffed to himself and squeezed his eyes shut. The debris on the ground rustled, then settled into silence. Lucien grimaced.

"It's too much," Lucien panted, his voice pained. "She's so strong."

"You are stronger," Henry said sharply. "She has only suffering at her disposal, but you have more. Reach past the pain. Find love or hope or sheer stubbornness to feed the magic."

Lucien's forehead wrinkled, and he looked defeated. But then he glanced around from Henry to Cassandra to Mary. He took a long breath and closed his eyes again, his face relaxing. Amy held her breath, pleading for him to find his strength.

The dry, brown leaves on the ground rattled and swirled into a vortex around the cellar opening.

"Go!" Domin grabbed Amy's hand and climbed with her through the opening.

They clambered through a grubby stone tunnel and landed under the dark trees of the Black Forest. The gold leaves hung limp overhead. Henry and Telesm tumbled through the portal into the forest, but Mary didn't follow. Amy understood; she didn't want to be there either.

"Will we be able to get out?" Amy asked, eyeing the cave-like mouth of the gateway.

"As long as the Dark Lady doesn't track us and seal it off," Domin said. "If she does, we'll have to find another exit. Perhaps Telesm and I should escape a different way to mislead her."

Amy nodded, her throat tight. So many ways this quest could go wrong.

Domin nodded to Telesm. "We will make an assault on the Dark Lady's treasury and try to gain the sword. While they are distracted, Henry and Amy will sneak around to take the horn."

"They'll be fools if they don't suspect what we're doing," Henry said.

"They'll suspect," Domin said, "but they'll still have to divide their forces to stop us."

"So, we only have to face *half* of the Unseelie Court." Henry crossed his arms.

Telesm flashed a mocking grin. "Don't think you can

handle it, human? Do you want to lay odds on which of us steals our object first?"

"No need," Henry said. "My object is the one that matters."

"Enough." Domin jabbed at Telesm. "We should be off before we're noticed."

The half-brothers jogged through the woods.

"They could at least try to act stealthy," Amy muttered.

"I'm sure they know what they're doing," Henry said. "What about us? We should sneak around the other way. Where do you suppose they keep the horn?"

"I haven't spent any more time here than you have," Amy reminded him. "Fitzhugh mentioned feasting. I think he was dropping us a hint. Though... I can't imagine Jane will ever be far from the horn."

Henry nodded, looking grim.

They snuck forward, weaving their way between black trunks oozing red sap and over a forest floor that crunched with old bones.

Shouting rose in the distance.

"That will be them," Henry said.

He motioned for Amy to move faster, and they jogged through the endless dusk of the Unseelie Kingdom until they burst out of the trees.

Before them stood a great hall of dark stone: not quite a castle, but a domed fortification with Gothic spikes rising from its perimeter to pierce the dismal sky.

"That looks like a feasting hall," Henry said.

Horrid creatures streamed out of it: red caps, trolls, and wyverns that Domin and Telesm would have to face.

Henry gave Amy a questioning look, and she nodded. She was as ready as possible. They darted for the hall, slipping inside the open doors. Henry motioned Amy behind one of the great pillars supporting the ceiling.

The horn sat on a dais in the feast hall, surrounded by half-finished meals of boar and ale. And Jane lounged by the dais.

"We won't sneak past her," Henry whispered. "I'll have to distract her."

Amy nodded.

Henry crept as close as he could before stepping into the open.

Jane grinned when she saw him. "Somehow, I thought I'd see you when I heard the racket outside. I knew you'd be jealous. Or did your queen send you for the horn?"

Amy held her breath, hoping Henry would avoid saying anything that would start a war between the courts—a war he would be forced to fight in.

"No," Henry said. "This is personal. Between you and me."

Amy snuck closer to the horn. A few shadowy creatures lurked in the corners, their attention fixed on Jane and Henry.

Jane grinned. "Yes. There's a connection between us, isn't there? Instead of fighting, you should join me. Think of what we could do together. I could offer you much more than that little human you've chosen as a mistress."

The temperature in the room dropped. Amy gritted her teeth. Henry and his temper. This was going to end poorly.

"Absolutely not," Henry said.

"Maybe if I kill her, you'll forget about her. You will eventually, of course. We are immortal, and she is only a brief flicker compared to the lives we will live."

Henry lashed out with a gale-force wind. Ice formed on everything the wind touched. Jane shielded her face, and the horn went slipping off the dais and into the shadows. Amy mentally scolded Henry. At least he had separated Jane from the horn, but now Amy was going to have to fetch it in the midst of a storm of ice and lightning.

The weight of Unseelie magic pressed around her, called to her. It would make her stronger, as it had for Fitzhugh. She could snap her fingers at Jane and whatever creatures still lurked in the hall. She could be powerful and capable. The Unseelie magic tickled her mind, begging her to open herself to it.

And it poured the taste of blood into her mouth.

She gagged and wiped her mouth on her sleeve. No. Unseelie magic would strip away her ability to feel anything positive. She would never touch it. She had to get to the horn without it. Henry was creating her distraction. Risking his life to do it.

Amy pulled her cloak up, casting her face in shadow. The Unseelie would notice if someone with positive feelings walked among them, but they would not notice more suffering. Her suffering was not a part of herself that she wanted. It was a bitter legacy left by her mother. But even suffering was part of life. The mistake the Unseelie had made was separating the suffering from the joy. Amy could walk through the suffering as long as she remembered the joy on the other side of it.

She drew the hood low and walked forward. She let herself sink into those darker memories that she hated stirring from their murky resting place. Mentally ran her fingers over them like someone plucking rotten fruit from the vine. Her mother's cruelty. Her late husband's belittling words. All of her own terrible mistakes and inadequacies. Pain, pain, pain. She hissed and gritted her teeth against how much the memories hurt. The Unseelie Fay did not notice her. She was as one of them. In pain and fear.

She stepped closer to Jane, who battled Henry with ferocious storm winds. Amy could feel the pain of others in the gale. So many people suffering, and she could not help them. It weighed her down. Made her movements slow. What difference did it make what she did? It was never enough. It was never perfect. And if it wasn't perfect, what did it matter? What did she matter?

She looked out from the shadowy recess of her hood. Henry was struggling. He felt the pain of the Unseelie magic as well. Amy might not be able to save everyone, but she could save her friends.

The silver horn lay forgotten against the wall. Amy snuck over and carefully lifted it. It was heavy and cold against her fingers. Much too heavy for its size.

Jane, focused on her fight with Henry, didn't yet notice that it was missing. Amy backed away. In the shadows opposite her, she caught glimpses of enormous creatures watching Jane's fight with casual amusement: giants, trolls, or something worse. They would crush her if they caught her.

The horn burned her skin with its bitter chill. She imagined summoning the Wild Hunt. Watching the black steeds and white hounds tear through the Unseelie Realm. Using the horn would trap her in the world of the Fay and the Hunt, never to dance again in London or ride her pony in the country. Like Jane, she would become less...real in the living world. But wouldn't it be worth it to end all the suffering the Unseelie Fay caused? Her mother would even be proud of her. She shifted her grip on the horn.

But suffering would still be part of life. The Faerie Courts would go to war over the horn, hurting the people she cared about. She tucked the horn under her arm, praying that she wasn't giving up her only opportunity to stop the Unseelie Queen, and slipped toward the exit.

Some of the dark creatures on the edges of the room stirred. They must have sensed her hope.

Henry glanced her way. He made a shoving motion, and a blast of ice pummeled Jane, freezing her feet and robes to the ground. He backed toward the door.

Jane shrieked, and lightning crashed into the hall, blasting chunks of ice to pelt the room. Amy ducked from one that exploded against a pillar behind her.

Jane spotted Amy, and her eyes went wide. "You! Return my horn!"

Amy gasped and fled out the door, Henry on her heels. He slammed it shut behind them and iced it shut. Jane shrieked like a wounded animal behind the doors.

"Run!" Henry said.

Amy did, still holding the horn, still uncertain if she had made the right decision.

Chapter Thirty-Four

Mary hung back when Amy went through the gate. She couldn't go through with her friends. She had to deceive all of them. Her stomach soured at the thought, but she clenched her fists. She would find her sister, whatever the cost.

Lucien stood back from the gate, his face lined with pain.

"I don't know how long it will stay open," he panted.

"I'm sure they'll be able to find a way out," Cassandra said, but she sounded like she was trying to reassure herself. Lying.

And Mary would have to lie as well—and more skillfully—for her plan with Lucien to succeed.

Jairus twirled his gun in one hand, watching the streets around them warily.

Lucien gave Mary a meaningful glance, then cleared his throat. "No, I should wait on the other side so I can open it for them when they return."

Cassandra opened her mouth then closed it again, obviously unsure of the wisdom in his plan. Mary trembled, preparing to trick the only people who had ever been friends to her.

Lucien didn't wait for permission from Cassandra or Jairus. He stepped up to the dark entrance and cringed in pain. Sweat rolled down his forehead. He took a deep breath and dove through.

Mary's heart caught. This was the moment—the point of no return.

"I don't think he should wait alone," Mary managed to squeak out.

She climbed through the gate and landed beside Lucien in the tangle of dark trunks.

Lucien hissed and glared at the gate.

"Does it hurt a great deal?" she asked.

"Of course. Unseelie magic is suffering, even pushing it back at them." He straightened, his face set in determination. "We don't have much time. Let's go."

Mary hung close to Lucien as they tip-toed through the bone-littered forest of the Unseelie Kingdom. In the distance arose a clamor of shouting and shrieking. No doubt Domin and Telesm's attack. At least the Unseelie Fay would be distracted.

"How will we find my sister?" Mary whispered, glancing past the trees with their dark, oozing sap as though Unseelie Fay might be lurking in every hazy shadow.

"I've seen a child wearing scrap like the one you have—tied over her hair in the kitchens. If she's not your...your sister, then she probably knows who is."

The banqueting hall was a great, spiky building of black stone, like a lurking beast on the edge of the forest. Mary paused to stare.

"Terrible, isn't it?" Lucien asked.

Mary nodded. "Let's hurry. Where are the kitchens?"

"Outdoors. Behind the banquet hall."

They snuck to the building. Wind howled through its narrow windows. Mary shivered. That had to be Henry.

"Hurry!" she whispered.

Lucien nodded. They broke into a jog, rounding the side of the prickly, domed building.

And they came face-to-face with a willowy Faerie lady with wide gray eyes and shining brown hair that swept down to the ground.

They stared at each other for a long moment.

The Fay's eyes filled with tears, and she held out a hand. "Can it be? Is it really you?"

Mary looked at Lucien, thinking he'd been caught, but the Faerie lady was staring at *her*.

"Me?" Mary asked. Had the Dark Lady warned them to watch for her? Did the Dark Lady even know that Mary existed?

The lady covered her mouth. "Darling, no one forgets her own child."

Lucien gave a start and stared between Mary and the Fay. "The Weeping Woman is your mother?"

"No!" Mary went cold, then heat prickled over her skin. This Faerie lady had to be mad. Mary shook her head as though she could deny the Faerie woman and make her vanish. "You don't know me."

"Oh, but I do." Panic entered the lady's eyes, and tears flowed down her cheeks. "What are you doing here? You should *never* come here."

Mary's hot-sick feeling resolved into anger. "*If* you are my mother, you...you threw me away. You have no right to tell me what to do."

The woman's expression fell. "Oh, my darling. I sent you

away so you could be free of this place. It is literally built on suffering. Can you imagine anyone wanting their child to live in such conditions?"

Mary's anger crumbled into confusion. Could this Fay be telling the truth? Mary was a Faerie changeling, after all. "You sent me away?"

"Our Lady, she found a human child she wanted. She came searching for an elf child to switch. I realized... I realized it was your chance to escape. So, I offered you for the trade. Was it... was it beautiful where you lived? Was the sky full of sunshine and stars? I almost remember their light."

Mary stared at her, not sure what to believe. "Why didn't you leave, too?"

The woman bowed her head, and more tears rolled down her cheeks. Weeping Woman indeed.

"I made choices...terrible choices," the woman whispered. "The pain here is too much a part of me. I cannot remember my name or...or what it was like to be happy, and so I can never be free, even if I left. You see, I cannot let that happen to you. You must go now before she finds you here."

"I cannot go without the child...the one she traded for me."

The woman blinked, and more tears leaked from her eyes—wide gray eyes much like Mary's. "The human child? But why?"

"You said this was a place of suffering. How can I enjoy my freedom if I know someone else is suffering for it?"

The elf sighed and dabbed away her tears. "There is so much goodness in you. I knew I did right. You will be like your father."

A thrill ran down Mary's spine. "My father? Who was he?"

"A human knight with elfin blood. He was...gentle. Yet brave and heroic. The only person who was ever kind to me. He is long dead now—died leading his men to safety—and his memory only another pinprick in my heart. But you must flee —live on!"

Her father had been brave. Mary rolled the idea around to study it, and it filled her with warmth even in that sunless kingdom.

"I'll flee as soon as I have the human child," Mary said.

The elf stared at her, the never-ending tears spilling down her cheeks. "Very well. I will help you for your sake, and the sake of your father. If *she* kills me for it, then at least I will have died for something that matters."

Mary stared at this woman who claimed to be her mother. Who was willing to die for her. The Weeping Woman possessed bravery as well.

"She is one of the kitchen girls," Lucien said.

The Weeping Woman looked at him as if surprised he could speak. He was a human changeling after all. They probably kept their eyes down and their mouths closed around the Fay.

"You are almost to the kitchens," the Weeping Woman said. "I oversee them, and I was going there to see if the next course is ready. The Court will be hungry after whatever battle they are fighting. But I will delay if they come back. That will give you a little time to escape."

"Thank you," Mary said. She could not yet think of this weeping Fay as her mother—not in place of the woman who had raised and nurtured her—yet she still felt a well of gratitude toward her, and a sympathetic connection.

She and Lucien headed for the kitchens. Humans of various ages worked around huge black ovens and open fires. They crafted the most amazing meal Mary had ever seen—like Christmas, but magnified by a hundred: boars dripping with glaze sizzled in pits, cauldrons of cider steamed over the fires, and great loaves of sweet bread topped with chopped fruit and nuts warmed above the ovens. Everywhere there was sugar— some of the children sculpted castles of the sugar: intricate, fairy tale designs so delicate Mary wondered how they didn't collapse.

"It is a celebration?" she asked Lucien.

He shook his head. "They eat this way every day. Sugar is their favorite. Have you ever seen a sugar plantation?"

Mary shook her head.

"Places of terrible suffering." He motioned toward a long, polished wood table where several girls worked. "She's over there."

"Thank you."

She didn't need him to tell her which girl. She recognized the scrap of cloth that matched the one her human mother had treasured. The child looked like what Mary remembered of her mother, though much younger—only ten or so. The girl had been allowed to age somewhat, then, but not to equal Mary's seventeen years. Though Mary could never know her own true age if she had lived in this place before being traded away. Her father had been a brave knight—her other father. There were still knights now, though they ran estates and joined Parliament and didn't seem particularly brave or heroic anymore.

Mary snuck up to the girl, ignored by all the changelings. Only then did she realize she didn't know what to call the child.

"Excuse me," she whispered.

The girl looked at her, confused. Elves weren't polite to changelings, but Mary didn't have time to explain.

"What is your name?" Mary asked.

"It's Sarah," the girl said absently.

Mary gestured to the sugar castle the girl crafted. "That's beautiful. It looks delicious."

Sarah looked confused. "It won't taste good."

"Why not?"

"It's what I do. I put my feelings into what I bake."

"I'm surprised they don't keep you happy then."

The girl wrinkled her forehead. "They hurt me when it's time to bake. They want their food to taste like misery." Suspicion entered her eyes. "Who are you?"

"I've come to take you away from here, if you want to leave."

The girl winced. "Of course I want to, but we'll never get away, and then they'll just hurt me more."

Mary's heart twisted. "I won't let them. They will have to hurt me before they can hurt you. And I will get you far away so they won't be able to touch you. Back to the human world."

"Is that where you come from?" the girl asked. "I've heard whispers about fresh-smelling rain and trees with leaves that are green and not gold. Are they true?"

"Yes. Are you willing to try?"

The girl nodded. "I am."

Mary took her hand. "Then let's go, quickly, before anyone notices."

The girl balked. "I have to leave the others?"

Mary looked at the faces of the children working over the fires. They ignored Mary, Sarah, and Lucien, each too lost in his or her own misery to have time for anyone else. Lucien gave her a helpless look and shook his head. They could not sneak so many children out at once, but Mary would never sleep well again thinking of their pain. She set her jaw.

"We have to go alone for now, but we won't abandon them. We'll find a way to save all of them."

She had no idea how she would keep that promise, but she would. She refused to believe that there was no help for the child victims of the Unseelie Queen's cruelty. Mary's parents—human and Fay—had been brave in their own ways. Mary would find her courage as well.

Amy followed Henry into the woods, feeling as though the whole Unseelie Kingdom was breathing down her neck. But they were almost to the gates.

Something moved in the woods in front of them, also running for the gate. Tingles ran over her skin as Henry drew in the energy around them, prepared to blast whatever stood in their way.

"Wait!" Amy called. "That looked like—"

Yes, it was Mary. And Lucien. Had the Unseelie changeling betrayed them to the Dark Lady? He carried something in his arms. A child.

"What are you doing?" Henry shouted, not slowly, but matching pace with Lucien and Mary.

"Saving my sister," Mary said through clenched teeth.

"Your..." Henry's eyes widened. "This is not the time!"

"Too late now," Lucien said.

Mary glanced at Amy. "I suppose you're very angry? But you can't be angry at her. She's just a child."

Amy shook her head and panted for breath. "No. It was foolish, perhaps, but brave."

Mary looked taken back by her response. And Henry was definitely angry. But a part of Amy was proud of Mary, even if she had been rash. It could not have been easy to sneak in and steal the child.

"Hurry!" Lucien called.

Amy met his eyes, saw the fear reflected in them. The Unseelie Queen would destroy a servant who betrayed her.

She looked forward, toward the gate, and her heart plummeted.

Fitzhugh was waiting for them.

He held out a hand and stopped Henry where he stood, pulling at his magic. Henry gasped and doubled over, sinking to the ground as he clutched his chest. But he rolled back up to his knees and pushed back, knocking Fitzhugh off balance.

Fitzhugh gritted his teeth. "A clever trick, but I will still kill you."

He clenched his fist, and Henry crumpled.

Lucien shoved the child into Mary's arms and charged at Fitzhugh.

The Unseelie elf dropped him to the ground with a gesture. "Foolish changeling. You should have stayed away."

"I'm not done with you—with all of you," Lucien said between clenched teeth.

Fitzhugh laughed and raised his hand, no doubt preparing to tear away the changeling's magic.

"No!" Amy shouted. The horn was heavy in her hands. If she blew it? Would the Wild Hunt destroy Fitzhugh? She did not want to harm an old friend, but she could not let him kill her current friends.

"Stop!" A Faerie lady with tears flowing from her eyes rushed forward, grabbing Fitzhugh's arm.

"There's no need to interfere here," Fitzhugh said, shaking the woman off with a sneer. "Go back to your weeping."

"You can do what you like to me," the woman said. "I won't let you harm my child."

"Your..." Fitzhugh trailed off and glanced at Mary, who held tighter to the little changeling girl and glared defiantly.

"My, that's interesting," Fitzhugh said. "But I don't care about her one way or the other. She's nothing to me."

The Weeping Woman held her arms out to barricade Mary and Lucien from Fitzhugh. She glanced back at Lucien, and her red-rimmed eyes widened. "But the boy is not nothing to you. You cannot harm him."

"This changeling? Just another human."

"No, you mustn't hurt him. One should always be true to blood."

"To blood? What does his blood matter to me?"

"It is also yours. Don't you see it? Don't you sense it?"

Amy stared between Fitzhugh and Lucien. And she gasped. Because she did see it. A resemblance that ran deeper than skin.

Fitzhugh scowled. "I have no children."

"But you do," the Weeping Woman said. "His mother was a woman from the French West Indies killed in the Revolution."

Fitzhugh's face softened into an expression lined with longing. "Nanette. But she—we—had no child."

The Weeping Woman clasped her hands as if in supplication. "She did. The Lady found that the woman was with child—your child—and thought the infant had potential. She took the woman and hid her and the baby from you, knowing you would object. But the child had too much human blood. No Faerie magic. And you had forgotten the woman, moved on. So, our Dark Lady kept the child as a changeling and tossed the woman to the revolutionaries."

Fitzhugh had gone deathly pale as the Weeping Woman spoke.

Lucien looked at Fitzhugh in disgust and cried out, "It cannot be true!"

But Fitzhugh just stared at him, his expression moving from anger and disbelief to wonder.

"Nanette," Fitzhugh whispered. "Oh, poor Nanette."

"No!" Lucien shouted.

He ran past Fitzhugh toward the gate. Fitzhugh stared after him, his posture stiff. In shock.

"Go!" Amy said to the others.

Henry stumbled to his feet and ran, and Mary put the child down and grabbed her hand, half-dragging the girl behind Henry. Amy ran on, cradling the horn. She looked back. Fitzhugh stood very still, watching them go.

Cassandra stood ready with her crossbow at the gate. She didn't know what had prompted Mary to leap through with Lucien, and it troubled her, but for now, she had to focus on protecting the others if—when—they returned.

The gate shimmered. Jairus tensed. Cassandra raised the crossbow, finger off the trigger for the moment.

Lucien dove through the portal, followed by Henry. Mary stumbled after them. And she was holding the hand of...a child. A little girl wrapped in rags and looking around in wonder and terror.

"What on earth?" Cassandra asked.

"Keep us covered!" Lucien said, the force of his words echoing in her mind despite her resistance to his magic.

Yes, she would ask questions later.

Mary and Lucien hurried for the street. A moment later, Amy raced through the portal, clutching the silver horn. Cassandra sagged in relief. They had succeeded.

"Shut it!" Henry called.

Lucien made a gesture, and the dark gate closed. He collapsed on the dirty street, gasping.

"What about the others?" Cassandra asked.

Henry paused to catch his breath. "They'll make it to Telesm's clearing. From there, I don't know, but they will be safe. The Dark Lady will be furious when she realizes what we've done, though." He straightened and turned to Lucien. "What kind of insane plan did you hatch back there?"

Mary pulled the child close. "He was helping me. None of you would help, and I had to save her. We have to save the others, too. The Dark Lady tortures them, and they are innocent children."

Jairus's expression hardened at that, and he tightened the grip on his gun. Cassandra looked at the thin, frightened child clinging to Mary, and her heart ached to think of more such children left behind.

Henry's anger dissolved, and he ran his hand through his hair. "I know. I know. We just... We're not strong enough to take on the entire Faerie Kingdom."

Cassandra put a hand on his arm. After what he'd been through with Titania, she could imagine how it hurt him to see others treated even worse.

"It will be difficult enough to protect this girl," Amy said. "If the Dark Lady comes after her, it will be a disaster. We can only hope she doesn't realize the child is gone with the other things we did today."

"My...my Faerie mother will cover our escape," Mary said quietly.

Cassandra stared. Much had happened in the Unseelie Kingdom.

Amy drew a deep breath. "There may still be consequences.

For everything we did." She glanced down at the horn. "And... and Lucien is Fitzhugh's son."

Cassandra covered her mouth and looked to Lucien, who pushed himself up to his feet and dusted off his knees, his eyes bright with anger.

"I didn't think even Fitzhugh was heartless enough to turn his own child over to the Dark Lady," Cassandra said.

"I don't think he knew," Amy said quietly. "I think... I think there will be consequences of that as well."

Chapter Thirty-Five

Henry kept a wary eye on the progress of the sun as they hurried back for the refuge of Amy's house. He wanted to grab Cassandra's hand, both to help her and to feel her reassurance, but she hung back from him. They loved each other, but it might not be enough.

And the Dark Lady would already be preparing a counterattack. Once the sun set, her powers would increase. It would be better if they didn't have the horn by then, but they would want Domin and Telesm's guidance on how to return it. Henry didn't know where to take it. He hoped they returned quickly.

A figure waited by the front door of Amy's house. Henry's worry faded for a moment, thinking it was Domin, but no—it was Fitzhugh.

Henry scanned the square. There had to be other Unseelie Fay about, lying in ambush. Jairus raised his gun, but Fitzhugh lifted his hands in a sign of surrender, and Jairus paused, glancing to Henry.

Henry put himself between Amy and Fitzhugh.

Amy stepped behind Jairus, clutching the horn. "We're not returning it."

"I don't want it." Fitzhugh said. He leaned against the door and patted the head of Telesm's stone dog—apparently unbothered by the spell meant to discourage enemies. "I'm here to help you."

Henry's first thought was that Fitzhugh was lying. But he was Fay—he couldn't lie.

"How?" Henry asked.

"Jane stole the horn from the land of the dead," Fitzhugh said.

"Are you volunteering to go there?" Henry asked.

"Hardly. But that's not the only way to return it. The Wild Hunt must yield to the winter when the harvest ends."

"So, Stewart can create winter and this ends?" Jairus asked.

Henry shook his head. "I could bring a storm, but that is not true winter."

"You need the Cailleach," Fitzhugh said. "The Hag of Winter."

"The Cailleach?" Henry asked. The Queen of the Winter Realm was at least as terrible as Titania, perhaps more so, because her kingdom never knew the softness of spring and the sweetness of new life.

"The Cailleach sometimes rides with the Wild Hunt," Fitzhugh said. "Give her the horn, and she can call the Hunt to order. But in the meantime, you have another problem on your hands."

"Do we?" Henry asked.

Fitzhugh glanced at Lucien, who glared at him in disgust. "Yes, my...my son, apparently, has helped turn your house into a refuge for changelings."

Amy blanched. "Does the Dark Lady know?"

"She does not, but she will find out when she is less distracted."

"And we're supposed to believe you're not going to tell her?" Henry asked.

Fitzhugh's lips curled up in disdain. "Despite what you think, I had no idea that my Nanette's child was in the hands of my Lady. I have been betrayed, and I do not take to that lightly."

"And what are you going to do about it?" Amy asked.

Fitzhugh frowned. "There are certain vows I have made. But I failed Nanette. I want to see...see *our* child safe from the Dark Lady. That can only happen if someone else—someone Seelie—takes the changeling under his protection."

"His?" Henry asked. "Do you mean the Lord of the River Vale? I don't know why—"

"Not him, you fool," Fitzhugh said, shaking his head. "I'm talking about you, Henry Stewart."

Henry stared at him, thinking he had heard wrong. Thinking it was some mockery that he didn't fully understand. "Me?"

"My hope diminishes by the moment," Fitzhugh said. "Of course, you! Can you think of anyone else with Seelie magic who is willing to stand up to the Lords and Ladies?"

"I am still under the control of the Lady of the Woods," Henry said bitterly. "And I hope someday to be free of all of them."

"You never will be. This is who you are now. Your only road to freedom is to master your own powers and break away from the Lady of the Woods. To become a Seelie Lord."

Henry's stomach churned. Fitzhugh couldn't lie, and he sounded so sure.

"I don't want to become one of them."

"It's either that or become a solitary Fay. Unless you wished to remain enslaved to them."

Henry ground his teeth. This wasn't what he wanted. He wanted to be free from the Fay, not to always be one of them. He'd always held some hope that he could somehow embrace his human side as Domin had embraced his daemon side. But daemons were creatures of magic, too, where humans were not.

"There's no escaping what the Fay have done to me, then." He couldn't even look at Cassandra as he said it.

"But if you became a Seelie Lord," Fitzhugh said, "You could right the wrongs that have been done to you and others."

Henry squeezed his eyes shut, then glared at Fitzhugh. "Why don't you become a Fay Lord, then?"

Fitzhugh pressed his lips into a thin line. "I can never return to the Seelie Courts, and I don't think I'm quite ready to overthrow my lady and become the Unseelie King, however much I might dislike her deception."

Henry glanced back to where Mary and Cassandra huddled protectively around the changeling girl. The child's eyes were wide with terror. They could not send the child back to the Unseelie Kingdom. Henry realized he would die before he let it happen. But could he give up everything he'd dreamed of to protect the changelings—give up Cassandra? And even if he did, was he strong enough? It was only Domin that kept Titania from killing him, after all, and even Domin probably couldn't protect all the changelings.

Fitzhugh raised his head as though startled by some far-off sound. "Give my regards to the Cailleach. I must return before my lady misses me."

He cast one last speculative glance at Lucien and hurried away.

Chapter Thirty-Six

The presence of the horn pressed on Cassandra, like a constant, dull ringing in her ears. She couldn't imagine how her more magic-sensitive friends could bear it. Or what kind of trouble it might draw to them. They had to return it, hopefully before another night fell. She kept glancing out the window for Domin and Telesm, but time did strange things in Elfland. Who knew how long until they returned?

Cassandra and Mary kept busy by fussing over Sarah in the drawing room, gently cleaning her face and hands and brushing out her short hair. The child stood very still, both frightened and intrigued by their attention.

"It's dark here," Sarah said. "Like in the other place."

Cassandra glanced at the sky outside and forced a smile. "It's cloudy today, but soon you'll see plenty of sunshine."

"What does it look like? Will it hurt my eyes?"

Cassandra tried to imagine never seeing the sun. "It might sting a little at first, but you'll become used to it, and it will feel warm on your skin."

"I haven't been warm much except when I was too close to the fires."

Cassandra wanted to embrace the poor girl, but her stiff posture warned Cassandra she wasn't yet ready for such displays of affection.

"I do like the green trees," Sarah said, wonder lighting her face as she turned to see outside.

"There are many trees where your...*our* father lives," Mary said.

"I have a father?" Sarah whispered. "What about a mother?"

"She died," Mary said gently. "But she loved you very much."

Sarah considered that solemnly. "I don't know what that feels like."

"You will learn," Cassandra said fiercely.

Annwn's hound padded into the room. Sarah glanced at the creature but seemed unconcerned by it. No doubt she had seen much stranger and more frightening things in the Unseelie Kingdom.

The hound growled.

Cassandra froze. Was the hound reacting to Sarah? She was not a lost soul to be taken back to the otherworld. Not if Cassandra could help it.

But the hound approached the window, head low and hackles rising along the ridge of its back.

Cassandra felt the wrongness, too, something more than the presence of the horn. A feeling that the sun didn't shine as bright as it ought.

A shadow passed over the square.

Jairus shouted a warning and raced for the door. Cassandra looked outside. Her sisters walked on the far side of the mostly-empty square. Behind them in the shadows moved a dark form like many black birds flying low in the shape of a crescent. Or a scythe.

The hound let out a terrible bay, starting as a deep rumble that resonated in Cassandra's chest and rising to a mournful pitch. It leapt at the window and through the glass as if it weren't even there.

Cassandra ran for the front door, cold clinging to her chest. Her sisters.

"It's the Sluagh," Henry hissed behind her. "Damned souls sworn to the Unseelie Court."

He sprinted out the front door after Jairus, who was already halfway across the square. Cassandra limped after them, her hands trembling as she armed her crossbow. She would not let the Dark Lady have her sisters.

But they were all too far from her sisters. Her sisters, who were oblivious to the threat swinging through the air to cut them down.

Annwn's hound bayed again and galloped for the Sluagh.

Georgina yelped and grabbed Sophie, pulling her behind the low iron fence lining the square. The hound leapt the fence and tore into the black cloud of the Sluagh. A horrible shriek echoed across the square, and the writhing black form broke apart into many bat-like shapes. Jairus fired at the ones closest to him, and the shapes swirled up into the clouds. The hound bounded off in pursuit.

Henry and Jairus reached the girls, each grabbing the arm of one and hurrying them across the square.

Jairus pulled Georgina into the house, her hair wild and her eyes wide with both fear and, Cassandra thought, excitement. Henry escorted a shaken Sophie inside. Cassandra hurried to embrace her sisters.

"Thank goodness you're safe," Cassandra said. "What were you doing out there?"

"We were coming to see you," Sophie said, her voice shaking. "To say goodbye before we left."

"I hate dogs." Georgina shuddered. "What was that?"

"An animal attack," Jairus said. "But you protected your sister. Well done."

Georgina caught his praise and flushed.

"I think we're due for another storm," Henry said wearily, and Cassandra wondered how much effort it took from him to keep all of London dripping wet and stuck inside.

Henry gave Amy a significant look. She looked confused for a moment, then her eyes widened in understanding.

"Oh, yes," she said to Sophie and Georgina. "You ought to stay in here until all of this has blown over. Maybe even make a house party of it. Then you can forget all that unpleasantness out there."

Sophie nodded, agreeable to Amy's suggestions, but Georgina looked confused.

Cassandra still felt cold all over, and now she couldn't stop her weak hand from twisting into a fist she couldn't open. Her sisters were in danger because of her as well.

"This is the strangest house party," Georgina said. "You all look miserable. And this cannot be normal for London. What's going on, Cassie?"

Cassandra looked to her friends gathered there in Amy's entrance hall: Jairus with his guns, Henry with his magic, Mary standing protectively in front of Sarah in the drawing room, Amy biting her lip. What was Cassandra supposed to say? Georgina resisted enchantments, and Cassandra didn't like pretending or lying to her sister. Henry met her eyes with sympathy and shrugged one shoulder. The choice was hers.

Telling her sisters more might put them in greater danger, but so might keeping everything a secret.

Cassandra took a deep breath. "There are strange things going on, as you've seen. Strange animals at large. Like something...something supernatural. We've found that iron and sometimes silver can stop the...the terrible creatures from attacking people."

"That's not funny," Sophie said.

"I don't think it was meant to be." Georgina met Cassandra's gaze. "I've had dreams. Nightmares, really. About things prowling in the shadows. I think maybe they're not just dreams."

Cassandra nodded slowly.

Sophie looked skeptically at the grand staircase and the gas lamps. "Are you saying this house is haunted?"

"No," Cassandra said. "This house is safe. It's more like London is haunted."

"What about Mother?" Georgina asked.

Cassandra's breath caught. "Is she out in the streets?"

"No, she stayed in to finish packing," Sophie said. "But she'll worry if we're not home soon."

"I'll send her a message," Amy offered. "Let her know that you're staying here and she should continue to rest."

Cassandra didn't think Amy's magic worked through paper, but her mother might be awed enough by Amy's title to listen anyway.

"We can't stay here forever," Sophie said.

"I know." Cassandra put a hand on each of her sisters' arms. "We think we know what the...the spirits want, and if we return it, there should be peace again."

That would have to be enough for her sisters. The rest of the truth wasn't her secret to tell.

Chapter Thirty-Seven

Cassandra saw her sisters safely installed in one of the upper rooms, then hurried downstairs to find Henry and the others in the drawing room. There was still no sign of Domin and Telesm.

"We can't wait any longer," Henry said, pacing across the soft rug. "Only, I'm not certain how to reach the Winter Kingdom and the Cailleach."

"Her kingdom is part of Elfland," Amy said slowly.

"But traveling through Elfland with the horn would be suicide," Henry said.

In the quiet, rain pattered against the window, and Amy's clock ticked in the background.

Cassandra thought back through the many lessons Domin had given her over the last year. "A gateway to Elfland can be opened anywhere, can't it? Isn't that how the Grigori had one in their dungeons?"

"Anywhere that the energies of a place align with the other

side," Amy said. "I hardly think my home resembles the Winter Kingdom."

"The Winter Kingdom's entrances are usually barrows," Henry said. "Places of death."

"All right." Jairus stood and gestured to the city outside the window. "So where can we find a barrow around here? Or a crypt, perhaps?"

"Oh!" Amy's eyes lit. "St. James Palace has a crypt."

"I don't think Queen Victoria is going to let us use it," Henry pointed out.

Amy frowned. "There are the new cemeteries the city built. Brompton has a catacomb."

Henry looked thoughtful. "Yes, perhaps. That's not too far. But this is assuming I can open a gateway there."

"I think you can," Cassandra said. "You have an affinity for the cold, like it comes easily for you."

"I suppose it does." Henry's voice was weary. "I'm willing to try. Hale, are you coming with me?"

"Wouldn't miss it," Jairus said with a grin.

"I'm coming, too," Cassandra said. "Domin taught me a little about the Cailleach. She's a feminine force—not just about death, but also rest and rebirth. I think she would talk to me."

And for her and Henry to have any hope, she had to be able to survive in his world.

Henry looked concerned, but he nodded. "Very well."

Amy chewed her lip. "I suppose I need to stay here to watch over the house. Oh! But I remembered something."

She dashed upstairs. Henry paced and Jairus readied his guns while they waited for her to return. Amy trotted back down the steps and pressed something into Henry's hands with a triumphant grin.

"What's this?" Henry held up a tiny vial. "Telesm's healing ointment? Did you take this from his rooms?"

"I remembered he brought it. You might need it, and Domin and Telesm likely won't."

Henry frowned. "There's so little left. Hopefully, none of us need it." He looked up at Jairus and Cassandra. "We'd better be off while it's still light."

Cassandra limped to the entrance to pull on a cloak and fetch her cane. She believed, based on what Domin said, that she would be able to help convince the Cailleach to aid them, but she worried that she would slow Henry and Jairus.

Amy held out a satchel for her. "You should carry this."

"Me?" Cassandra didn't want to touch it. The power of the horn within buzzed in her ears.

"To present it to the Cailleach." Amy offered the strap of the satchel. She lowered her voice. "You won't be tempted by it."

And if Cassandra was found with the horn, she wouldn't start a war between the Faerie Lords and Ladies. She was just a human, beneath their notice. She accepted the satchel and slung it across her chest. No matter how she adjusted her cloak, she couldn't hide it well enough. Her hands turned clammy at the thought of the creatures who would happily kill her for the treasure she carried.

Henry ran a hand down the edge of her cloak to smooth it, brushing her arm and sending a warm jolt to her chest. She smiled at him, and her racing pulse steadied. She wasn't alone. Just to be careful, she hid her crossbow in the satchel as well.

They set off into the gathering gloom. Henry offered his arm, and Cassandra grasped it, longing to be close to him, yet feeling ill knowing that it was just tormenting both of them. Henry hailed a hackney coach, and they climbed in to rumble on through the evening traffic for the cemetery. It was probably only slightly faster than walking, but Cassandra was glad to stay dry and save her strength for whatever they would face in the Winter Kingdom. Jairus toyed with a silver bullet. Henry stared out the window at the rain, but when he caught Cassandra's glance, he reached over and took her hand.

She didn't pull away.

As they entered the western outskirts of the city, the carriage jolted. The coachman shouted something at the balking horse.

"I think we have company," Jairus said. "The Unseelie host have found us."

Henry nodded. "We'd better walk now."

They exited the carriage and paid the apologetic coachman. Little could he know it was their fault and not the horse's, but at least he didn't seem to be the type to abuse his animal. They hurried away through the rain. A deep sense of dread settled over Cassandra—something from outside herself—from the Unseelie monster hunting them.

They rushed past townhouses, recently built, for the open space of the cemetery. Cassandra's cane clicked over the pavement.

Jairus stopped and turned back, shotgun raised. Henry slowed, too. A dark form cut through the sky toward them. The Sluagh was back—smaller, but still a terrifying darkness hurtling toward them.

"Go!" Jairus said. "I'll hold them off."

Cassandra hesitated, but Henry tugged at her arm. They had the horn. They had to be rid of it or the attacks would not stop. If only they had been a little faster, if Cassandra hadn't come with them. But Jairus was a priest of sorts. Who better to face a horde of damned souls?

Cassandra let Henry pull her along. They found the long slope leading down to the catacombs. Henry stopped in front of the great wooden doors.

"We don't go through those," he said. "I have to make the portal in a liminal place like this. Only, I'm not sure—"

Cassandra squeezed his arm. "You can do this. You understand the elements. They listen to you."

He gave her a faint smile and then stepped aside, concentrating on the door. Cold rose around them. Henry's breath came in frosted plumes, and he shut his eyes, wrinkling his forehead in concentration. The cold intensified, and Cassandra shivered and drew her cloak tighter.

Behind them, Jairus shouted a warning.

The air in front of them shimmered, and the door dissolved into a dark passageway. Henry grabbed her hand, and they rushed forward into the gateway.

It turned into a long tunnel lined with stone, like the mouth of an ancient barrow yawning open. Before them, the blasted branches of a hawthorn hung low over the entrance, the sharp thorns reaching out, the red berries bright as fresh blood against the white landscape beyond.

"Death and rebirth," Henry whispered.

Cassandra nodded, trying to focus on the rebirth aspect. She tucked her cane under her arm and clutched Henry's hand for balance, then stepped down into the dimness. A pale glow rose around them, the reflected light of a gauzy, clouded sun on a field of white. Cassandra pulled her cloak tighter and pushed on, her boots crunching over powdery, fresh-fallen snow.

Snow drifted gently from the clouds and muffled any outside sounds. A few birds sang and darted among the hawthorn trees, whose limbs hung with bright red berries. She relaxed her grip on Henry's hand, enjoying the contrast between his warmth and the cold in the air. The chill gave their cheeks a rosy flush.

"I thought a kingdom of winter would be a terrible place," she whispered, and it seemed the hush of the snow would keep her secrets quiet and safe.

Henry exhaled a great plume of air like a dragon breathing smoke. "It's a part of nature. Of life. It's not good or bad, I suppose."

Cassandra reflected on that. The darkness was a time for rest and renewal before everything would be born again in the spring. And they certainly did not want the harvest to last forever—especially not when souls were the object of the hunt.

"How do we find the Cailleach?" Cassandra asked.

"I imagine she will find us. Though she will be more likely to speak to you."

Cassandra took a deep breath of stinging cold and drew out the horn. It felt heavier than it looked, and she wished she could push it away, but instead she cradled it.

Henry released her hand slowly, leaving her to limp forward uncertainly. She prodded the snow with her cane, picking her way over the blanket of white. Birds gathered around a tree in the distance laden with winter berries. Something about that felt right, so Cassandra made her way toward it. She was distantly aware of Henry trailing well behind. Other animals watched from the woods, especially deer browsing for winter forage. Cassandra thought she spotted the white stag among them, but she couldn't be sure.

A white hound with red-tipped ears bounded forward, tongue lolling. Cassandra smiled and reached out a hand.

"You're safe, then!" she said, scratching the hound behind his strange ears.

Cassandra noticed the figure of a man watching her from

the shadows of the trees. He was old but not weak, with his gray beard neatly trimmed and arms still strong and well-muscled after many years of labor. There was something familiar about him, like she had seen his image somewhere before. Not in newspapers or book plates, but in the crisp chill of the autumn breeze, the rustle of dried leaves, the brilliant colors of a sunset.

Jairus had called the Lord of Annwn a grim reaper, but Cassandra realized not everything had to be grim about the spirit who guided the dead.

With a shiver, she looked away.

"Do you fear to look on him, maiden?" asked the rusty voice of an old woman.

Cassandra looked up, startled, to find a cloaked and bent woman watching her. She swallowed. "I...I thought it might be...bad luck?"

The old woman chortled. "Luck has nothing to do with it, child. Look or don't, it won't change the ending. There is no man nor woman who escapes the Lord of Annwn's call. No Faerie nor changeling, either. The lords of the earth try to flee, but they find no escape and must bow low before him. But the ancient and suffering sometimes find peace in his company." She looked at Cassandra, her face lit by the soft glow coming from the snow. The light reflected in her eyes seemed to be that of distant stars—ancient ones that no mortal had ever viewed.

"That seems sad," Cassandra said.

The old woman smiled, revealing many missing teeth. "You think it so? But you have a mortal perspective. You see the things you know crumble but not how they rise to build something new. Nothing lasts. Yet everything lasts."

"That is, perhaps, too much for my mortal mind to understand." Cassandra hesitated, but she dared not approach that quiet figure in the woods, so the Cailleach it would be. "I am here on a quest. I seek to return Annwn's horn to the Queen of Winter. Are you she?"

"Do I look like a queen?"

"I don't know. But you speak like one. You...you feel like one, if I may be so bold."

"I like bold. Bold but gentle. I sense those things in you. You were kind to the hound when he was lost and confused. And the white stag has told me how you protected him."

"It was terrible of Rushford to shoot him and leave him wounded!"

"Yes. Death is part of nature, of life, but needless suffering is an abomination."

Cassandra held out the horn. "There is needless suffering now. The Unseelie Fay unleashed the Wild Hunt on London. We beg you to end that suffering. To bring rest and order. You, who may ride with the Wild Hunt and call winter to end it."

The Cailleach bowed her head in acknowledgment and took the horn, her hands icy where they brushed Cassandra's. "I do wish to see order restored. When I blow the horn, those nearby will reap the whirlwind. I would advise you and your friends to be far when that happens."

Cassandra's eyes widened. "Thank you, my lady."

She curtseyed as well as she could and hurried back to Henry.

"We need to leave," Cassandra said. "We don't want to be here when she blows the horn, and I don't think she'll give us much time."

Henry took her arm, and they hurried back for the gateway. They emerged from the catacomb opening, the autumn air crisp but inviting. The storm had stopped. A faint light hung over the cemetery, but all was still and silent.

"It's just before dawn," Henry said. "We've been gone all night."

"Mr. Hale?" Cassandra asked, panic fluttering in her chest.

They hurried to the top of the ramp, which gave them a wide view of the cemetery. There was no sign of the Sluagh, and no sign of Jairus.

"It couldn't have carried him off," Cassandra said.

"No," Jairus said behind her. "It couldn't have."

"Mr. Hale!" she cried.

"True blue, through and through. I was able to hold that thing off, and then it suddenly wound itself up and went flying off. I would guess when you handed over the horn?"

"Yes. The Cailleach has it now," Cassandra said.

"We need to get back to London," Henry said. "The Cailleach will bring the Hunt to heel, but the trouble there isn't over."

They all nodded their agreement. There were no carriages about that time of the morning, so they walked back to Amy's house.

But that's not where Cassandra's thoughts were. Nothing lasts forever, yet everything does. She would die someday. So would Henry. Did she really want to give up what happiness she might have enjoyed because she didn't know how far apart those two events would occur? She and Henry might bring danger to each other, but they were in danger separately as well. Would it be better to face the challenge together?

Chapter Thirty-Eight

A knock sounded on Amy's front door, breaking the early morning stillness. She bolted up from the sofa where she had dozed off. Were her friends back? But if so, why would they knock? She tip-toed into the entrance hall, its familiar outlines muted and blurred by the predawn shadows.

The knock came again, more insistent.

"Isn't it common to open a door when someone knocks?" Lucien asked behind her, yawning and scratching his curly head of hair.

"I don't know who it is," Amy whispered.

"There's an easy way to find out." Lucien frowned at her hesitation. "You don't trust the spell? It's supposed to keep away those who wish you harm."

Amy let out a long breath. "Of course."

Still, she returned to the sitting room to peek out the window. A man walked toward the door, then suddenly turned and walked back into the street again. Agitated. Then she caught a glimpse of his face. Robert Ashby. The sun hadn't quite risen, so he wasn't coming to court Sophie Weaver.

Amy sighed and went to open the door.

"What do you want?" Amy called, a little harsher than she meant to.

She understood Domin's words now. She had forgiven Robert for the role he played with the Grigori, but she didn't quite trust him.

Robert jumped and looked guilty. He cleared his throat, backing up a little. "I, uh, I thought maybe you were looking for Mr. Rushford."

"Did you?" Amy asked. She directed her will and her magic at him, trying to force him to tell the truth. It wasn't guaranteed to work, though.

"I... I did gather that from Fitzhugh, yes. And I thought if I helped, I might get closer to Sophie Weaver. Do you think...do you think she still could care for me? I know I've made a terrible mess of things. I was stupid, and I'm sorry for the...the pain I caused. My mother is in denial, and my sister is even worse. My father was a monster. But I don't want to be like him. And I like Sophie Weaver."

Well, that certainly sounded like he was telling the truth, more than he probably intended to confess to Amy.

"I'm not in Miss Sophie's confidence," Amy said.

"I know." Robert looked over his shoulder. "May I come inside? I want to make amends, and I think I have something useful to say, but not out here."

Amy considered. He had worked with the Grigori and with Fitzhugh. They could still be manipulating him, even if he didn't realize it.

She smiled when a solution came to her. "The garden in the back. I will meet you there."

He nodded and went to find his way to the back of the house. Amy went through and met him climbing over the wall to get in. He was determined, at least.

"Well, what do you have to tell me?" she asked.

He looked around nervously.

"This garden has certain protections on it," Amy said. "No enemy will see or hear what you say here."

None of Amy's enemies, anyway. She didn't know who the young man was so afraid of.

"I've seen Rushford," he said, still keeping his voice low. "Or rather, my mother did, at first. She practically attacked him, asking what he knows of...of my father. It was a humiliating scene. Rushford pretended not to know her and hurried away, but it was him."

Amy considered that. It could have been a shape-shifter or someone using a glamour. Not Domin, because Domin would have played along, but Domin wasn't the only one who could alter his appearance.

"Very well," Amy said. "Is that all?"

Robert shook his head vigorously. "I followed him. I saw where he's staying."

"Really?" Amy asked skeptically.

"Yes. We were in Covent Garden. I followed him to the Strand and saw him slip in the back of the Lyceum theater."

Amy's heartbeat picked up at that. Of course! A theater. It was sophisticated enough for the Grigori, and a perfect place for the Leannan to find victims or to feed off the emotions of the audience members. But Amy did not trust Robert and didn't want to give anything away.

"How do you know I would find him there again?" Amy asked.

"I watched all night," Robert said. "I recognized others of Rushford's associates as well, coming and going."

"And did they recognize you?" she asked. "Because if they did, you might have scared them off."

"I don't know," Robert admitted. "But I don't think so."

"Well, thank you for bringing me this information. I will think on it."

Robert hesitated, stood, clasping his hands. "I want to redeem myself. I truly do. If there's anything I can do to help—"

"Thank you. I'll keep that in mind."

She waited while he left, putting on a calm face, but her mind buzzed with this information. They might know where the Grigori were, if Robert could be believed. And the Grigori might have spotted Robert and be ready to move somewhere else. She didn't know how long until Domin and the others were back. She would have to consult Mary. And even Lucien, much as she wasn't sure she trusted his opinions. She didn't fully trust her own mind, but they needed to make a decision quickly.

She found Mary and Lucien in the drawing room, their heads bent over a new crossbow that Mary was building. They looked up at Amy expectantly.

Amy sighed and sat on a chair near them. "We might know where to find the Grigori."

Mary's face brightened. "That's good news! The others will return the horn, and then they can be rid of the Grigori, too. We won't be in danger anymore."

"We don't know when the others will be back, and we might need to act quickly."

"Oh." Mary looked distinctly less enthusiastic about that.

"The Grigori may be hiding in the Lyceum. A theater near

the Strand. Robert Ashby claims he saw them there, and while I don't entirely trust him, I do think the information is worth checking."

"They could be trying to lure you in," Lucien said.

Amy rubbed her forehead. "I know. But if we walk into a trap knowing it's a trap, does it give us the advantage? I'm afraid if we wait for the others to return, the Grigori may move elsewhere, and then we'll have to start the search all over again. I'm not sure what's the best thing to do."

Lucien shrugged and glanced down at the crossbow on the table.

Mary's gray eyes were troubled, but she lifted her chin. "I... I'll do whatever you think is best."

Amy groaned inwardly at Mary's trust in her. She didn't want to get Mary hurt. Or lead her down a dark path as she had with Fitzhugh and the Gunpowder Plot. "We might be able to deal with Rushford, but what about the Leannan? We don't have the hound anymore."

"Didn't they say if we could resist her temptations, we would have power over her?" Lucien asked.

"Yes," Amy admitted. "But that's risky. If we fail, we die. Though, the Grigori must have some way of controlling her or she would have destroyed them. If only we knew what. I think... I think we at least have to take advantage of the chance to see what they're doing."

Mary's shoulders relaxed at that. "Just spy on them, then?"

"Unless...we find the opportunity to assassinate Rushford," Amy said, feeling sick at the words. "Then, should we do it?"

It was like the Gunpowder Plot again. Killing had not been the right solution, though it had seemed like it at the time. But that had been a scheme to blow up all of Parliament. Innocent people would have died. Innocent people were dying now, and if she could get rid of Rushford, she might be able to stop it all.

Mary looked down at her hands. "I made my crossbows for killing Fay. The bad ones. But they would work on people, too."

"I won't ask you to be the one who does it," Amy said. "If it comes to it, I will pull the trigger. And I will accept the consequences if I'm apprehended." Because this wasn't a Faerie creature they would be killing; it was a human with power and connections. Maybe, as a wealthy woman, she could avoid being hanged for the crime. But if not, it would be worth it to save the Fay—or, at least her friends—from the Grigori's reign of terror.

"I'll come," Mary said quietly. "In case...in case you miss."

Amy hesitated over that. She looked down at the rug, her eyes tracing the lines of the vining floral pattern that looped around themselves again and again. Amy didn't know if any of this was wise. Her plans were always wrong, but she couldn't see any other way.

"Very well, if you wish," she said finally. "Lucien, I will ask you to stay here and tell the others what happened, in case they return soon and can help. We'll avoid the Leannan and focus on the Grigori. We need to go now, when there won't be many other people around."

"Better chance at escape?" Lucien asked, an edge to his voice.

"Less chance of innocent victims being in the way," Amy retorted. "We're not going to let anyone be hurt."

Mary was deathly white, but she pressed her lips together and nodded her agreement.

Chapter Thirty-Nine

Amy stepped outside just as the first light poured over the square. She had secured their smallest crossbow in her elaborate bustle. Mary followed close behind, her own weapon concealed in a basket.

Amy's scalp prickled with the sense that someone was watching. She held her hand out to stop Mary and scanned the square. It was quiet, empty. A few birds flitted in the trees, and droplets from the previous night's rain shone in the grass. Amy sensed no magic nearby. That meant no Domin or Telesm, either.

They continued on through the misty morning, cloaks hiding their faces. If anyone was around to watch, the two women might have appeared to be ghosts gliding through the dawn.

The mists were thicker near the Thames. The Lyceum's grand portico with its many Greek columns loomed from the haze, making Amy feel small. The street and building were quiet, as

Amy had hoped. Later that day there would be actors rehearsing and the stage crew and musicians getting ready for the night's show, but now, the building was a sepulcher to performances past.

A thump behind them made Amy jump and reach for her crossbow.

There, in the murky, early morning shadows, she spotted a figure in a white suit. Spring-heeled Jack.

He tipped his hat. "Off 'unting, are we?"

"What makes you ask that?" Amy asked.

"Most pretty lovies don't go shopping for ribbons at dawn, or with crossbows 'idden in their bustles."

Amy gave him a withering look.

He laughed. "Don't be sour. Maybe old Jack can 'elp. I 'ate them Grigori as much as you do."

Amy glanced at Mary, who offered no answers, and sighed. "We think the Grigori might be in the area."

"So, the time's come for a fight? But where's Domin and your other nice friends?"

Another question Amy didn't want to answer, but her Seelie magic wouldn't let her lie directly. "We're just spying things out. We have to act quickly. We're not entirely sure what we'll find here."

"Well, I've never promised to be loyal—it's not in Jack's nature—but I can 'elp spy right enough." He glanced at the Lyceum. "And you never know with theater what's real and what's not. Who's just playing a part."

Amy shot him a suspicious glance, but she felt the same way. It made her doubly nervous to step inside.

"Oh, don't fear," Jack said. "Old Jack won't be coming in with you. I'm much too obvious, even among the acting crowd. But I'll find my own part to play, never you fear."

With that, he bounded to a high window sill and then above the mists.

"I don't like him," Mary said.

"Neither do I. Let's move quickly."

Amy and Mary walked around the back, trying to look like early-rising theater devotees or tourists. Amy checked several doors, but they were all locked.

"I can help," Mary whispered, pulling the tools out of her pocket.

She deftly picked the lock, and they slipped inside. Amy let the door shut behind them, leaving it unlocked in case they needed to leave quickly.

Amy didn't sense anyone near, but the place was thick with emotions from performers and audience, the real and the pretend mingled until there was no distinction between them. Now, where would they find Rushford?

"Down," she whispered to Mary. She had a sense that the Grigori and the Leannan were in the bowels of the theater. It seemed appropriate.

They made their way through the empty corridors, dark and eerie without the crowds thronging the passages or the actors preparing to go onstage. As dead as a tomb. Amy shivered and tried to push such thoughts aside.

"Who's there?" called a deep male voice.

Amy whirled to see a man watching them. He wore the doublet and ruff of Queen Elizabeth's reign, and in the shadows, her first thought was that he was a ghost—a reminder of her past mistakes come to confront her. But no, he was an actor, of course. She put a hand to her fast-beating heart. She needed an excuse with some magic behind it.

"Oh, you startled me! Are you an actor here? How

exciting!" Flattery. Pushing the man to feel at ease, which was difficult when she wasn't at ease herself.

His face relaxed somewhat, but he still looked wary. "I am. But the theater isn't open to visitors right now. Even such lovely ones."

Amy forced a giggle and worked her way around the truth. "Oh, but we're here to see Mr. Rushford."

He raised an eyebrow. "You're one of Rushford's people? I see. I suppose that's a different case, then. Follow me."

"Hang back," Amy warned Mary in an under voice.

Mary nodded and let herself fall behind while Amy peppered the man with questions about the theater and flattered him excessively, hoping to convince him to continue being helpful.

They reached a staircase at the back of the theater. It went down, deep into the darkness below. It was exactly the kind of place Amy expected to find Rushford, but she hesitated, not wanting to go into the dark alone. She caught Mary's eye, now far behind them in the corridor, and shook her head. Mary should not follow her here.

"Rushford is down there?" Amy asked, pushing her longing for the truth into the question.

The man tilted his head. "Not at the moment, but the Leannan Sidhe is."

Amy's gaze jerked back to him. He was grinning coldly, and he had shifted to block her escape.

"What?" she squeaked out.

"Our new muse. Why do you think our theater is so successful now? The Leannan will make us gods upon the boards. All of London will worship at our feet."

"I'm not here for the Leannan," Amy said, her stomach turning cold.

How many people did the Leannan have in her sway? Amy's pulse hammered in her throat. She had made a foolish, rash decision once again.

The man smiled. "Yet I'm certain the Leannan will be interested in you."

The man raised a hand as if to strike Amy. He gave a jerk, and a crossbow bolt appeared through his arm. He screamed and whirled to face Mary, who stared at her work with a mix of triumph and terror.

"Run!" Amy shouted to Mary.

She drew her own crossbow, but the man knocked it aside with his uninjured hand. The gesture threw Amy off balance, and she stumbled back. Her foot came down onto nothing, and she flailed her arms, smacking one of them against the edge of the stairwell. A horrible, sickening feeling filled her as she fell. A half-formed thought begged Mary to escape, and then a sharp pain sent a flash of colors across her eyes, and darkness swallowed her.

Chapter Forty

Amy awoke to a throbbing headache—to aches in her neck, back, and arm—and a sense that something had gone very wrong.

"I didn't expect you to survive that fall," said Rushford somewhere nearby. "You are stronger than I gave you credit for. But Fay heal quickly, do they not?"

They did, if their energy wasn't too far spent, but between the headache and her disdain for Rushford, Amy didn't bother answering. She forced her eyes open a crack—enough to see that she was on a dirt floor behind iron bars.

One of Amy's plans had finally gotten her killed. Of course, eventually one would. At least she had not given up. She could give herself credit for that. Domin would be disappointed, but he would know that she had tried. Even better, *she* would know she had tried.

And Mary wasn't there, so only Amy would pay for her foolishness.

Rushford sauntered over and looked down at Amy through

the bars. "I've already taken your blood to study. A great deal of it, since you won't be needing it for much longer anyway. You are more Fay than any of our other recent guests, and unlike them, you know about your Faerie blood. Maybe you can answer some questions. I might let you live longer."

Amy's skin felt cold and clammy, and her stomach churned, though whether because of Rushford's words or her injuries, she couldn't be certain. "I won't help you."

"You've already helped me. I might need fewer victims to experiment on if someone gave me some answers. You don't want to be responsible for more deaths, do you?"

The pain in her head lanced, but then she recognized the lie. She had blood on her hands, but none of it came from Rushford's victims. "You are responsible for the deaths, not I."

Rushford grabbed the iron bars. "How much Fay blood does it take to use magic? If we added your blood to one of the changelings who lack magic, would it unlock their abilities?"

Amy squeezed her eyes shut. Rushford was mad, and he made no sense. She had heard of desperate physicians giving blood from a healthy patient to a dying one, but magic was even more personal than blood. Of course, Rushford didn't know that. He thought they were one and the same.

She let her head loll to the side and opened her eyes to stare at him, his face mostly in shadow. "Are you trying to...to transfuse magic?"

"Clever little elf. Yes, I've determined that magic is all about bloodlines, and with the right blood infused in our veins, humans can do magic as well. We have had some...unfortunate reactions among our people who have volunteered to experiment, but I believe we will succeed." He rattled the cage door. "I just don't understand the percentages. Some of the people we collected with high levels of Faerie blood couldn't do any magic. And Henry Stewart can do magic, though he is more human than Fay. Maybe we need him—his blood. Fitzhugh said he has royal bloodlines, and I certainly owe him for the last time we met."

Amy groaned. "You can't steal magic by stealing blood. You can't steal magic at all."

Rushford narrowed his eyes. "It's bestowed, then."

Amy's stomach tightened. She had said too much. But her thoughts tumbled around like beans in a jar. "It's a curse."

She didn't need to tell Rushford what the Fay speculated among themselves: that perhaps the first Fay were those beings who refused to choose sides in the war between light and dark angels, banished to earth to watch the war play out until they decided where they stood—and to pass their cursed, in-between state on to their descendants.

Rushford snorted. "Power and immortality are strange curses. No, what you call magic is a gift. An ability. And, as a part of our world, they are abilities that can be mastered by study. By human science."

Amy was too tired and too pained to argue. Let Rushford chase magic, just let him do it without killing again. Maybe, if he realized Amy's blood wouldn't help him any more than any other blood he had stolen, he would let her live.

She wet her cracked lips. "No matter how much blood you steal or how many Fay you kill, it won't bring you magic. You should count yourself lucky not to be bound by it. To be free."

"Bound by it?"

He stared at her, thoughtful. It frightened her. If only she could make him believe her, but she didn't have the strength to use magic against him. He was so strong-willed, it might not work regardless.

"You don't need me," Amy said, trying to put some

persuasion into the words. She believed them, after all. "You might as well let me go."

He laughed. "No, dear lady, I can't do that. The Leannan is hungry, and I must keep her happy. She has not been as helpful as I had hoped, but she does have her uses. She will come to see you soon."

Rushford left, a door clicking shut behind him. Amy let her head sink back against the dirt floor. The cool of the earth felt good against her aching scalp. The dirt was old, compacted, long cut off from the energy of sun, wind, and rain, but it was still alive and part of the natural world. She relaxed and let its weak power rise into her.

The door to the room creaked, and she forced her eyes open. A woman walked into the room—a tall woman with pale skin and eyes such a soft blue, they were almost silver. She wasn't beautiful, but she was arresting, with her strange eyes, wide mouth, and sharp cheekbones. A man followed behind her, and she turned to him.

"Open the door," the woman said, her voice low and soothing.

The man unlocked the iron bars and swung the door open. The woman stood well back from the iron. Then, the man left Amy alone with the woman. The Leannan Sidhe.

As soon as the man was gone, Amy forced herself to sit up. Her vision spun, and her stomach gave a lurch, but she would not face potential death helpless on the ground. Perhaps she could bargain with the Leannan—one of her own kind.

"I don't know what Rushford is doing to keep you here," Amy rasped, "but maybe I can help you escape."

"To go where?" The Leannan tilted her head.

Amy tried to think. Somewhere the Leannan would do less damage. "Elfland."

The Leannan looked at her with those strange, silvery eyes, then she laughed, a musical sound like little bells ringing. "You cannot break his hold on me. We have an arrangement. He offers me souls in exchange for whatever information they give me."

If Rushford had been able to resist the Leannan's enticements, she would have to serve him. And since the Leannan couldn't give Rushford the thing he most desired— the magic he obsessed over—he might have conquered her. Amy had no dreams of being an artist or musician. Perhaps she could resist as well.

"I won't give you anything," Amy said, scooting back from the Leannan, hoping the iron bars would keep her outside the cage.

The Leannan grinned, showing off perfect white teeth. "Oh, you will eventually. It is easier, I admit, with the artists who only want a muse. I draw their creativity to the surface. They enjoy a brief but stunning career while I feed off their emotions, and they die happy. Fay don't often make good meals for me because they are not rich in creativity or emotion, but you have enough human in you that I think I can offer you something."

"You can't offer me anything I want."

The Leannan stepped past the iron bars, wisps rising from her like smoke when she got too close to them. But she ignored whatever pain that caused and leaned close to Amy, inhaling as if Amy were a flower.

"Ah, you want love. Poor dear. It's one of the most common human longings, and yet the most powerful. Humans are so strange. I wonder how you came to be so like them?"

"I would rather be like the humans than like the Fay."

"You want to grow old and suffer and die?" The Leannan flashed her a predatory smile. "I can easily provide that for you."

"No!" Amy said, alarmed. "Though, I would be willing to pay that price if...if it also meant I could enjoy love like some humans do."

The Leannan studied her curiously, then her eyes lit. "A dream of love! That is what I can offer you. I will help you step into the perfect fantasy—the man you long for holding you in his arms, whispering words of adoration in your ears. You will die in his embrace."

As the Leannan spoke, Amy's mind drifted. Domin held her tight against his chest, his steady heartbeat sounding in her ear. All was safe and right. Her anxiety faded. She just had to relax into his arms forever.

A flash of pain brought her back. "No! I don't want anything tainted. False."

The Leannan laughed. "All love is false. All is tainted by selfishness."

"The Fay know nothing of love." Amy narrowed her eyes. "You have had countless lovers, but you never cared for any of them. Caring is antithetical to the Fay."

Antithetical to the Fay. The thought rang through Amy's swimming head. The Fay, like nature itself, were above petty feelings. They wouldn't know what to do with them. The Leannan consumed creativity, stole its energy to survive, but without ever understanding the emotions behind it—the true power they contained. Even her victims with Faerie blood were not Fay. They did not know how to manipulate emotion. But Amy did. If only her head didn't throb so—she couldn't concentrate.

The Leannan stepped closer. "I don't need to care. I only have to weave the illusion that someone cares for you and then steal the dreams you create of him. Love is only a fancy, a day-dream humans imagine, after all."

Amy's chest ached. Was love only an illusion for her? Maybe it was impossible that anyone could love someone so flawed. Her swirling thoughts went back to the night at the Weaver's house when Henry's bargain with Queen Mab had nearly destroyed her. Domin had come to her rescue. Despite his disdain of his Faerie abilities, he had tried to use them to divert her pain. But the pain had been too much even for him, spilling out of him and amplifying to hurt the others in the room as well.

Amy was not as powerful as Domin. She could not control emotions as he could—her own or anyone else's. But maybe she didn't need to control them. Maybe she needed to let them loose.

The Leannan's power was a strange, hypnotic thing. It called her to relax, to trust the Leannan, to put everything in the Fay's hands—even the energy that gave her life. But Amy held onto the emotions swirling around her. The Fay understood pain and humiliation. Those would do little good against the Leannan. Instead, Amy found memories of her friends past and present, both warm and bittersweet, and she pushed them out toward the Leannan.

The Faerie lady gasped, and her eyes widened, no longer quite as silver, but light blue. Amy hesitated. Had it actually worked? A brief hope of victory flickered in her chest. Amy shut her eyes and took advantage to press more feelings on the Leannan. She gave the creature enemies and strangers. She gave her Domin. She made her know what it was to care even as her heart broke, to long until the desire was a crippling ache, to hope when despair tried to claw away all feeling. What it was to be part human. All the emotions that lay behind the creativity the Leannan desired.

The Leannan stood frozen as the deluge of feelings washed over her, stunned into stillness.

Amy slowly rose to her feet. Hope filled her, and also fear, battling over the knowledge that even if this worked, Rushford would likely kill her. She let the Leannan have those emotions as well.

The Faerie creature's eyes darkened, her irises dilating and her eyes growing deeper blue with every moment.

Amy stumbled past her and grabbed the iron bars of the door. They burned her hand, a horrible searing pain. She gave the Leannan that, too. Then she slammed the door shut, and the latch fastened with a satisfying click.

Amy opened her throbbing hand and stepped back from the cage. The Leannan still stood, frozen. It wouldn't last. The emotions would fade or the Leannan would find a way to consume them. And then she would open the door, willing to hurt herself just as Amy had done. That meant Amy only had a few minutes to find her way out of the theater with a furious Leannan Sidhe on her trail.

Chapter Forty-One

Henry ached with weariness, and Cassandra leaned heavily on his arm. Even Jairus's normally quick steps had slowed. But they were almost to Mayfair and the safety of Amy's house. There was still no sign of the Wild Hunt, but the wind whispered to Henry of winter.

A familiar figure on the street caught his eye.

"Domin!" Henry said.

Domin strode toward them, followed by...Lucien? The changeling wore a hat pulled low over his face. Henry's stomach twisted. Something was wrong.

"You returned it?" Domin asked, his voice reaching them from down the street.

Henry helped Cassandra forward to meet him.

"We gave it to the Cailleach," Henry said. "Fitzhugh suggested it, and it worked."

Domin glanced at Lucien. "Yes, circumstances are shifting in the Faerie Courts. But for now, we need to get to the Strand."

"The Grigori?" Jairus rested a hand on his pistol.

Lucien spoke up. "A man came to the house and said he'd seen them at the Lyceum. Amy and Mary went."

Cassandra gripped her cane. "Alone?"

"They were only going to spy, but that was several hours ago," Lucien said.

"I left Telesm to tell you when you returned, but I didn't want to waste any time going after them." Domin looked toward the Strand.

"We're coming, too," Jairus said, though his voice was weary.

Henry glanced at Cassandra, and she nodded.

He took her arm, and they hurried as well as they could behind Domin, Lucien, and Jairus. Henry thought it strange that Domin had taken the changeling instead of his brother, but perhaps Telesm didn't want to be involved.

Henry's feet tingled with pain by the time they reached the Strand, but the sun was still low. The streets were quiet, most of the shops and theaters not yet open and their denizens sleeping off their revelries of the previous night.

"Oy, lovies!" Spring-heeled Jack loped toward them with his unnaturally long strides.

"Jack!" Henry called. "Have you seen Amy and Miss Leland?"

"If that's what you call the pretty one and the awkward one, then I 'ave indeed. They went to the theater early this morning to find them Grigori, and they 'aven't come back." Jack fixed a toothy smile on Domin. "I'm glad to see you 'ere now, old friend."

"It may be an ambush," Jairus said.

"Just so!" Jack bobbed from foot to foot, his eyes flashing orange. "But I warned you, I did. Now, I'd say we can put the past aside and be bosom pals again, eh, Domin?"

"Hardly," Domin said coolly.

Jack glowered at him. "When I think on it, you've never been a very good friend to me, 'ave you? Well, you're on your own now."

Jack bounded away.

Domin huffed. "The Leannan is probably here, too. A theater is a good hiding place for her."

"If we can bring the Cailleach here, she'll remove the Leannan." Henry took a deep breath of air laced with the distant scent of snow. "Maybe I can summon a winter storm, and that will capture the Cailleach's attention. It could be dangerous, though." How often in the past had he hurt people with winter storms?

"More dangerous than leaving the Leannan free?" Jairus asked.

Henry pressed his lips together and didn't respond.

"The storm might work." Domin rattled the door and looked at one of the windows high up in the stone facade. "And we need to find a way inside. Miss Leland could have opened a door for us."

"This is where I can be helpful," Lucien said. "I can convince someone to let us in if we get their attention—and a sudden storm will likely bring someone to a door or window to look."

"Very well," Domin said. "But then you should stay out here. The Grigori will still want you."

Lucien shook his head. "I have unfinished business with them."

"You don't have to—" Henry began.

"You don't understand," Lucien said, keeping his eyes down. "The Dark Lady put a geas on me. I *do* have to confront their leader. I couldn't before because they had me gagged, but it's been itching at me ever since, and it will eventually drive me mad if I don't."

"And you didn't say anything about this geas?" Jairus asked.

"Why would I? I just needed to wait until you found him for me, since you wouldn't let me go to him myself. Now is the time."

Domin sighed and looked to Henry. "Summon the storm."

Henry turned his face to the wind, then looked down to meet Cassandra's gaze.

Her eyes were full of sympathy, but she squeezed his arm and nodded. He could do this without hurting anyone.

He closed his eyes and felt the press of winter around the edges of autumn. He called to it, and it responded as though it had been waiting. A cold wind howled down the streets, and eddies of snow whirled around the buildings.

But something was off. A furor gripped the wind, and the clouds churned overhead, out of Henry's control. Hail pelted them. Cassandra gasped and shielded her face.

"Stewart?" Jairus called.

"It's not me," Henry said through gritted teeth. He tried to reach the wild edges of the storm and calm them, but they slithered away from him.

Thunder grumbled overhead, like a deep, maniacal laugh.

"Henry Stewart," Jane called.

She galloped through the curtains of snow on the back of her black stag. Her blonde hair hung loose and bedraggled around her shoulders, and her eyes blazed with raw hatred. She could not dismount in the mortal world. After riding with the Wild Hunt, Jane was trapped.

"You have taken something from me," Jane snarled. "You will return it."

"It's returned to its rightful place," Henry called over the wind.

"Then all of your friends will suffer!"

Jane raised her arm, and the hail redoubled, penny-sized balls of ice shattering on the streets. She threw her head back and laughed as the storm battered her.

Domin, Jairus, and Lucien pressed against the stone facade of the theater for shelter. Cassandra shrank closer to Henry, shielding her head with her arm.

Cold coursed through Henry's veins, the fury of winter flowing into him. Jane would not be allowed to hurt Cassandra or any of his friends. Frost crackling over the ground under his feet. His bones were ice, his breath the storm, ready to freeze Jane's blood and shatter her and everything around her.

A gentle pressure on his arm brought him back. Cassandra's hand. Yes. This wasn't who he wanted to be. He had let Titania control him in the past; he wouldn't let the storm do the same. He had to become his own master if he was going to protect anyone.

He let out a breath that plumed white around him. With a sweeping gesture, he extinguished the hail, and snow fell again.

Jane howled in frustration, and thunder rumbled above them, echoing in Henry's chest. The wind redoubled, lashing sleet through the city.

"Inside!" Domin shouted over the wind. "We have to find the Grigori."

Jairus and Lucien followed him to the front of the theater, but Cassandra stayed. Stayed by Henry's side, trusting him. Keeping him from losing himself in the storm.

Henry seized her hand, pulling her near to shelter her from the worst of the wind. The storm roared around them, but

Henry pushed back. A cyclone of snow rose above their heads. Henry shoved it toward Jane.

Jane shouted in alarm and pushed the icy funnel back so it hovered between the two Tempestarii. It tightened and rose higher, like a serpent spewing ice over the city. The temperature plummeted, and frost coated the surrounding buildings.

Henry kept Cassandra close. He forced the cyclone up, and the funnel unwound itself into a mass of clouds. The winds calmed, and the sleet turned to a thick fall of snow.

Jane's snarl carried through the billowing white that fell around them, but the snow blinded Henry.

"Where is she?" he whispered.

Cassandra pulled her crossbow from the satchel and turned so she was back to back with Henry. The wind plucked at the edges of her cloak, flapping it against Henry. He scanned the sifting curtains of white.

Something black whisked past them. A crow. The Morrigan reveled in this chaos.

Cassandra cried a warning. Jane charged, and her stag knocked Henry down with a swipe of its antlers. Jane raised a sword. Henry couldn't risk reigniting the fury of the storm. He grabbed his little iron knife.

A bolt from Cassandra's crossbow flew crooked in the wind, glancing off Jane's hand. The Unseelie changeling hissed and dropped her sword into the snow.

Henry scrambled for the weapon, but the stag kicked at him. He rolled away from the creature's hooves and stumbled to his feet.

"I need a real weapon," he panted.

Cassandra frowned at her little crossbow, then grabbed her cane, which she'd dropped into the snow. It glittered with hoarfrost. "Use this. Not as a cane, I mean, but see how it's coated with ice?"

Henry grinned his understanding, and he took the cane. At his touch, ice crackled up the length of the rowan wood, forming a sharp point at the tip. More of spear than a sword, but the pale light glinted off its edge. Henry advanced on Jane. She hesitated at the sight of his new weapon.

Over the hiss of the wind, a distant horn sounded.

Jane's eyes narrowed. "Who bears the horn?"

"The Cailleach," Henry said. "She will bring the Wild Hunt back to its proper order."

"No!" Jane turned her stag for Henry.

He raised the ice spear and slashed at the stag, turning it aside. Cassandra fumbled to reload her crossbow, but before she could draw it, Jane cried out in pain. The stag tossed its head and veered. An iron bolt protruded from Jane's back.

Mary stood in the shelter of one of the doors, her crossbow still leveled at the Unseelie changeling.

Jane turned toward Mary, but then Cassandra fired, hitting the black stag.

"The Wild Hunt approaches," Henry shouted over the wind, "and you no longer command it."

Jane howled, bringing a fresh pelting of hail, but she turned her stag and fled into the white and gray flurries of the storm.

"Inside!" Henry called, beckoning for Mary as well.

They crunched through the snow, the icy wind stinging their faces. Henry guided them to the open front doors of the theater. Domin and the others had made it in, then. Henry's nose and fingers tingled when he stepped into the relative warmth of the dark building. Cassandra shook the crust of snow from her cloak. She trembled, though whether from cold or terror, Henry couldn't be sure. He pulled her close, trying to warm her, and she sagged against him, resting her forehead on his shoulder.

Mary scurried up behind them, crossbow still in hand.

Cassandra released Henry and smiled at Mary. "Good shot."

"I was still afraid, but I couldn't let her win." Mary returned the smile, then her expression fell. "They have Amy. She told me to run, but maybe I shouldn't have."

"You did the right thing," Henry said, shaking off the cane as its icy tip dripped onto the floor. "Let's go help the others."

Chapter Forty-Two

Amy stumbled up from the basement, clinging to the banister for balance. She only made it a few steps down the corridor before one of the Grigori spotted her and called for Rushford.

Amy stopped and leaned against the wall, her head still aching. Why couldn't they cease shouting and simply let her go? All she wanted was to lie down and rest for a few minutes.

Rushford walked down the corridor, carrying a gun and flanked by several of his men. Spring-heeled Jack bounced behind him.

Amy fixed her weary gaze on Jack. "You're a traitor, then?"

Jack smiled. "A survivor. Your lot couldn't stop these ones, so I 'elped them with where to find Faerie-born."

Rushford gestured for Jack to be quiet and focused on Amy. "You escaped the Leannan," he said, sounding more curious than annoyed. "How?"

"I gave her what she thought she wanted," Amy mumbled. She should have danced around the truth, but the pain behind her eyes pulsed when she tried to think.

"Interesting," Rushford said. "I'm not sorry to have another chance to speak to you. You said that magic is a curse. That it binds you. But if you defeated the Leannan, your magic must be more powerful than I had suspected. I wonder if you can give me what I want as well."

Amy chuckled weakly. "Even if I could, it would end even worse for you than it did for her. I will never help you."

"You are a foolish elfling," Rushford said, creeping closer to Amy.

She couldn't fight her way through Rushford's men, and her efforts against the Leannan had left her too empty to charm her way past them. There was a single window in the corridor, too high for her to escape through. But if this was how it ended, she didn't regret dying to help her friends. At least she knew that she had finally done something worthwhile. She could hold her head high.

Amy pushed herself away from the wall. "No, I'm not foolish. I'm resilient."

She could speak the words. They were true.

A terrible wind roared past the windows, and hail clattered against the glass. Rushford paused, and his men winced at the ferocious gale.

Henry.

Amy allowed herself a small smile. "And I'm not alone anymore."

The slam of iron on iron echoed behind her, from downstairs. Her smile faded. Oh, yes, the Leannan was angry. Amy backed against the wall, not certain which threat was more pressing: Rushford or the Leannan.

A sheet of wind-driven snow slammed into the window, distracting Rushford. The Leannan climbed the stairs toward Amy, her face twisted with a snarl.

In the distance, a horn sounded, long and low and full of mourning. The Hunt rode, but who held the silver horn? Perhaps they would claim Amy, too. Its cry washed over her, and she couldn't fight its allure anymore, sinking into the peace it promised.

The Leannan reached the top of the stairs, her eyes almost completely silver again, and her lips curled to show sharp, white teeth. She fixed her pale gaze on Amy and reached out as if she would forgo magic and simply strangle her.

Rushford's men shifted to either flee or intervene, but Rushford held up a hand. "Wait. We may learn something from this."

Another note on the horn, its wail riding over the wind. Amy stumbled back from the Leannan's outstretched fingers.

The sound of rushing footsteps echoed off the walls, and Domin, Jairus, and Lucien ran around the corner at the far end of the corridor behind Rushford and his men. Amy gasped and glanced from them to the Leannan's deathly glare.

Domin looked past Rushford and Jack and fixed his attention on the Leannan. "Your time is up."

The Leannan studied Domin, then grinned at Amy. "So, this is the one—the one who does not return your love. You should have let me weave a fantasy for you. At least you might have died happy."

Amy wished she could melt into the floor and disappear right there. Domin might have respected her enough not to pry into her feelings, but of course the Leannan would reveal her secrets. Amy couldn't bear to look at Domin, certain the Leannan's voice had carried down the corridor.

The horn sounded again, ringing in Amy's ears. The baying of hounds rose over the fury of the storm, then faded to a whisper. The Leannan's savage grin faded, and worry flickered in her eyes. She looked to the window.

Annwn's hounds burst through the wall as if it weren't there, white fur bristling and red-tipped ears pricked forward. After all, what were human walls to death?

The Grigori shouted and stumbled back, and Jack sprang behind Domin and the others. Only Rushford stood still, watching Annwn's pack with interest.

The hound Amy's friends had kidnapped from Annwn led the pack. It bounded between Amy and the Leannan, hackles raised.

The Leannan raised both hands and looked around for an escape, but there was none.

The hounds leaped, and the Leannan screamed in rage. She grabbed hold of one hound as if she could push it back or perhaps drain away its life. The others latched on to her with flashing teeth. Cold wind whirled down the corridor, lashing Amy's face with ice crystals before circling around the Leannan and the hounds. The white cyclone hid the Leannan, and Amy felt the distinct pop of a Faerie doorway opening.

Then, the Leannan was gone along with the hounds.

The only sound in the corridor was the wind outside, which calmed to a gentle shooshing.

"Fascinating," Rushford said. He gestured to one of his companions. "Take notes on that incident for later study."

Rushford raised his shotgun. Amy cried out, her feet too tired and heavy to lunge for the barrel swinging toward her friends.

Domin shoved Lucien to the floor. Jairus's hand flashed to his revolver, and he fired. The shot took Rushford just below his shoulder. Rushford yelled, and his shotgun went off.

Jairus dropped his gun with a shout. Blood blossomed on one side of the American's neck and shoulder.

Domin started forward, his teeth bared. But Jack pulled a metal shard from his white suit. He stabbed it deep into Domin's back.

Domin stumbled, an ashen color seeping over his face.

"You never should 'ave turned your back on me, old friend," Jack hissed.

Jack leapt down the corridor, away from the fighting.

Jairus fumbled after his fallen gun, his steps unbalanced and his blood dripping to the floor.

Rushford raised the shotgun again, aiming his iron shot at Domin.

"Stop!" Lucien pushed himself to his feet. "Don't move."

The magic in Lucien's words hit Amy, strong enough to freeze her for a moment. She gasped. The Dark Lady hadn't discarded Lucien when she sent him to the Grigori: He was a weapon, one of the most powerful changelings Amy had ever encountered. He hadn't bothered using his ability on any of them since that first day, and Amy had almost forgotten what he could do. Silver-tongued indeed.

Rushford didn't move, his gun held in mid-swing and blood oozing from below his shoulder to seep across his shirt. The other Grigori stood frozen in place.

"Drop the gun," Lucien said. "You know magic is a more powerful force than any concoction of gunpowder."

The gun clattered to the ground.

"That's right," Lucien said. "Humans are weak, and the Fay are strong."

But his words lacked conviction. He probably believed them when he left the Faerie realm, but he had seen and learned since then. He was human, too, after all. And Henry had shown him how to fight back against the Fay.

"What you are doing is pointless," Lucien went on, and Amy could feel him trying to press more power into the words. More belief. "You can never defeat the Fay. Give up. Give up your meaningless life, and throw yourself into the Thames as penance for your presumption."

What a terrible weapon the Dark Lady had created in Lucien. If he still believed his words, they would have killed as certainly as a gun. But he was acting under a geas and not from conviction. Rushford shuddered and glanced down at the fallen shotgun. Lucien's power over him was slipping.

Amy scrambled for the gun, but her aching body obeyed clumsily, and she was too slow.

Rushford grabbed the gun and swung the butt around to connect with Amy's still-aching head.

Light exploded across her vision. The pain erupted through her head and then turned to a numb pressure that left her blind. She reeled into the wall and slid down. Cold. Everything was so cold. Another gun fired, or perhaps two. Was that Henry's voice? The baying of Annwn's hounds echoed in her memory. Or were they real? Amy wasn't certain anymore, and the dark was quiet and peaceful. If only it wasn't so cold.

"Your ear is gone for certain," Henry said.

Her ear? Her head felt split open, but her ear was fine. No, Jairus. Jairus had lost an ear. Maybe more?

Amy groaned and forced her eyes open. She sat with her back against the wall, its support keeping her upright. Her friends were blurry shapes in the shadowy corridor. Cassandra —Amy *thought* that was Cassandra—knelt next to Jairus, holding something against his head.

"The elixir," Mary said.

"Oh, yes, I have it," Henry said. A pause. "There's only one drop left."

"I don't need that ear," Jairus slurred. "I've got another, and I've had enough of magic potions. But Domin's back is still bleeding."

Domin leaned against the wall, his shoulders slouched.

Henry faced him. "Why don't you heal yourself?"

"Jack had a piece of Telesm's blade that destroys magic," Domin said, his voice slow and weary. "The one I stabbed him with. It's brittle. It broke back then and left Jack with that shard, and it broke again today and left another piece behind."

"We need to get it out," Henry said, a note of panic in his words. "Then you can heal."

"No. It's just above my heart. I don't know if I could heal fast enough if you cut that deep. It's already eating away at my Faerie magic."

"Then we use the elixir," Henry said. "I'll cut out the iron and give you the last drop. Hale will recover, just with some scars."

"Yes, I suppose we must." Domin hesitated. "Where's Amy?"

Amy managed a weak groan. They needed to help Domin, not worry about her.

But Domin sank to the ground beside Amy and took her chilly hand in his warm one. The only warmth she felt as cold iced its way through her veins. Why was it so hard to keep her eyes open?

"What happened to her?" Henry asked.

"A blow to the head," Domin said. "Elves can usually heal from such injuries, but if she used a great deal of strength fighting the Leannan... Yet, she is strong." He sounded uncertain. And Domin had chosen his daemon side. He could lie.

Amy's eyelashes fluttered, and she tried to make herself focus. Domin's face was near hers. He looked at her with an expression Amy couldn't decipher. She should have been embarrassed that he knew what she felt for him, but it didn't seem to matter so much anymore.

Domin squeezed her hand. Reassurance flowed into her. Pride. Admiration. Amy gazed at him, confused. He was using his Faerie magic, letting her feel what he felt. What had the Leannan offered her? That she would die in a dream of Domin's embrace? This was better.

"Fight, Amy," Domin whispered. "Cling to that spark."

She wanted to stay there forever, holding his hand. She wanted to be as strong as he believed her to be. But an odd lightness flowed through her. She was drifting, and she couldn't make her hand tighten on his. The spark was fading. But he had been right: it was precious. The joys and even the failures. She wished she could keep it bright.

Henry knelt by her and made an odd noise. "That wound is... Miss Weaver, I need a needle and thread. No, that won't be enough..."

Everything was so cold now. Her eyes were open, but she only saw the Twilight Vale. She couldn't feel Henry's prodding at her head or Domin's hand on hers. She was leaving them behind. Everyone walked the Twilight Path alone.

"Amy!" Domin's voice chased her, but she could not answer.

Amy sighed out one last breath. Her friends were safe. She finally had done well.

Something touched her lips. A farewell kiss? No, something

cold. A different cold than the numb chill that gripped her body. A living cold that stung.

She gasped. Prickling flowed through her veins, like the hot needle sensation of limb that went numb and revived. It concentrated in her head, a blinding pain that stole her breath and her vision. She cried out, wished it would stop. Then the pain subsided, and she could see the worried faces of her friends gathered around her. Domin held the empty vial.

His face was so pale.

"Domin!" she whispered. "No! You should have let me go. Now you're trapped with a blade in your heart."

Domin smoothed her hair off her forehead, his fingers damp with her blood. "I have already rejected my Faerie nature. If we cannot find a solution, I can survive without it. But I did not want to survive without you."

Tears filled Amy's eyes, and she was still too weak to wipe them away. They trickled down into her blood-matted hair. "You won't be able to use magic."

"I can still sense my link to Henry. My daemon abilities. For now, that is enough."

Amy and Henry exchanged terrified looks. The blade would keep eating away at Domin's magic. After it consumed his Faerie magic, would it destroy his daemon magic as well? Eventually, his link to Henry might not be enough to keep him alive.

Chapter Forty-Three

There was no triumph in the group that limped back to Amy's house. Cassandra's heart was leaden in her chest, and her eyes ached at the bright light of the morning sun reflecting off the snow from Henry's storm. She helped a still-weak Amy stay upright, while Henry supported Domin. Gauze wrapped Jairus's right arm and the side of his face. Blood had already seeped through, but he pressed his lips tightly and walked on. Mary and Lucien kept step with him in case he stumbled. Cassandra suspected nothing—and none of them—would be quite the same after this encounter.

Telesm met them at the door. His eyes widened at the sight of his brother's bloodied shirt.

"What happened?" Telesm ushered them inside and shut the door firmly behind them.

"The Leannan is gone," Domin said. "The Wild Hunt is restored to its proper order. Rushford and some of his men escaped, though."

"But what happened to *you*!" Telesm looked tempted to shake his brother.

"Jack stabbed Domin with a piece of the magic-eating blade," Amy said quietly. "It's lodged near his heart."

Telesm made an odd sucking noise, like all of his breath had been stolen. He turned on Henry. "The elixir. I'll get it. Then you can treat him."

"Too late. It's gone," Henry said dully.

Telesm's eyes flashed with panic and then rage. "Gone? This was why I brought it. I would save my brother—"

"Then it's good you weren't there," Domin said. "The elixir went to a worthy purpose. I will...manage."

"Idiot! If a piece of the blade is still in you, what do you think will happen when it's done eating away your Faerie magic?"

"I don't know," Domin said.

"Neither do I! It might devour the rest of you."

"Can you make another elixir?" Amy asked, her eyes brimming with worry.

"Do you know of any unicorns remaining?"

Amy slowly shook her head, her gaze fixed on Domin.

"I'm taking you to rest, and I'll patch up what I can," Henry told Domin. He looked over his shoulder at Jairus. "You as well. Can you manage the stairs?"

"Sure thing," Jairus said, though his voice was weak.

Domin didn't object to Henry's help, which Cassandra took as a bad sign. Jairus negotiated the stairs by leaning heavily on the banister. Telesm shuffled behind them, rubbing his temples.

"Domin," Amy whispered, the word full of fear.

"Mr. Stewart is helping him," Cassandra reassured her friend. "And Telesm."

Amy groaned. "If I hadn't been injured... If he hadn't been helping me..."

"Stop," Cassandra said. "Jack did this. And Rushford. You stood up to them. You're not responsible for any of it."

Amy sighed. "You're right. But I hate it. I hate that I can't do more."

"I know," Cassandra said. "But we're not done fighting."

"It will be dangerous when they find out Domin is weakened," Amy said. "Dangerous for all of us. And Rushford is still out there."

Cassandra's throat tightened. Titania might come after Henry, or the Dark Lady could attack them—especially when she discovered they were harboring refugee changelings from her court. And Rushford would never stop. She squeezed Amy's hand. "We'll stay together, protect each other."

"What about me?" asked Lucien. He shuffled his boots over the rug in the entrance hall. "I'm sorry to eavesdrop, but I have to know. What's going to happen to me?"

Mary, who had been hesitating at the bottom of the stairs, turned to hear Amy's answer.

"You're staying with us, of course," Amy said.

"But I deceived all of you. About the geas."

Amy laughed weakly. "You're not the first to make that mistake. I'm not saying we'll trust you completely, but we're not going to throw you out. You're an outcast like us now."

Lucien eyes widened and lit with something like hope. "Thank you. I'll help. I know how to work hard. And I'm not injured."

"See if Mr. Hale needs help for now," Amy said. "If you see Cassandra's sisters, convince them they're tired and want to stay in their room today."

Lucien nodded eagerly and hurried upstairs.

Cassandra pressed her eyes shut at the reminder about her sisters. Even with Amy and Lucien's help, they were going to have questions that she didn't know how to answer.

Amy started up the stairs, and Cassandra and Mary hurried to follow on either side in case she stumbled. At the top, Amy swayed, and Cassandra grabbed her elbow. Cassandra turned for Amy's room, but Amy pulled away to enter the chamber Domin shared with Telesm.

Domin sat on the edge of the bed while Henry cleaned his back. Cassandra met Henry's eyes, and his expression was grim.

Telesm gave Amy a nasty look from his post by the window, but her gaze stayed focused on Domin.

"Amy?" Domin's brows drew together in worry.

"Domin, I... I don't know what..." Amy swallowed, and her eyes shone with tears.

"There's no need to speak of it," Domin said softly.

Amy squeezed her eyes shut and nodded. Cassandra sensed Amy had wanted to speak of more than the elixir, but it would have to wait. She helped Amy to her room, where Amy sank into her mattress, her expression dazed.

"I can help Amy," Mary whispered.

"Thank you." Cassandra rubbed her eyes. "I should check on my sisters and...and..."

And what? She wasn't certain what to do next. She needed to protect her family, help protect her friends, but she didn't know what to expect or how to prepare. Everything was shifting. The past and everything she knew were crumbling before her eyes, and she couldn't even grasp at the pieces as they fell.

"You need sleep, too," Amy said gently. "Tomorrow will be a new day."

Cassandra let out a slow breath. "Yes."

Everything crumbles, but it turns into something new. The sunset would bring night and the peace of sleep for all of them, and then a fresh dawn.

Cassandra left Amy to Mary's care. She would have to face her sisters the next morning, navigate her way through a conversation of half-truths, but they were safe for the moment.

As safe as any of them.

She walked to the back of the house to stare out at the garden. The roses shed the last of their soft petals, and the berries on the hawthorn tree blushed red. Jane's pillows lay in the gazebo where she had abandoned them, and the table waited with its map, the fallen chess pieces dusted with snow.

Cassandra stepped outside and carefully brushed off the pieces, standing them in a circle around the Lyceum theater on the map. The Leannan would not claim another victim. The souls she had cut down could rest, but Cassandra vowed not to forget them.

Domin had paid the heaviest price for banishing the Leannan. His connection to Henry was a lifeline now. So, if Cassandra put Henry in peril, she put Domin in mortal danger as well. That was a heavy burden. But *she* wasn't a burden. She had stood by Henry when he faced Jane. By helping Henry, she helped Domin, Amy, and their other friends. It didn't have to be selfish to love. In fact, it was the opposite, because she would never put her well-being before Henry's.

A crow landed on the hawthorn tree, turning its head to watch Cassandra with one shiny black eye and then the other.

"I won't let you have any of them," she said to the bird. "You've taken enough."

She swept the chess pieces up with her strong hand and limped inside to deposit them in the library.

Familiar footfalls made her heart beat faster, and she turned to find Henry in the doorway.

"Domin?" she asked.

He ran his fingers through his hair. "He seems well enough for now. He can't change shape. Can't heal himself, though he should heal normally from the more superficial wounds. Over time...I don't know."

Cassandra took his hand, ran her fingers over his. "We'll face it together. We're stronger that way."

"You think so? The danger—"

"The danger is there no matter what we do. We can't let that keep us apart. Our friends, I mean, but also you and me." She thought of the silent figure watching them in Winter Kingdom, biding his time—not an enemy, but an inevitability. "I don't know what we'll encounter next, but I know I want to be by your side, whatever it is."

"Really?" Henry's eyes brightened. "You don't mean... Cassandra, are you saying you'll marry me?"

She smiled at the sound of Henry—her Henry—saying her name. Her heart pounded faster, flushing her with warmth in spite of everything else.

"Yes, Henry," she said. It felt so right, she was more certain just saying it. "We may have to keep it a secret. It won't be easy. But, if things are going to be difficult, I'd rather face the hard times with you than apart."

Henry broke out into a grin. "And I thought I was the reckless one."

To prove he wasn't, Cassandra pulled him closer and kissed him. He returned the kiss enthusiastically, pulling her in so close she felt like they could melt together. And for just that moment, everything was perfect.

Epilogue

Mary kept a firm grip on Sarah's hand as she led her changeling sister along the dusty road into Drixton. She breathed deeply, enjoying the scent of autumn trees and wood smoke in place of London's thick stink from coal fires. Sarah gawked at the Old Woods and the birds scavenging in the fields.

The farmers preparing their fields for winter didn't notice them, of course. Mary was still Mary, and people paid her little heed, but she didn't mind so much now. She had helped her friends and rescued her sister, and the people of the village did not seem as important.

"I never believed the stories about blue skies and other good things," Sarah whispered.

"It's not all good," Mary warned her. "There's still work to do, and not everyone is kind, but it will certainly be better than *there*."

Sarah nodded somberly. "And I have a father. Perhaps he will even like me."

Mary stopped, forcing Sarah to stop as well. "He will *love* you. You will see."

The girl's eyes were wide and uncertain. Mary's heart broke for her. But Sarah was safe now. She could begin to heal.

"Oh, is *that* real?" Sarah asked, pointing to something moving in the trees.

Mary caught a flash of white and antlers among the autumn colors. "The white stag? Yes, it appears in these woods some times.

"I hope *she* never finds out."

Mary looked down at Sarah. "Is she looking for it?"

"Oh, yes. Always. It's a messenger. A guide."

"It has helped my friends and me in the past," Mary said.

"Then the Fisher King likes you."

"The Fisher King?" Mary asked.

"Yes. He's the one who keeps the land and its magic healthy. He sends the stag. *She* wants it."

Mary shivered. If the Unseelie Queen wanted it, that had to be bad. "Come, don't worry about that now. We're almost home."

"Home," the child repeated.

They reached the shop. Mary guided the girl in by the front so she could admire the window displaying their father's clocks and wind-up toys.

Sarah's eyes went wide and she let her mouth hang open. "This is where you live?"

"It's where you live now. I'm sure our father will teach you to help him, just like he did for me."

"Everything I cook will be happy now," Sarah said.

Mary smiled. Sarah's ability was an odd gift, but at least not a dangerous one like Lucien's. It would benefit their father, and hopefully Sarah as well.

They stepped into the shop, and the bell over the door rang. The scents of wood shavings and oil rolled around Mary, and the ticking of dozens of clocks greeted her. It was good to be home.

Her father came out from the back. He looked weary—older—but his thin face brightened when he saw Mary.

"You've come home," he said, his voice cracking a little.

Mary gave Sarah's hand a gentle squeeze. "I told you I would. I had to...to do some things, but this is still my home. And I've brought someone."

Sarah had been reaching tentatively for a carved toy horse, but she pulled her hand back as if afraid she would be punished.

"Who is this?" her father asked gently.

"This is Sarah," Mary said. "Your Sarah. The ones the Fay took from you."

He froze, his eyes meeting hers. Then he stared at the girl, who looked up at him tentatively. He slowly fell to his knees, stirring up tiny flakes of wood shavings to float and glitter in the sunlight.

"Sarah," he whispered. "Can it really be?"

"I stole her back," Mary said. "She had this."

She held out the scrap of cloth from her mother's blanket, so threadbare against her fingers now that she was afraid it would fall apart. Yet the echoes of her mother's love still clung to it. Those echoes would outlive the threads that had captured them.

Her father took it with trembling hands, his eyes brimming with tears.

"Thank you, Mary—my Mary," he said, then looked to the girl. "My little Sarah. You know, I only held you a few times before...before they stole you. You were so tiny. Look how grown up you are now." His voice cracked. "Your eyes are sad."

"So are yours," Sarah said quietly.

Their father looked like he wanted to embrace the girl, but he had the wisdom to sense it was too soon. Sarah was like a wild creature, not quite ready for so much affection.

"We will learn to be happier together," he said. He glanced up at Mary. "All of us?"

Mary sighed. She had thought so, too, but Sarah's comments about the white stag had made up her mind for her. "I will stay for a short time, but then I have to return to London. There are other children who are still trapped, and my friends need my help. But Sarah will be safe here. Keep her hidden. Like you did for me."

He nodded, relief and understanding flowing between them. "I'm so proud of you," he said. "I was proud even before you left, but look how you're growing up."

Mary reached out her arms, and her father stood to embrace her. Sarah watched in wonder at this simple, healing show of love. Mary wished she could stay safe in the shop forever, listening to the gentle, eternal tick of the clocks. She was more frightened of what was out there than ever. But now she knew she could face it, and that for the people she cared about, she had to.

Notes on Lore and Limps

I have tried to keep the lore in this book faithful to Celtic and sometimes broader European folklore, though I have mingled Irish, Scottish, Welsh, and even some ancient Nordic and Continental folk traditions. The Fay were thought to be fallen angels, the restless dead, or demoted gods and goddesses from pre-Christian times depending on who you asked, but everyone agreed they were dangerous.

The Wild Hunt appears in various forms throughout European folklore as a stormy night manifestation of powerful beings or the dead. I chose to tie it to the Fay and to Annwn, its hounds, and Welsh tales of the Otherworld. I drew my descriptions of the otherworldly island fortress mainly from a medieval Welsh poem about one of King Arthur's exploits. Lore about corpse roads and visits to the Otherworld helped round out that section of the story.

Spring-heeled Jack is too much a part of Victorian London's lore for me to leave him out of this book. The many accounts of him agree that he was tall, appeared to breath fire, and could jump amazing heights. Perhaps he was some kind of Victorian acrobat and prankster, but the stories about him are very strange. I decided a fire elemental backstory fit him best and wove a history involving him and Domin (which I hope to flesh out more someday).

Tempestarii was the title given by medieval people to weather mages, though it is a mouthful. I have tied their powers to other lore about the power of royal blood and birthright.

The Alexandra Limp was a real fashion trend in 1869 and 1870 as a result of Alexandra, Princess of Wales developing a permanent limp following a fever. She also later developed deafness, giving her something in common with both Cassandra and Georgina. Cassandra's injury was caused by a spinal stroke (a stroke in the neck or back, cutting off blood supply and damaging nerves) resulting from scarlet fever, though medicine at the time would not have recognized those details. Strokes are often associated with the elderly, but they're not uncommon in younger people. Still, neither Princess Alexandra nor non-royal girls with limps probably enjoyed having their disability imitated as a Victorian fashion trend.

Also by E.B. Wheeler

British Fiction:

Born to Treason

The Royalist's Daughter

The Haunting of Springett Hall

Wishwood (Westwood Gothic)

Moon Hollow (Westwood Gothic)

A Proper Dragon (Dragons of Mayfair 1)

An Elusive Dragon (Dragons of Mayfair 2)

A Subtle Dragon (Dragons of Mayfair 3)

Cruel Magic (Iron & Thorns 1)

Utah Fiction:

No Peace with the Dawn (with Jeffery Bateman)

Letters from the Homefront (Utah at War)

Balm for the Heart (Utah at War)

Bootleggers and Basil (in *The Pathways to the Heart*)

Blood in a Dry Town (Tenny Mateo Mystery)

A Company of Bones (Tenny Mateo Mystery)

Nonfiction:

Utah Women: Pioneers, Poets & Politicians

Mysteries of the Old West

Mysteries of the Middle Ages

Juvenile Fiction:

The Bone Map

Alejandra the Axolotl and the Big Mess

Acknowledgments

I took far longer than I had hoped in crafting this second book in the Iron & Thorns series, but I wanted to do justice to the characters' stories, so thank you to my readers for their patience. I hope you find it worth the wait. My heartfelt thanks to The Writers' Cache and UPSSEFW for their support and critiques as I worked on this book, and especially to Dan, Karen, Lauren, and Melanie for their detailed feedback. I also appreciate the many experts and reenactors who have shared their knowledge about historical details in person and online. As always, thank you to my husband and kids for their ongoing support.

About the Author

E.B. Wheeler is the author of over a dozen books of history, historical fiction, and historical fantasy, including Whitney Award finalists *Born to Treason* and *A Proper Dragon*, and YA Fantasy Whitney Award winner *Cruel Magic*, as well as short stories, magazine articles, and scripts for educational software programs. She has a B.A. in history with an English minor from BYU and graduate degrees in history and landscape architecture from Utah State University. In addition to writing, she sometimes consults about historic preservation and teaches history, and she loves gardening, folk music, reading, and exploring the West with her husband and kids.